MAGICA

1

RISE OF THE CULT

M

E. S. MAGILL

MAGICA

1

RISE OF THE CULT

Scribes & Scribblers Publishing
Gramarye Press
2023

Scribes & Scribblers Publishing 2023
Gramarye Press
Phoenix, AZ

⌒

Title: Magica: Book 1 – Rise Of The Cult
Author: E.S. Magill
ISBN: 978-1-961502-06-2
Genre: Fiction | Urban Fantasy | Paranormal Family Thriller
Supernatural | Suspense

⌒

BOOK COVER AND FORMATTING | GR Book Covers
GRAPHICS | www.depositphotos.com
AUTHOR PHOTO | Byron Medina

www.esmagill.com

For my mother Aurora,
who always believed in me.
You would have loved this.
I'm sorry it came too late.

M

PART 1

M

CHAPTER 1

HOME CALLED TO LAVINIA. SHE FELT IT IN THE PIT OF HER STOMACH—
that need to be done with work and far away from irate library patrons and
chewed up books. There was a pull to be safely alone in her cottage, curled up
in her favorite oversized chair with her cat Salem nestled on her lap.

...and something else she couldn't quite put her finger on.

The work week had been long and tedious, and now standing precariou-
sly at the top of the library ladder trying to shelve the last book, freedom
seemed within reach. All she had to do was slide the book in place, and her
shift would be over. Praise the goddess. But like the entire uninspired week,
this last book was making things difficult for her. Its slot was to her right
and out of reach by just inches. Every time she thought she had it, the slot
seemed to move over, teasing her. She cursed not being born with telekinesis which would've allowed her to float it into place. That, however, wasn't
within her scope of powers.

What she needed to do, and should've done, was climb down and move
the ladder over, but she didn't and wouldn't. Annoyance boiled in her veins.
At this point, it was a matter of wills. She wasn't going to let this crummy
week win. Her legs trembled in her effort to reach. If she leaned a little more
to the right and stretched her arm—

The heavy tome slipped from her hand. Gravity kicked in and tried to
pull Lavinia in the direction of the plummeting book. Her body angled
away from the ladder, arms flailing like she could flap her way out of this
predicament. At the last second, she jerked herself back to center, grabbing
for the rails, her heart racing.

"Lavinia."

The book hit the wood floor with a thud.

"That could've been your head," Eleanor said.

Lavinia looked down at her fellow librarian and mumbled, "Sorry."

Eleanor picked up the weighty tome with two hands. "You risked getting hurt, or worse." The way Eleanor said *worse* gave it substance, and the word hung in the air like a portent until it dissolved into a wisp that floated away. "What were you thinking?"

"I was thinking about getting home to a mushroom pizza and a bad movie with flying sharks or shambling zombies." Lavinia loved schlocky B-movies with bad acting and even worse monster costumes.

"Do you have a date tonight?"

Lavinia shook her head. It was another Friday night alone since the love of her life broke up with her years ago, and she hadn't found a person who could equal Sylvie Mills. It would've been nice though to have someone to share pizza and a few laughs with.

"I was going to ask you for a favor."

Lavinia groaned to herself. She knew what was coming because lately it was the standard routine. "Sure. What is it?"

"Sophia tasked me with repairing a couple of books but," Eleanor held up her arm and looked at her watch, "I need to pick up the twins from orchestra rehearsal. Could you please stay and take care of them for me? I'll owe you one."

There it was. Just because Lavinia was single, all the other librarians didn't think twice about asking her for favors regarding their families.

"James usually picks up the kids, but he left this morning on another business trip."

Lavinia didn't want to work late. A crackling fire and her cozy fall pajamas beckoned her. She turned her head away and bit her lower lip, mulling it over. Just because she didn't have a partner or kids, didn't mean they could all impose upon her.

"Please, Liv. You'll understand when you have your own family one day."

Lavinia cringed. She hated hearing that line. Her mother said it to her. Her sisters said it to her. Even her grandmother harangued her about being single. Maybe this one time she should dig in and say no, but Eleanor was still explaining her predicament. "The kids are waiting, and there's a storm heading our way. I don't want to leave the twins stranded. I'm so worried."

There it was, again. The thing Lavinia could never object to—children. She thought of Eleanor and her four kids and traveling husband. Eleanor who came in to work every day with dark circles under eyes, ragged nails, and stains on her raincoat. Lavinia looked at her perfectly manicured hands. Leaving the sigh out of her voice, she agreed to stay. "But first, can you?" Lavinia wiggled her fingers.

"Thank you, you're a dear." Eleanor turned the book vertically and whispered a word into its spine. It lifted from her hands, hovered in the air, and then slid easily into the vacant space between two others.

Lavinia scowled at the slot and the book before following Eleanor to the circulation desk.

Eleanor gathered her coat and purse and then stared hard at Lavinia. "You're not going to pull any more stupid stunts and get yourself killed or maimed once I leave. Right?"

"Promise."

"Okay, I've got to get going." Eleanor glanced at her watch again as she hurried toward the library's twelve-foot double doors. Her heels clicked on the marble floor like a stopwatch counting down.

Lavinia picked up a tattered book. "Is this the one?" She waved it around as if that made it easier for the other librarian to see.

Eleanor squinted at the book being held out to her and gave a thumbs up. "See you Monday and lock up after me."

Lavinia stood in the quiet, book still in hand. Her eyes lifted to the motto painted in gold leaf above the doors: *Sapere Aude*. 'Dare to know things through reason.' Or more simply interpreted by Kant, 'Dare to know.'

"Yeah, I *know* I could be heading home right now if it wasn't for other people's kids and families." Lavinia knew she had to give it a rest and stop griping. Family was important and not something a person could just ignore. Still the tug to get home that night was strong. She didn't even know what the urgency was about. It wasn't like anything, or anyone, waited for her there, but she knew she needed to be at home curled up on the couch.

She dropped the book on the desk and herself in her chair, ready to complete the projects Eleanor had left out.

One of the entrance doors creaked, startling Lavinia. Eleanor stuck her head through the gap. "You didn't lock up."

Lavinia plucked the keys from the drawer.

"Liv, I didn't come back about the doors. I wanted to say thank you. I know it's an imposition, and you're dying to get home." She gave Lavinia's arm a sweet squeeze. And here was the Eleanor who was kind and supportive.

"You're welcome. Now go. Get out of here." Lavinia smiled at her friend. "Pick up your kids and have a nice weekend."

Eleanor nodded and left. Once the door swung closed, Lavinia locked it.

She tossed the keys on the counter and picked up the first book needing to be repaired, *Circe's Love Spells* by Septimus Quill, most definitely a pseudonym. Once again, she settled into her black leather office chair. The tea she'd made hours ago had turned cold. She uttered a short spell, waved her hands over its surface, and blew into the cup. That was one of her talents she loved. No microwave needed. She could harness energy with her words and hands. But would she trade that ability for telekinesis? She took a delicate sip and found the temperature as she liked it. Not right then at least.

She flipped through the Circe's, admiring the quality of the spells. Men couldn't do magic, and Quill most likely acquired the incantations from witches he knew. That was the problem with witchcraft. Few ancient books were penned by women because they couldn't risk having evidence lying about incriminating them. Women kept their knowledge in their heads and spread it with their tongues. Still, the *Circe's* was a record of magic that would have been lost if not for men like Septimus Quill. She found the ripped page toward the middle and used mending tape to repair it. The book was a copy. Rare and valuable volumes were stored in a vault in some far-off location known only to the Mothers of Hecate.

The last book she needed to work on was Reginald Scot's *The Discoverie of Witchcraft*. The boards were detached, and the book needed a complete reback. This was a job beyond her scope. On Monday she would send it over to the library's professional binder. Before putting it away, she stroked the embossed cover and lifted it to her nose. She loved books—the way they felt in her hands, their musty smell, the beauty of an artfully bound volume. She paged through the Scot.

In it he argued that people's beliefs in witches and magic was based on superstition and ignorance, and therefore they shouldn't believe in such things. His argument was factual: What nonmagicals believed about witches was based on misinformation. Scott wanted to stop the burnings, hangings, and torture the witch trials inflicted upon so many, primarily women. Scot, however, knew both witches and magic were real, but saving lives was his goal.

Writing the book was a risky move on his part because it could have revealed his own beliefs. Lavinia had read that Scot belonged to a heretical sect of Anabaptists known as the *Familia Caritatis*, the Family of Love. Its followers believed in nature ruling the world, education, and free speech, but unlike other sects, the Family of Love didn't proselytize, unwilling to risk persecution for heresy. Outwardly, they conformed with society. Lavinia found it unfortunate that rational and positive religious groups like Scot's didn't outlast the zealots with their bizarre, hate-filled beliefs. Scot may have been trying to do good in a roundabout way by writing *The Discoverie of Witchcraft*, but his was a society of finger pointing, lazy thinking, and prejudice. In the end, the book might have even caused more harm than good, angering James the IV of Scotland and most likely fueling his obsession with witchcraft.

Lavinia shook her head. Scot's world was much like today's because nothing ever really changed. All these books and all the other books in the world, now and throughout time, were filled with incredible wisdom and knowledge, but mankind still insisted on acting stupidly. She closed the book. That was enough. She wasn't going to solve the world's problems tonight. She slid the Scot into a book pouch along with a note.

She could finally go home. All she had to do was make a quick tour of the library to ensure that everything was ready for Monday.

It was now past seven. The stained-glass clerestory windows that hugged the ceiling along the west wall were black with night. By library standards, the Witches Library would be considered small, but what she lacked in size she made up with beauty. Mahogany bookshelves detailed with columns and carvings of acanthus leaves and acorns lined three of the twenty-foot walls. Taking up the greater part of the floor space, rows of bookcases lined up like soldiers about to march into battle. Library tables and leather armchairs filled the rest of the room, now empty of patrons.

The bookshelves held a millennia's worth of knowledge. They catalogued every plant and mineral known to witches and their uses for life and health, and a few even for death. Some books contained the histories of the supernaturals who lived in the shadows of the nonmagicals. Lavinia picked up a nearby book and thumbed through the pages, pausing at a drawing of a dragon. The dragon shook its head and began to exhale. Lavinia snapped it shut. Some, like this one, held spells and curses on their very pages, and it took a master witch to know how to open those books without letting the magic escape. It saddened her to think she would never have the time to read all the books she wanted to read.

The entrance doors rattled. Eleanor seriously couldn't be returning to check up on her again. Lavinia steered the cart to the front. They shook again. "Eleanor, hold on." The oak was thick and dense, and anyone on the other side wouldn't be able to hear her, yelling out was just a habit. She'd left the keys on the circulation desk but now couldn't find them. She pushed around catalogs and papers searching for them. The keys jingled. There they were. "Coming, Eleanor."

The doors blew open. The blast knocked Lavinia off her feet. Her head connected with the edge of the circulation desk, and she tumbled into darkness.

≈

Lavinia groaned, her head throbbing. She tried to raise a hand to feel her forehead but couldn't move her arms. She looked down to find chains crisscrossing her chest and arms, and duct tape covering her mouth. Something moist slipped down the back of her neck. The concussion made her dizzy, and she found it difficult to focus on anything.

Fumes stung her eyes, and she blinked rapidly to ward off the burn. It was then she saw the logs piled around the chair she was bound to. What was going on? Strangers in white robes stood on the other side of the circulation desk, each with a torch, faces hidden by deep hoods. Who were these people? All she could think was the inane thought that they shouldn't have fire in the library. Lavinia struggled against the chains, trying to free her hands. She couldn't do magic if she couldn't move them.

An older man raised his arms above his head. "O Heavenly Father," he intoned, "only your word is the true knowledge. Man has polluted your Garden with his filthy science. They have blighted the earth with cars and electricity and mining and all other atrocities against nature. Your faithful flock of Abecedarians have come to purge this evil."

Abecedarians? Lavinia studied the robed figures surrounding her. The coincidence was odd. She'd just been thinking about Anabaptists, and here was a sect the exact opposite of the Family of Love. No, not sect. The Abecedarians were a cult, fanatics who believed any knowledge not of God's and documented in the Bible was heresy. Their two favorite targets were scientists and witches. She knew she had to get out of there right then. Even though her feet were bound, Lavinia pushed against the floor, trying to topple the chair, but in every direction, logs hemmed her in.

The man tilted his head and spoke heavenward. "The witch filth has damned your Garden, Lord. They have taken your knowledge and assumed it for themselves. Only you can heal the sick, Lord. Only you can perform miracles, Lord. Only you can mend the world, Lord." The acolytes hummed as the man spoke, their torches spluttered and licked at the air like hungry living things.

Lavinia's phone in the pocket of her linen pants vibrated. This morning she had fussed over her outfit, intending to wear black slacks but her hand kept reaching for the baggy cotton pants she only wore in the summer. She had given in to the compulsion and was glad she did. The pants had oversized pockets, and her phone lay along the outside of her thigh. She jiggled her leg trying to work the phone out.

The old man droned on. "The world is changing. The Abecedarians' time has come. The scientists, witches, and free thinkers are the pestilence of this age. We, the Abecedarians, are ready to step up and assist in the cleansing. We will return the world to its natural state."

The vibration stopped. *No, no, no.* Maybe they would call back. She prayed for anyone to call, even a spammer.

"We have come here to destroy the Witches Library as you destroyed the evil of Sodom and Gomorrah."

Lavinia looked up at the old man. Did she hear him right? Destroy the library? She resumed jiggling her leg until the phone plopped out on the stone floor. There was a feature she had never needed to use: the Emergency Call button. It was at the bottom of the home screen, beneath the number pad. She kicked off her shoe.

A hand reached down and picked up the phone. Lavinia tried to protest but the gag muffled her objections. The person laughed. Lavinia struggled to turn her head to see who was standing behind her, but the person remained out of sight.

"The witches can no longer hide," the old man said. "For decades people have consumed the lies of New Age beliefs. They accepted Wiccan indoctrination, and even worshiped in the Church of Satan. That tide has thrust aside religion and traditional beliefs. But a prophet rises amongst them. I, Noah Corwin, will lead your people to the Holy Land. We end this blasphemy here." He pushed back his hood. His eyes were blind, only white orbs in his head, but when he looked at Lavinia, it was as if he was peering into her soul.

Her flesh prickled in fear. Her eyes skittered across the dozens of torches, down to the gas-soaked logs at her feet. They weren't serious. They wouldn't—

But she knew they would. She needed to find a way out of this. She couldn't breathe, feeling as if she was going to suffocate. Then she laughed, a morbid-hysterical sound that spoke to the irony of her physical reaction to being constrained and frightened. Suffocation. That's what the witch burners did as an act of mercy, suffocate their victim.

Calm, she told herself. Her breathing evened.

"Girl, fetch the *Librum Hecate*," the person standing behind Lavinia said, the one who had taken her phone. Lavinia cocked her head. The voice was familiar.

A small figure scampered across the room, nearly tripping on the hem of the too large robe she wore.

The book they wanted was the most sacred of the witch texts, and it lay in a special glass cabinet in the middle of the room. This was an original on temporary loan. Lavinia watched as the young woman touched the lock, the case opening for her. She was a witch. This surprised Lavinia because it didn't make sense. The Abecedarians abhorred witches. The girl struggled with the *Librum*, which was almost too big for her to carry.

"We have come to cleanse the world of the witches and their lies. And the world will be pure," Corwin prayed.

Now that they had what they came for Lavinia knew time had run out. The gasoline fumes nauseated her, and she feared vomiting. She tried speaking a spell, but the gag made it impotent.

Half the acolytes left the circle and headed deep into the library. Lavinia turned her head trying to see what they were doing. They dipped their torches to the books. Pages caught, spluttered red, and then curled up to die.

Not the books. Anything but the books.

Ashes, lifted by the fire's draft, fluttered around the room like gray moths and up to the clerestory windows as if they could escape. This wasn't about saving just herself anymore. She jerked her body forward and back, trying to loosen the binds that trapped her. The fire marched across the rows of freestanding stacks, and the blaze consumed the carved acorns and leaves that adorned the tops of the fluted columns, embers dropping to the floor.

Corwin nodded to the woman, the one who had taken her phone, to step forward and speak to the librarian. Unlike the others, the woman's cloak was black, the hood shrouding her face created the illusion that Lavinia was looking into a pit of oblivion, and not being addressed by an actual person.

"Sister, you were warned. You were given the chance to stop your sin against God. Now look what you have come to. It was wrong to be brought up in this sinful world of witchcraft. You brought this upon yourself."

The woman addressed her as Sister, which meant she was also a witch. That voice, she knew it. The librarian pulled against her restraints. Despite the gag, Lavinia kept mumbling spells in the hopes one would catch.

"Sister, you have done more than sinned against man. You have blasphemed."

They stepped forward with their torches. The witch held out a hand and one was passed to her. She leaned over the circulation desk, closing the distance between them. The woman pulled her hood back. Their eyes locked. Lavinia knew this woman. This was a person she hadn't seen in years. Hadn't some tragedy befallen her?

"There is no escape."

Lavinia's protest came out as muffled grunts. The woman smirked at her. Angered, Lavinia rocked the chair side to side. The chains loosened across her chest, and for a brief second Lavinia saw her escape as possible. She pictured her hands freed, pulling the gag off, and conjuring the deadliest spell she knew against this traitorous witch and all her cult scum.

Cold malevolence settled on Lavinia. "Now that wasn't very nice to think." The witch read her mind.

The torch tipped toward her, and the flame brushed across her cheek like a warm hand.

"I'll tell the Magica you said hi."

The witch then dropped her torch onto Lavinia's lap. Her screams exploded around her gag as the fire scorched her skin. The time she fell off her bike and skidded on her bare legs and arms for yards across an asphalt road flashed through her mind.

The rest of the acolytes threw their torches onto the logs piled around the librarian's chair. The fat under Lavinia's skin bubbled, bursting and peeling away from muscle and bone. The heat melted the tape, finally freeing Lavinia's mouth and tongue, but it was too late.

The stink of burning human flesh filled the room. Several acolytes coughed, but Corwin inhaled deeply.

As the library became engulfed in fire, the Abecedarian acolytes surrounded Corwin and rushed him to the exit. But the witch stood at the edge of the librarian's desk despite the threat of being burned.

The girl carrying the *Librum Hecate* waited for the witch. "Get out of here, you stupid girl." Clutching the tome to her flat chest, she did as she was told.

Only the witch and the librarian remained in the burning library. She extended her hands to Lavinia as if offering salvation. Instead, the witch drew the magic out of the librarian's body. The magic flared white, arcing towards its new host. Lavinia's body turned into a charred husk.

The flames licked at the motto over the door: *Dare to Know*. The witch paused and turned around to have one last look. "Oh, they will know soon enough."

Chapter 2

Maggie Towne was at a crossroads. She couldn't decide between getting on with her day or crawling back into bed. Part of her wanted to pull the covers over her head and go back to sleep. She sat on the edge of her bed and listened to the house cooling after the fiery energy of school-day preparations. All morning the word *Mom* echoed through rooms. *Mom, where's my shoe? Mom, there's no bread. Mom, did you sign the permission slip? Mom. Mom. Mom.*

Minerva, her eldest, had volunteered to drive the younger ones to school and then take the wet laundry to the laundromat. The dryer had broken down five days ago, and the service company told her they couldn't get anyone out there right away, maybe the following Thursday. Something was always breaking down. Two months ago it had been the upstairs plumbing at $1259.77 and then the car needed $3901.01 in repairs. Her budget was figured to the penny because money worried her, a holdover from childhood trauma.

The other part of her, the good mom part, poked her. Get up, it said. Keep moving. Momentum would motivate her.

Maggie told it to shut up and let her rest her eyes for a few minutes. She fell back into bed, her head sinking into the downy pillow. It felt so luxurious, and she sighed. She was glad she could count on Minerva for help, even though it made Maggie feel very guilty.

For the past month her super mom status had been slipping, resulting in this inertia. Good mothers kept going, she chided herself. They don't let little things like exhaustion and backaches stop them. Yes, she should get up. There were so many chores to be done that she had neglected in the past month—bills to pay, bathrooms to clean, and meals to prepare, though to be honest that had been relegated to her oldest son.

After everything that had happened, she had set aside her career and most of her witch responsibilities and thrown herself into mothering. She promised the children and herself she would be the best mother anyone ever had, but at that moment all she wanted was to lie here and have one more hour of sleep. The house was empty. Who would know? Maggie fluffed up her pillow and snuggled in. So warm. So comforting.

After a couple of minutes, the mattress felt hard under her hip, and she rolled onto her other side. The position wasn't right. She adjusted the pillows and flipped back to her left side. That was just as uncomfortable. Then she rolled to her back and stared up at the ceiling. The house was too quiet. It pressed against her eardrums. Close your eyes, Maggie, and think about sleeping. Sleep would feel so good.

Visions of dirty socks and frozen dinners tormented her. Her eyes popped open. Nothing. That extra bit of sleep she was chasing would not be caught. She threw back the covers and struggled out of bed. If lolling-about wasn't in her cards, she would muster the energy to be productive, to be a good mother.

"Up and at 'em," she told herself. "Let's manage the first three gets of every successful day: Get up. Get a shower. Get dressed." When was the last time she'd showered? Her auburn hair was feeling oily. And when was the last time she indulged in a pedicure?

She caught a glimpse of herself in the full-length mirror near the dresser. These were the same yoga pants and sweater she'd worn yesterday, maybe even the day before yesterday. "Ugh. Maggie, you are looking and feeling your mom years."

On the way to the bathroom, she bumped the dresser. One of the framed photographs toppled over and slid to the wood floor, shattering. She flinched and took a step backwards away from the glass shards. The last thing she needed was to cut her foot because Minerva would have plenty to say about that too. Maggie skirted the glass and went to the hall linen closet to retrieve the broom and a dustpan. After the mess was cleared, she picked up the frame and turned it over. That dark pit she tried to avoid reopened in her gut.

In the photograph her husband Richard was tossing a ball to Michael, their youngest son—her husband so handsome and Michael just three, a ball of energy. She thought of them every day, wishing them still alive. Their murders were still unsolved two years later.

Her life had been perfect, but in minutes evil destroyed it. No one had answers for her, and she resorted to using the Magica to hunt down the killers. Months passed with no success, and the only outcome was a path of unforgivable destruction. Out of guilt for what she'd done, she retreated home and turned her energies to protecting her children, even trying to keep them at home with her. They pushed back, actually demanding to go back to school. She couldn't blame them, staying home with a grieving mother wasn't healthy.

Come on, Maggie. It hurts but keep moving. She sighed and returned the frame to its place amongst the photographs of her other children. She would need to remember to buy a new frame. Good luck with that, she told herself. Remembering anything these days was impossible. If she didn't write it down, it didn't get done. No, a new frame was important. This was something she would remember.

The shower and clean clothes refreshed her. She even dried and curled her hair. Today wasn't going to be a messy bun day. She would marshal her strength and be the good mother. Good moms made dinner, not pawn them off on their teenage son. She headed downstairs. The weather had turned chilly, and the children would appreciate comfort food. She wondered if there were ingredients for a stew.

First though, she wanted to draw her morning tarot card, and she detoured to her office whose décor was in the currently fashionable dark academia style which had always been her aesthetic even before it became trendy. Her desk sat opposite the door, and behind the desk was a wall of bookshelves packed with books. To the right was a bank of windows dressed in velvet green curtains and overlooking the back of the house. To the left was a wall of dark cabinetry and apothecary drawers that contained everything from diamond dust to snake skins. Situated in front of the cabinets was her sacred altar. Armchairs and a loveseat occupied the rest of the room.

She retrieved the deck from the cabinet where she kept all her tarot decks, but the one she preferred for daily readings was her trustworthy Rider-Waite. She admired other decks, their artistry and inspiration, but Rider-Waite was utilitarian, like a good kitchen knife.

With the cards in hand, she settled at her desk, a massive wooden table with a trestle base that came from an ancestor, a sixteenth century witch, who passed it on to her daughters who passed it onto their daughters until it reached Maggie, the current living daughter. In the future, her girls would inherit the treasured item. She loved the idea of so many hands touching it, leaving behind grime and body oils. The table was imbued with the DNA of dozens of witches and that made it powerful. She shuffled the tarot deck thrice and then fanned them out onto the desk before her. Her fingers danced over the cards as she thought about her day. What did it require of her? Where would it take her? She drew.

Strength: a young woman in a white gown stroking a lion, the infinity symbol over her head. This was the card of determination and power. It signaled stamina and persistence. She had only to overcome her fears and tame raw emotions. The card was a good sign. She recognized her own will conquering the pain of lost loved ones. She didn't see tarot as predictive, but more akin to therapy. The most uncanny thing about the cards is that people drew the same ones over and over, the universe revealing specific messages. This card told her to get a move on, so into the kitchen she went.

She assembled a beef stew in the jumbo-sized slow cooker—a frozen London broil (because bothering with chopping and searing the meat first thing was a waste of time), two seasoning packets, vegetable stock, rutabagas, carrots, onion, and celery, and the ever-magical bay leaf, her favorite. She searched the pantry for the ingredients to make cornbread. All the containers were empty. The cornmeal, flour, and sugar were all depleted. Canned goods were down to black beans. The more she rooted around in the pantry the barer she found it.

She had no idea what the kids had been eating. She made note of pantry items to replenish and then checked the fridge and freezer. Armed with a list, she was ready to battle the grocery store. Then she remembered one more thing to add, a new frame. A quick stop at the discount store to purchase it first because keeping Richard and Michael ever present was important to her. After that, she would head over to the grocery store. The weather predicted afternoon rain, so on her way out she grabbed her hooded cape.

Maggie settled into the driver seat of her six-year-old Land Rover that needed an oil change, despite the recent repairs. Minerva would be pleased she was going out into public. Since the murders, Maggie felt uncomfortable going into town. She knew the people of Rockill judged her. Small towns were like that, but she needed to get groceries. She started the car and headed down the driveway. She thought about the children and how supportive they had been through everything. They deserved a decadent dessert. Brownies with ice cream would go over well. She wondered if she could remember two more items without having to pull over and add them to the list. Yes, she could. She wasn't totally vapid these days.

Only when she pulled into the market's parking lot did she realize she forgot to go to the discount store first and that she'd left the list on the kitchen counter.

Chapter 3

Benson Scott hadn't intended to go to the grocery store and fall head-over-heels-infatuated-at-first sight. He'd spent the morning in court testifying, and since he wouldn't be needed for the afternoon session, the judge released him. Instead of grabbing lunch or going back to the police department, he decided to make good use of the extra time. He took pride in being efficient.

He was still dressed in his court suit, which drew the attention of the women doing their shopping. They considered his face first and then scanned his left hand for a ring. He exuded New York City poise and charisma, and the women imagined him opening car doors for them and inviting them to candlelight dinners—then their thoughts turned to things a little spicier. Benson lacked any self-conscious vanity and was oblivious to the fact that he'd suddenly become the center of attention.

He liked to think of himself as logical and pragmatic, which made him well-suited to being a police detective. He had a plan for everything, including grocery shopping, which meant starting on the perimeter with produce, meat, cheese, and dairy. By the time he did that he was too exhausted to shop the inner aisles, where cookies and chips tried to tempt him. With list in hand, he steered his cart into the store, heading first to produce to get some cauliflower, Swiss chard, and onions.

And then it happened. A force struck him, draining all those rational, positive attributes away.

He looked across the piles of tomatoes and apples and a swoony intoxication swept over him. He felt drunk and stupid. Sounds around him were muffled, and his vision narrowed and blurred at the outer edges. He had to look at his feet to make sure he wasn't floating. The beautiful woman who caught his attention stood on the far side of the produce section. Only stands of red peppers and zucchini separated her from him. He couldn't help staring. She looked as if she had risen from bed, or like Venus from the ocean, with tousled hair and a glow. She picked up a red pepper in her graceful hands, felt its texture, and then raised it to her pert nose to smell if it was ripe.

Benson stood entranced.

Someone near him cleared their throat. A shopping cart knocked into his. "Excuse me, sir."

His cart was blocking the aisle. "Oh, sorry about that." He moved to the right, allowing the woman to pass. She glanced over to see what he was staring at and wrinkled her nose as if she smelled something off.

His heart's desire moved onto melons and lemons, and he followed, keeping one or two stands between them. He didn't want to come across as a stalker. Tinkling chimes signaled the start of the misters over the delicate parsley and Bok choy. The fine water diffused through the air, forming a halo about her. She looked up at him across the apples and smiled. He ducked down.

The sound part of his brain tried to muscle in and remind him he was acting like a ridiculous teenage boy. Go talk to her. What would he say? Try, hello. Sometimes he hated his rational mind. He pretended to tie his shoes before standing up.

She'd moved on to fruits. His heart thumped so loudly in his chest he was afraid others could hear it, and he looked about to see if anyone noticed. A woman in a ponytail and sweatshirt rolled her eyes at him. Two moms with toddlers huddled conspiratorially near the zucchini. People were staring at him. He steered his cart toward fruits.

His bella placed two melons in her cart. Her simple actions spelled him. He had to talk to her. Had to approach her. Had to find out if she would have dinner with him or coffee or the rest of their lives. Easy there, boy. This was crazy. He couldn't just go up to some random stranger and declare his feelings. Take it slow, buddy. Start with coffee or a cocktail before a proposal and honeymoon. One step at a time.

She headed for the last-of-the-season pumpkins, and he maneuvered his cart to keep her in his line of sight.

This was ridiculous. He was a forty-three-year-old police detective. He'd come here to do his grocery shopping, not fall in love. Then get back to it, he scolded himself. He focused on his list. When he looked up, she was gone, and he panicked. He couldn't lose her.

He took a corner too fast and bumped a display of bagged nuts. The whole thing tipped to the left. Bags of nuts lay about on the floor, and he kneeled to collect the mess he'd made. When he stood, he saw her on the other side of a mound of yellow bananas. She grinned and shook her head. He tried putting the bags back on the wire hangers, but they kept slipping off. A bag hit the floor, and walnuts scattered in every direction. Reddening, he started picking them up. He couldn't leave a mess. Someone could slip.

"Clean up in produce," the loudspeaker voice announced to the entire store. "Are you okay?"

The woman with the auburn hair was speaking to him, and here he was down on all fours rounding up errant walnuts, not the most gallant first perception he wanted to make. The idea of meeting her thrilled him.

He looked up. His witty response dried in his mouth.

What he saw first was her belly, very round and projecting from her flowy peasant blouse. He found himself staring hard as if presented with a situation that didn't fit the scenario he'd painted. It perplexed him. And that was when he realized she was pregnant, at least eight months, or more. With the vegetables and fruits piled high on their stands, he hadn't seen her below breast level. All he noticed was her radiant face and her ample bosom. Now he knew the reason for her ampleness.

"I'm good. More embarrassed than anything." Way to go, idiot. Fall for a pregnant woman. He felt like a pervert.

"I think the speed limit for taking corners in the produce section is like one."

"Yeah, I was in pursuit of a tomato, and I was trying to catchup." He couldn't believe that had just come out of his mouth. What was he thinking? Maybe it wasn't too late to run away.

She laughed, and it was the most beautiful sound he'd ever heard, deep and real. It was cream poured over peaches. And now standing so close to her he could smell her, vanilla and cinnamon as if she had been baking pastries just minutes earlier. Despite her state, Benson still felt bewitched. Caution had entered the picture though. He couldn't hit on a pregnant woman, and most likely a married one, even though her left hand was missing a ring. Her fingers were probably too swollen, buddy.

"Well, if you aren't injured, I'll let you get back to your shopping or hot pursuit."

"Yeah, sure. Thank you." That's it? He was just going to let her walk away? This Raphaelite goddess was about to disappear forever. Go after her, man.

No. Ridiculous, he couldn't pursue a pregnant woman.

His cart had a mind of its own and followed her. She stopped to examine the wide array of yogurts. She tilted her head as if listening and then continued to butter.

He'd been made.

Benson swung his cart left into an aisle out of her sight, but it veered too far to the right, slamming into a pyramid of coffee cans. The clatter of fifty metal cans crashing to the floor caught the attention of everyone. He should run, abandon his shopping, and run. No, he had to do the right thing. He kneeled and started collecting cans.

She peeked her head around the corner. He looked up and shrugged. She had to think he was a degenerate or at least weird.

"You know," she said, "that's twice now I've encountered you on your knees in the last five minutes. If I knew you better, I would swear you were trying to propose to me." The mischievous sparkle in her eyes made Benson put down the cans. If she only knew.

"Clean up on aisle 8." Benson winced at the storewide broadcast.

The coffee cans continued rolling down the aisle, but Benson gave up on trying to right the mess. "I know this is forward and most likely inappropriate." He inhaled for courage. "They have a great tea bar here in the co-op. Will you have a cup with me?"

At first, she looked surprised but then nodded. "Sounds good to me. I just have to pay for this."

A store employee appeared, and Benson left behind the coffee display and his cart. "I'm Benson."

"Maggie."

While she went through checkout, he found them a table. An amused grin spread across her face as she approached him. He saw her belly and didn't care. He positioned her cart at the end of their table.

"You certainly left a path of destruction," she said as he pulled a chair out for her.

"Do know that I am horrified by the whole thing. I swear I am never this clumsy." They ordered tea—Earl Grey for him and a non-caffeinated herbal for her.

"Can I infer that you're a police officer from the tomato joke?" she asked.

"Just call me Detective Chuckles." Dear god, something was wrong with him. Pivot, man. Pivot to grown-up talk. "I moved here about four months ago from the City." He put his cup down. "I'm sorry. I hope you don't think I'm depraved for asking a woman in your condition to have tea." Benson tested the waters. "Your husband is lucky to have a beautiful woman like you and a little one coming along. Your first?"

She sipped her tea. "This is my seventh child."

Hot tea spewed through Benson's nostrils, splattering Maggie's white blouse. "I am so sorry." He stood and hurried away. Maybe he should keep going, out the doors, to his car. Instead, he returned with a glass of water and napkins. She dabbed at the tea-colored spots. He wanted to help but decided he should just stay on his side of the table.

"And my husband died two years ago."

In his head he tried to make the math work—her husband gone two years and if she was eight months along. Probably in vitro but he wasn't going to pursue that conversation. "I am so sorry about your shirt. And your loss."

"It's okay and thank you. I haven't laughed like this in a long time."

They spent the next hour talking about their lives. Her dewy skin and soft pink lips melted him. He noticed the other shoppers giving them surreptitious looks but shrugged it off as small-town behavior.

Alarm crossed her face. "What time is it?" She didn't wait for an answer before struggling to her feet. "I have to get home. The kids are back from school and wondering where I am."

He walked Maggie to her car but didn't want her to go. Should he ask her out? He glanced at her oversized baby bump. It was crazy. Whoever heard of someone asking an expectant woman on a date? But when he looked into her eyes, he felt himself get warm. He loaded the bags in the back of her vehicle. Pregnant. Six kids at home. No husband. What was he thinking? For the first time in his life, he wasn't. It was all feeling.

"Have dinner with me," he blurted. "I make incredible spaghetti." He looked around for his own cart. "We can go out to eat. I've been dying to go to Fork & Honey."

"How about you come over to my house," she said. "I've got a stew simmering in the slow cooker."

He accepted the invitation, and she texted her address to him. She drove away, and he felt a pang of sadness. He scolded himself for being impetuous, but when he pictured Maggie's auburn hair running through his fingers, he sighed. It was time for him to get back to work.

When he headed for his car, shoppers stood at the store's entrance eyeing him. He didn't care. He had a date.

CHAPTER 4

She couldn't figure out if what she'd just done was crazy. On the drive home, Maggie tried to convince herself that inviting a man, a stranger, to dinner was normal and sane. She wasn't blind to Benson's crush. Even after he realized her pregnant state, his eyes still had that dreamy quality. She knew he wasn't under a spell because in her condition that just wasn't possible. His feelings were real. He made her laugh, and she needed that more than anything right then. It didn't hurt he was handsome too—athletic build, dark brown hair, and that scar that ran from his cheek to his chin and a small one on his forehead, like he was regularly in knife fights, was very sexy. His clumsiness could be chalked up to being nervous. She hoped. What the kids would think concerned her, and more importantly, Minerva's possible reaction made her neck muscles tight.

Clouds like dark barrels rolled across the sky, and in the distance the first nine-pin rumble of thunder made all those in the Hudson River Valley pause and consider Irving's famous somnolent character. Maggie wanted to make it home in time to unload the groceries while it was still dry. Her house was the last on the lane, five miles from Rockill, separated by ten acres from her nearest neighbor on the west side of her property, and on the east side edging the river itself. She turned left into the driveway right before the road dead ended at the Hudson River. She pressed the button on the rearview mirror. The gates had a slight malfunction and opened slowly. She put the Rover in park to wait. If the zombie apocalypse ever happened, they would be overrun and all die.

She rarely minded and liked having a few quiet moments to contemplate life, like forced meditation. But today, reflection made her uncomfortable when she thought about what she'd just done. Maggie's misgivings had nothing to do with Benson and everything to do with her own mother. Was inviting a man into her home two years after the death of her children's father something a good mother did?

Maggie had lived in this house for over twenty-five years, and she never took it for granted, considering what her childhood had been like. She loved every inch of the property. Oak trees planted three hundred years ago lined the driveway creating a leafy tunnel. A hillock blocked the view of the house from the road, keeping it private. Once over the rise, the house emerged from the ground like a living thing. It was originally built as a simple Colonial in the 1700s and then later updated to a more sophisticated Georgian. Her owners over the centuries lovingly added wings to each side, keeping the house symmetrical. The front façade was now complemented with a portico of a pediment supported by columns, gifted by a generation from the Federalist period. Another family added the wrap-around front porch and second floor balcony. The house stood stately, inspiring visions of Christmas parties in the main salon and summer picnics on the lawn. She knew she romanticized the house too much, tending to overlook peeling paint and leaky pipes. The house had been handed down from one generation to the next, but Maggie almost missed her opportunity. As a child, she knew nothing of this house or its occupants.

Her mother had inflicted homelessness on Maggie as a child. Winnie fancied herself a free spirit witch, working as a medium in a traveling carnival during the warmer months and shacking up someplace rent free when little Maggie had to attend school. She had sworn that when she had children, she would be the best mother ever, and her children wouldn't suffer like she had. They would live in the same house their entire lives and have their own rooms. Her children would eat nutritious meals and have a mother who loved them more than she loved herself. This house allowed her to do the thing she promised herself ever since her childhood, to give her own children a decent and secure life.

The gates were now open, and Maggie drove through. Once again, she had to put the Rover in park and wait for the gates to close. She insisted that Samuel and Minerva, and guests, wait as well. They'd had intruders on several occasions. Most were just curious supernaturals wanting to see the Magica. A couple—well, there had been trouble then. She should've had a repair company come out and fix the gates. It was on her long list of improvements. The gates inched closed behind her, and she returned to her reverie.

∾

On Maggie's eighteenth birthday, her mother died in a car crash. Maggie had been waiting at the restaurant Winnie promised to treat her to. Her mother never took her anywhere, and Maggie felt that maybe things were changing. She felt grown up on that day, dressing the part—a skirt and a light-blue sweater-set found at the Goodwill. For an hour, she paced outside that restaurant, her stomach and anger grumbling. There was only one place her mother could be, the place she spent the better part of every day and evening. The bar was only a few blocks away, and she marched down there ready to confront Winnie.

Maggie heard the fire engine sirens before she saw them. Flashing blue and red lights spotlighted the accident. It was her mother's car, a beat up mini-van held together with bungee cords and duct tape, now sandwiched between a light pole and an over-sized pickup truck. Only one fire engine and police car were on scene. Patrons filtered out of the bar and milled about on the sidewalk to gawk. Maggie stood amongst them, trying to make sense of the twisted metal. Her eyes passed over the yellow tarp near her mother's car. She stepped off the curb and headed for it.

A police officer stopped her, telling her she had to stay back. *That's my mother.* He waved a firefighter in a red helmet over who came and expressed his condolences. Her mother hadn't survived. Maggie wanted to see her. He warned her about the blood and injuries, but she insisted on seeing her mom one last time. Someone yelled, and the captain excused himself to help his firefighters who had shifted their focus to helping the injured in the truck.

The officer escorted her over, and Maggie walked up to the edge of the yellow tarp. She hadn't seen the blood seeping from under it, and it grazed the tips of her dress shoes. She took a step back. Later, she would have to scrub the blood off them. When Maggie said she was ready, the officer eased the tarp back from her mom's face. She asked him if she could stay with her mom until they took her away. He shrugged and left to direct traffic or take statements.

Once alone, she knelt next to Winnie. If it wasn't for the gash on her forehead, she would've thought her mom sleeping. Maggie wondered why she wasn't crying. Weren't you supposed to mourn the dead, especially your own mother? She stared for another minute, waiting for something to happen, and when nothing changed, she did the only thing that came to mind, she whispered, *Goodbye, Mother,* and pulled the tarp over Winnie's face. Maggie's indifference troubled her, but more practical matters pressed her.

The driver's door hung open. Inside she found her mother's purse and dumped out its contents: a cell phone; a debit card, the kind you get as a gift; and two twenty-dollar bills. No bank card or credit card. Maggie didn't know how she was going to live off $40 and whatever was on the card.

She walked up to the police officer who'd helped her and thanked him. She then had to beg one of her mom's bar friends for a ride back to the trailer they were squatting in.

The next day Maggie used her mother's cell phone to call the funeral home the ambulance had delivered the body to. The director told her cremation would cost $2000. Maggie knew what she had to do. After school, she went to the bar and demanded her mom's bar buddies ante up, since they got more of her time than she did. Her anger and magic twisted into a compelling knot, and she came away with an extra $300. She could eat now and not have to rely on scavenging food from the trashcans at school.

Her mother never taught Maggie about her powers, and her magic was always haphazard and ineffectual. She considered what happened at the bar a fluke. Back then, Maggie didn't even know she was the Magica. Winnie had never told her. A week later, she brought home Winnie's ashes in a cardboard box.

Even though she was still in high school, Maggie was eighteen which meant nobody from CPS would come looking for her like they had in the past. She was responsible for herself, which wasn't new, just more official. The car was totaled, and she lived miles from town in a wooded lot. If she took an after-school job, how would she get home? The school bus got her into town and back home, but the town wasn't the kind of place that had public transportation. And then what about the weekends? She was trying to be frugal with the little money she had. She still needed to supplement her meals with food she took from school. Most days she was cold and hungry. She didn't know what she was going to do. High school ended in two months and then she was free to go wherever she wanted. She had no idea where that might be.

As she was doing her homework, a voicemail came from the local hardware store that served as the shipping and copy store for the small town: *Your box is full. Pick up your mail.*

Maggie rummaged about the trailer until she found the keys she'd taken from her mother's purse. The ring held about a dozen keys, and she flipped through them until she found one that looked like it belonged to a mailbox. She didn't know what all the other keys were for since Winnie hadn't owned anything worth locking up—as far as Maggie knew.

She snuck out during lunch so she wouldn't miss the bus after school. The store was downtown, a few blocks from the high school. The clerk directed her to a bank of mailboxes on a far back wall. Her mother's was stuffed with junk mail and a single envelope, linen paper and elegant, addressed to her, not her mother. Maggie had never received a piece of mail in her entire life—not even a birthday card. She took the envelope outside to the bench under the window. Maybe it was from her father. She always fantasized he would come for her one day, explaining that Winnie had stolen her from him. In Maggie's fantasy, he whisked her away to a better life. She'd never known her father, and Winnie never volunteered that information. Maggie took out her keys and slit open the flap.

It contained a check for $7,000.

She sat staring at it, trying to make sense of all the zeros.

There was a letter too:

Dear Ms. And Miss Towne,
Now that Maggie has reached the age of majority the quarterly checks will be made out to her so that she can assume responsibility for her own care as an adult.

There had been more, but all Maggie could focus on was what that quarterly number amounted to yearly—$28,000.

Shacks without electricity. No plumbing. Shoes and clothing from thrift shops. Living with strangers. Being left alone most nights as Winnie went out carousing. And the men she brought home. All the nights Maggie went to bed hungry. She choked on her sobs. Several people walking by asked if she was okay. "Now I am," she had said. Her mother had been keeping a secret from her for years, well, forever in fact. Maggie hadn't wasted a tear over Winnie's death, but this... These tears were for her mother's ultimate betrayal.

～

"Now I am." Maggie said the words aloud as she swallowed the pain from all those years ago. Stop, Maggie. That was a long time ago, but the pain of the past was always sharp, ready to cut through the veneer of the present to expose all the darkness of a life once miserably lived. Clear it away. She waved a hand as if shooing away an irritation and said, "*Ocultarse.*" Nothing happened. Of course, what was she thinking? Her powers were on hold.

She didn't like relying on spells to forget the past, but those memories from her childhood felt as if someone had taken a hot branding iron and stamped them on her mind. If only the good and positive were as easy to conjure as the painful. She was still stuck with her dilemma. Did bringing a stranger and a man into her home violate Maggie's principal objective of protecting her family? She knew she wasn't the kind of mother Winnie had been, which was no mother. So was inviting a man to her home wrong?

The first raindrops pattered across her windshield like the tiny feet of scurrying mice. In the tradition of her ancestors, Maggie had added to the house—an up-to-date kitchen with its own porch and a covered breezeway connecting the house to an exterior garage, the former carriage house. She pulled the Land Rover around back, aiming to get inside before the storm hit.

She didn't make it. The gale-like winds drove the rain vertically, making the breezeway, covered or not, useless. She grumbled, wishing she'd built an enclosed structure. Buckets of water sluiced from the sky. She tried to jump from the vehicle, but it was more a slow slide out of the driver's seat, her belly catching on the steering wheel. She waddled to the back door, but it wouldn't budge. The thing tended to swell in damp weather.

Maggie beat on the door. "Kids, kids! Let your mother in."

Luka, eight-years-old and the youngest, appeared to her rescue. Her hair and clothing were already drenched. "The groceries," she wheezed. Luka rushed out to the car, and Samuel, second child and recently turned eighteen, was right behind him. Maggie waited for her eldest daughter to appear.

"Mother! Where have you been?"

And there she was, her first born. Twenty-two going on forty-two. Minerva had graduated from college the previous spring but was unsure what her next steps would be. This worried Maggie. Minerva was a notorious homebody and if left to her would remain at home indefinitely. Her daughter insisted she was only staying to help Maggie with the family and the final months of the pregnancy, but Maggie suspected there were other issues troubling her eldest.

"Are you trying to kill our baby sister? Let's get you dry." Minerva grabbed a towel from the laundry room and wrapped it around her mother's shoulders.

Becca & Betsy stood in the middle of the kitchen all too happy to watch everyone scamper about. "Girls, help with the groceries, please." They rolled their eyes at the same time.

Becca was the third and Betsy the fourth child. At fourteen and thirteen respectively, only eleven months separated the two. They were almost identical. In the old days, they would've been referred to as Irish twins, but Maggie didn't think that term was used anymore. She often wondered if perhaps they might be twins. She had a nagging suspicion her egg had split in two, but Betsy decided to stay behind because having an older sister close to her age would be nice.

The girls removed the groceries from the soggy bags. "Mom," they said in unison, "the flour." Rain had soaked through the paper bag.

"Transfer it to its container, girls." Maggie headed for the stairs. "Samuel, could you please make your wonderful cornbread muffins? And, everyone, help tidy up the house. We're having a guest tonight."

Minerva, who was leading the way to her mother's room, stopped suddenly. Maggie's belly crashed into her daughter's back. "What?" Minerva blinked like a surprised owl. "Who?"

"A nice man I met in the produce section." She went around her daughter. Maggie knew what was coming.

"Mother, have you not noticed that you're nine months pregnant? You can't pick up strange men in the— Well, anywhere." Minerva stood with hands on hips, looking incredulously at her mom.

"Don't be silly. I didn't pick him up. It's not a date. He's funny and handsome."

"But Mother."

Maggie proceeded to her bathroom. "He's a police detective, Min. Not a serial killer." She stuck her head around the corner just as Minerva's mouth was about to open. "And don't 'Mother' me again, dear. I'm a grown woman who can make her own choices."

Maggie heard Minerva leave the bedroom with a string of gripes in her wake. People talk about the joy of watching their children grow up, but rarely does anyone mention the wonder of their children becoming adults. Minerva could be a delight but she thought her mother was embarrassing and going senile in her old age. Forty-four was not old. In fact, Maggie had never felt more womanly or more seductive in her whole life. She sloughed off her wet clothing and stood before the mirror admiring her long legs and strong arms. There was the belly, though. She laughed and rubbed her hands over the shiny orb.

Another girl. Maggie wished her husband could be there to share in this. He'd visited her several times after his death, which was how she ended up in her current condition. After their little surprise, Richard stopped visiting. The Sisters of Mamitu conveyed the message to Maggie that the Passed frowned upon such things. "It's okay, little one. You have a very large family who love you so much. See how your big sister worries about you?" Maggie missed Richard. She never got to say goodbye before they restricted his moving between realms.

After a quick shower to warm up, she finished her hair and make-up. She chose black velour pants and layered it with a t-shirt and her favorite sweater. Downstairs, Samuel was vacuuming and Minerva dusting. In the kitchen, Luka and the girls were debating something consequential only in the minds of children. It was the great *maple syrup versus honey* debate that always occurred when cornbread was on the menu.

Becca & Betsy had the ingredients for a green salad on the counter, and they argued with their little brother as they cut up tomatoes and cucumbers. Both girls were concerned with nutrition. Maggie kissed their heads, thanking them for helping out. She went to the fridge for her favorite snack, Hansen's garlic and dill pickles. It was the only thing that satisfied her constant hunger.

"Mom, did you ask the man if he was vegan or vegetarian?"

The cold pickle crunched as she bit into it, the garlic and dill dancing in her mouth. She loved these so much she feared the day they would be discontinued, which happened with just about all her favorite things. "His name is Benson Scott, and I didn't think of it, girls." Maggie checked the slow cooker. A fork pierced the meat like a knife through butter. The time was now 5:30, good for adding the peas.

Betsy diced red peppers. "To be on the safe side, we decided on a salad as well. It complements the stew. Right, Becca?"

"Yes, salad complements stew, and cornbread with honey." Becca glared at Luka.

"Mom, tell them it's gotta be maple syrup," Luka whined. "And I don't want any salad."

Betsy rolled her eyes. "Salad is good for you. Becca, remember those French fries I had last weekend?"

"Yuck, your face was a disaster for days. I avoided standing next to you for fear of that one pimple," Becca said.

"Kids, finish cleaning the kitchen. Mr. Scott will be here at six." She yelled the last part loud enough for everyone in the house to hear.

"Fine. Whatever," Minerva huffed on her way to the laundry room. "I think this is a bad idea. Dating men when you're pregnant."

"It's not a date," Maggie repeated as she took a bite of pickle. "How did the laundry situation go this afternoon?"

"You're changing the subject, Mom."

"Mom, Luka is now setting the table," Betsy yelled from the kitchen.

Her tone hinted that something unacceptable was occurring. "He told us we needed to have a theme for our guest," Becca said. Both girls shook their heads indicating that they just didn't understand creatures like Luka.

Curious, Maggie went to the dining room. Even though the room was quite formal, she insisted dinners be eaten around the table. With its seating for twelve, the table accommodated the entire family and any visitors they might have. A built-in China cabinet occupied the wall near the room's double doors, and a long sideboard took up the opposite wall with a mirror and several paintings hanging over it. A bank of tall windows overlooked a cut-flower garden. The final wall held the original colonial fireplace, as the dining room was once the home's kitchen. A green tablecloth covered the table, and red napkins flanked wide, red bowls on white plates. Candles of various sizes occupied the center of the table.

Luka entered the room with two fir tree boughs. "Look, Mom. I wish the dryer was working so I could dry them. Don't worry. I wiped them off with a towel."

Maggie now knew why the dryer had stopped working. Comments about electricity and fire danger came to mind, but she stopped herself. The house hadn't burned down so she let it go. After Samuel was born, she decided worrying too much about children wasn't a good idea. They found their way. She would broach the subject of safety another day, but now wasn't the time.

Luka placed the boughs amongst the candles. At least they were battery operated. "There. It's got kind of a log cabin feel. Can we light the fireplace?"

She hugged her son to her, smothering his head with kisses. "It's wonderful, Luka." He had been her youngest child for six years, until Michael came along. Luka relished the role of big brother, but after Michael's death, Luka found himself not knowing whether he was still a big brother or the baby of the family once again. The death of their father and youngest sibling took its toll on all the family members.

Maggie stood at the windows looking out as the rain cut the house off from the rest of the world. Water amassed in puddles that would take days to dry out. In the house, they were all warm and dry and happy and waiting for their guest. If he came. The weather might put him off.

Maggie prayed she wasn't making a mistake inviting this man into her home.

CHAPTER 5

"Mom, he's here!" Becca & Betsy stood at the bay window overlooking the front of the house, peeking through a part in the sheers. "And you should see his car."

Maggie stood between her two daughters to have a look for herself. His car surprised her and simultaneously worried her. Benson didn't come off as the Playboy type. She reminded herself they'd only met that day, and his behavior in the store probably wasn't indicative of who he was. He pulled the silver Corvette behind her Land Rover, and again she questioned her decision to invite him over. Well, it was too late. He was here now.

The children stood behind her as she opened the door. She liked the way he dressed—slacks, not jeans, a sweater and a collared shirt, plus a tie. He held a grocery bag in one hand and flowers in the other. He looked past her to her brood. If that didn't scare him off, she'd take that as a good sign. He smiled at all of them. Samuel relieved Benson of the paper bag, while Becca & Betsy accepted the flowers on their mother's behalf. Glass bottles in the bag clinked making Minerva scowl.

"I come bearing sparkling cider. The flowers are for you." He watched the girls carry them off.

"Welcome to my home. Let's go to the kitchen," Maggie said.

The kitchen bustled with activity. The flowers went into a vase, and Luka asked Benson for his jacket. The children ping-ponged around the kitchen finishing the salad and plating the cornbread. He stood amidst all that activity like he was at the center of some mysterious vortex of forces. Maggie thanked him for bringing cider and asked Samuel to take down the good glasses. She called all the children to her. The whirlwind of activity came to a stop as they gathered around the kitchen island. They each took a glass, and Maggie made a toast. "To new friends." They clinked glasses.

"Kids, this is Mr. Benson Scott. Benson, this is Minerva and the oldest." The young woman scowled at him. "And this is Samuel." The young man reached out and shook his hand. "And this is Becca & Betsy. They're not twins." They stood behind their mother and smiled. "And this is Luka. He's eight." Following his big brother's lead, he shook Benson's hand.

"Thank you for inviting me over."

They sipped at their drinks. The moment started to stretch into an uncomfortable silence.

Maggie felt the awkwardness of having a stranger and a man in their kitchen. Maybe Minerva wasn't wrong. "Well, I think we're all starved. Let's get started. Benson, we're informal tonight."

The children burst into action as if holding in all that youthful energy was too much. Maggie reminded them to turn off their phones and leave them in the basket in the kitchen. Becca & Betsy shepherded Benson to the dining room where he remarked on the size of the table and the fireplace. Everyone collected their bowls and trooped back to the kitchen to serve themselves stew.

Benson laughed. "That's huge. I don't think I've ever seen a cauldron slow cooker. Got any witches around here?" Becca & Betsy giggled, and Minerva threw them a look.

"Big families need big pots," Maggie said. They ladled up their stew and went back to the dining room.

At the table, salad and cornbread were passed around, and Benson chose two muffins. Luka and Becca & Betsy watched him butter both, then reach for the honey. Becca & Betsy cheered. He looked from the girls to Luka. "Could you please hand me the maple syrup. Thank you." He dribbled honey on one and maple syrup on the other.

Luka raised his arms in triumph.

"That's a draw, Luka," Betsy said. "Mr. Scott used both."

"Did I do something wrong?" he asked.

Luka spoke up, "We were debating whether cornbread should be served with honey or maple syrup."

"I can never decide so I use both." He winked at Maggie across the table. He knew what the kids were up to and had made both sides happy. This pleased Maggie.

Dinner proved to be a success, despite Minerva's warnings. The children talked sailing with Benson since the house sat fifty yards from the Hudson River. Richard had taught the kids once they could walk. Becca & Betsy and Luka lamented the rain, or they would have dragged Benson to the cove off the river where they had a boathouse with a sailboat and a motorboat.

Minerva quizzed their guest on his occupation. She demanded proof he was a police detective. He showed her his badge, but when that didn't quell her skepticism, he pulled up the department's website on his mobile. For Becca & Betsy, his bachelorhood was a thing of fascination. "You've never been married?" the two kept repeating. "And you don't have kids." He insisted he'd never been and had no children either.

Maggie felt sorry for the myriad directions Benson found himself pulled, but she was happy for her children. It had been a long time since an outsider had stepped foot into their house. She thought things had been going well for the last year and didn't realize until now how much grief had affected them. Tonight, there was a great deal of chatter and laughter.

"That was the best meal I've had in a long time," Benson announced, after having not just seconds but thirds. Maggie was pleased by his appetite. "Let me help in the cleanup." And even more pleased that he didn't take it for granted that the women would be obligated to wash dishes.

"Nope, we've got it," Luka said.

"Are you sure?" Benson asked. Luka nodded and started stacking plates.

While the kids cleaned up, Maggie and Benson settled in the living room. "Thank you for inviting me. And I apologize again for being such a freak in the store. I was just intrigued by you."

She placed her hands on her stomach. "And then a little dismayed?"

"Let's call it surprised." They both laughed. "Okay, I confess, a little dismayed. Only because I thought you were married. Your kids are pretty great. But I thought you had seven."

It was a topic she dreaded, but this time she didn't feel the need to hold the truth back.

"Michael is my sixth child. Michael and my husband Richard were murdered. The killer was never caught."

Benson winced. "I am so sorry. And I shouldn't have pried."

"It's fine. Not easy to talk about—"

Luka flew into the room. "Mom, we have the dessert stuff on the counter. Can we start?"

"Dessert? Wait for us." Benson helped Maggie off the couch.

In the kitchen the kids were debating whether the rain would stop that night or in the morning. Becca swore the weatherperson predicted tomorrow, and Betsy supported her sister. Samuel insisted the rain would continue through the night. At that moment a bolt of lightning sparked across the night sky. Immediately a rumble followed the light show.

"That's right over us," Luka said. The rain let loose again, sheets of water slapping the roof and windows.

"Good grief," Maggie said. "Benson, you might be trapped here tonight. That dip a half mile back on the road floods. You won't make it with your car. We have plenty of room for you."

Pounding at the front door startled everyone.

"Thunder?" Becca & Betsy asked.

They looked at one another.

The pounding started up again.

Samuel set down his ice cream bowl. "I'll get it, Mom."

Maggie followed him to the foyer. "Samuel, wait." Whoever it was hadn't come up the driveway because the gates were closed. She turned to Minerva who shook her head and shrugged. Benson stepped beside Maggie, his tension like a rubber band.

Again, the door rattled as someone tested the handle.

With the violent storm and the late hour, no one should be at her front door. All she could picture was a menacing threat waiting for them. Her husband and little boy came to mind and that horrible day. Then all the other villains she'd encountered over the years popped in her head. Samuel couldn't be the one to answer the door. "I'll do it."

"No, Maggie," Benson said. "I'm sorry for stepping in, but in your condition, I think you should let me."

Even though she'd just met him that day, she was glad Benson was here. And it wasn't strange to have this man in her house, like Minerva said it was.

"Please help."

"Oh, it sounds like a child," Maggie said. "Go ahead, Samuel." He pulled open the door.

A young woman stood on the front porch, water dripping from her thin coat and straight hair. She was trembling.

"I need the Magica," the girl screamed. "They're after me." The girl looked over her shoulder, went rigid, and then collapsed.

Benson rushed in and caught her before she hit the floor.

Chapter 6

The police detective in Benson took over. He scooped up the stranger and looked to Maggie for direction.

"There's a guest bedroom down here." She led the way.

He placed the girl on the bed. She was slight, just shy of five feet tall, and slender. Her rain-soaked clothes clung to her, accentuating her frailness. Her teeth chattered.

Minerva arrived with towels. "Good," Maggie said, "we need to get her dry and warm. Becca & Betsy, she's a little smaller than you girls but please find a pair of sweatpants, a t-shirt, and zippered hoodie." She turned to the males in the room. "Gentlemen, we will need for you to wait in the kitchen."

"She said someone's after her," Benson said. "I'll take a look outside."

"There are rain slickers and boots in the laundry room," Maggie said. "And be careful."

"Mom, the girl asked for the Magica," Minerva said once they were alone. "In front of Benson. He's going to ask."

Maggie threw a blanket over the semi-conscious girl. "Min, we need to get these wet clothes off her and warm her up. I think there's an electric blanket in the closet."

Becca & Betsy returned with the change of clothes and clutching their cell phones. Maggie took the clothing and asked them to stay with Luka. "Mom, just so you know the internet's down." That was unfortunate because no internet meant that cell service would be sketchy.

"Girls, do you know her?" They both said they'd never seen her before. Maggie hugged them before they went upstairs.

"Mother, he's going to ask questions."

"Not now, Minerva. Let's take care of this first. Help me get her out of these wet clothes. They're bringing down her body temperature." For the girl's modesty, they changed her with the blankets covering her and wrapped a towel around her damp hair. They settled the girl beneath the crisp sheets, down comforter, and the electric blanket.

"Mom, who do you think she is?"

"I don't know, Min."

The girl's shivering stopped, and she settled into a calm sleep.

Benson returned. "I didn't see anyone, but the rain's coming down hard. Someone could've been out there, and I wouldn't even have known it. But we should be cautious. I asked your son to make sure all the doors and windows are locked. I also put in a call to my department." He held up a backpack. "I found this on the porch."

"The police won't be able to make it out here in this weather. That wash down the road will be flooded," Minerva said.

"That's what I told them. They're not sending anyone. I just wanted them to know that we might have a minor child here and that someone might be after her." Maggie agreed that was sensible.

"Do you know what she was talking about? She said she needed the Magica." Minerva made a face at her mother and left the room. "Did I say something to upset her?"

"No, Minerva is sensitive. She'll be fine."

Benson nodded. "So what's this Magica? Did she get your name wrong? And why was she asking for you?" Maggie waited for him to end the interrogation. "Sorry, that's the cop in me."

Thunder rumbled over the top of the house, followed by a whiplash of lightning. The house lights flickered. The storm intended on holding them hostage.

"Well, I think she's going to be fine. Her pulse is strong, and she's breathing easily. So I don't think she's in danger from a medical standpoint, but we'll keep an eye on her."

"Did you find any identification?"

"No, but girls don't tend to carry wallets in their pockets." She pointed to the backpack still clutched in Benson's hand. "Might be something in there to help."

"Can I have my bag?" The voice was weak.

They were surprised to find the girl conscious.

"My bag." She reached for it. "Please."

Maggie and Benson looked at one another, trying to decide the best course of action. Maggie shrugged. "Sure." He handed it over.

The girl hugged the damp backpack to her like a life vest. If she was a runaway, everything she owned was most likely in that bag, and her attachment to it would be strong.

"Hi, I'm Benson. Can you tell me your name?"

The girl closed her eyes and drifted back to sleep.

"Looks like we're going to have to wait to find out who she is." Maggie stood and stretched. "For now, let her sleep."

They found the kids in the living room. Samuel was adding another log to the fireplace. The fire crackled and made the room glow. Maggie's back ached, the baby unsettled by the excitement. All she wanted to do was plop on the couch and put up her feet. She knew Benson was dying to ask questions because that was who he was, a police detective. Maggie had her own questions but procuring answers was going to get messy and complicated.

"Kids, it's bedtime."

"But Mom," Becca & Betsy said like a pair of bookends.

Luka turned and left. As the youngest he knew it was no use arguing with his mother.

"No buts, girls. This is a matter for adults."

"So why does Samuel get to stay?" Becca said.

"Your brother is officially an adult. You, ladies, have a few years to go. Scoot."

"Fine, Mother." The girls linked arms and headed upstairs. That was the second time in one day she'd been 'Mothered.'

After the younger children went to bed, the adults discussed the mystery guest. As if she'd overheard them, the girl appeared at the entrance to the living room looking less like a drowned raccoon and more like a Dickens orphan. The backpack hung from her right shoulder. While she was worried, Maggie also felt protective. Whoever this girl might be she was younger than Minerva and only a few years older than Becca & Betsy.

"Dear, you should have called out. Come sit by the fire." Maggie pointed to an ottoman near the hearth. "Samuel, can you please get her a cup of chamomile. And Minerva, can you bring her a lap blanket. I'd get it myself, but I think I'm wedged into this corner of the sofa. Thank you."

The girl sat down and tucked the backpack between her feet. Samuel brought her tea, and she smiled at him. Maggie took that as a good sign.

"I'm Maggie. This is Minerva and Samuel. And the gentleman on the couch is Detective Scott," Maggie said, hoping that by making things familiar the girl wouldn't be frightened.

At the mention of the police officer, the girl's shoulders hunched, and she drew her feet closer together, keeping the backpack between her legs. "You didn't have to call the police."

"Detective Scott was here for dinner as a friend, but he did contact the police to let them know a minor showed up at our door."

"I'm twenty-years-old. I know, I look young."

Benson cleared his throat. "Can we start with your name and if you have an ID."

"My name is Heather. I'm sorry but I don't have an ID." She said the word as if it was a foreign concept.

Of course, the girl ran off without it, or never had any. "So how did you end up here?" Maggie asked. Benson took notes on his phone.

"I came along the edge of the river, from the north." She smoothed the blanket over her lap. "They were chasing me. I had to stay off the roads."

"Who was chasing you? I can notify the police if someone has hurt you," Benson said. Maggie was surprised to hear concern in his voice rather than a police officer's tone.

"No, please don't do that!" Heather's eyes grew large. "They haven't hurt me." Her voice became steadier. "I ran away."

He spoke kindly to the young woman. "It's okay to contact police when you're in danger. I know you want to protect your family. I've seen this before. People trying to escape a bad situation. You don't want your family hurt in the process—even though they might have hurt you." Heather nodded and cast her eyes to the floor. "But I won't contact the police until you tell me."

Hearing Benson's gentleness, a soft warmth opened in Maggie's chest. She made a good call inviting this man into her life. Maybe the goddess had guided him here tonight for this very reason. "Can you tell us who's after you?" Maggie asked.

The girl bowed her head and turned mute. Maggie couldn't help but think of a turtle who believed if it hid its head no one could see it. "Who's after you, Heather?"

She shook her head and turned her body sideways. The glow of the fire flashed off the side of the girl's face. Maggie shivered. Something in the moment troubled her, but the feeling drifted away before it could take hold.

Benson leaned toward Heather and held his palms out to her. "Heather, we can only help you if you tell us who's after you. Please."

"I'm afraid."

"But you said they haven't hurt you," Samuel said.

She glanced over at him, her eyes flooding with tears. "They could. I don't want to go back there."

"You're over eighteen. You don't have to do anything you don't want to do," Maggie said. "Who's after you?"

Heather mumbled something.

"The what?" Benson asked.

"The Abecedarians," the girl whispered.

"Mom." Minerva jumped to her feet.

The name felt like a blow to Maggie. Maybe she heard incorrectly. "Heather, I don't think I caught that."

"The Abecedarians."

"Mom." Minerva's voice went up an octave.

Suddenly this wasn't just about a young woman running away from a bad homelife, which was bad enough. If the Abecedarians were involved, this had become something worse.

"What did she say?" Benson asked again.

Maggie ignored everyone around her. "Heather, that group was—" She wanted to say destroyed but instead chose her words carefully. "We haven't heard from them in quite some time."

"I just couldn't take it anymore." Heather put her face in her hands. "I had to get away from them."

"What's she talking about, Maggie?"

Maggie stayed focused on Heather. "Who's heading the group now?" She'd almost said cult.

"No, no. I can't tell. He'll know!" The girl stopped talking and turned away from her.

Pushing hard wouldn't help the situation. As to who the leader might be, Maggie had her own suspicions. She would have to wait and see before saying anything. "Excuse us." She motioned for Benson to follow her into the kitchen, out of Heather's hearing range. "The Abecedarians. They're a cult, a radical group," Maggie explained. "They don't believe in human's acquiring knowledge. They believe the Bible is all people need to live by."

"Like the Amish?"

"No. Very radical. However, they have related origins. They do live without electricity, cars, phones. Lots of book burnings. Their animus is focused on scientists...and teachers." Here Maggie paused, unsure of how much to reveal, specifically her role in it all.

"A cult?"

She could see he was trying to connect this girl, a cult, and her. "Yes, a cult." He had questions but now wasn't the time. "Let's go back."

When they returned, Heather was sipping her tea, her hands were shaking. Samuel and Minerva watched her from the other side of the room.

"Why come here?" Maggie asked.

"This is the only place I could think of for protection. You have to protect me." Then the girl added, "You're duty-bound."

A brick to the head would have surprised Maggie less than what the girl had just uttered.

"What?" Benson said, looking at Maggie. It had become his fallback word.

Minerva opened her mouth to say something, but Maggie warned her with a look. She proceeded warily. "You just said you were with the Abecedarians. You would only be asking for duty-bound protection if—"

"Mother, not in front of—" Minerva glanced at Benson.

What was it with her kids today? None of them thought she had the ability to make a logical decision. "Heather, what do you mean by that, me being 'duty-bound'?"

"I'm a lineage witch, and you're the Magica," the young woman said.

The atmosphere in the room turned somber, while the tempest outside turned volatile. The wind battered at the walls of the house like a beast wanting in. Maggie felt Benson looking from her to the girl and back to her. Minerva's face turned red, while Samuel folded his hands in his lap.

Minerva broke the tension by crossing the room and peering down on Heather. "I don't believe you. The Abecedarians wouldn't tolerate a—" She looked uncomfortably at Benson again.

Maggie had spelled her children so that they'd never reveal their family secret, but Minerva as an adult had outgrown these limits. Maggie was both proud and perplexed that Min took the secret to such lengths.

"Witch," Maggie finished Minerva's sentence.

"Mom, in front of a stranger?"

She understood her daughter's reticence to reveal a thing so personal and sacred, but Minerva's reaction felt excessive. "Perhaps he's not a stranger anymore." She looked at Benson who looked back at her as if question marks were dancing around his head.

"My mother renounced witchcraft when she joined them. I was just a small child. I was raised as an Abecedarian. I didn't know any different." Heather drew the blanket tighter around her shoulders as if it could protect her. "I'm scared and tired. Can we talk about this tomorrow after I feel better?"

A flash of lightning knifed the sky outside the picture window. The house rattled as if someone had picked it up and shook it. And then the lights went out. The fire's amber light kept the room from plunging into blackness. Shadows danced on the walls.

"Why is she talking about witches?"

"Mom."

"Because we are, Benson," Maggie said matter-of-factly. His eyebrows jumped to his hairline, his mouth hanging open in disbelief.

Minerva stormed from the room, her mother's response the last straw.

Maggie felt exasperated. A stranger, a young girl, had washed up at her doorstep demanding protection. Benson kept wanting answers. And Minerva was angry at every decision she made. She'd had enough. "Well,

Mother Nature's made the decision that we need to call it a night. Samuel, is it okay that Benson bunk with you?"

"Actually, Maggie, if you don't mind, I'd like to stay out here to keep an eye on things, just in case something happens."

She agreed and asked Samuel to round up sheets, blankets, and a couple of pillows for their guest.

"Maybe, we should talk?" Benson suggested.

Maggie patted her huge belly. "I think we're tired. All this can wait until morning." At first, it seemed he would argue. Instead, he let it go and helped her to her feet. She was relieved he respected her decision. Right now trying to explain everything was going to take more energy than she had.

Heather hung back for a second. "Thank you, Magica." She rushed back to the guest room.

Maggie said goodnight to Benson before he could ask another question. Samuel with his hands full of bedding passed his mom on the stairs. Maggie pulled him in and kissed his cheek. "You're the best kid." He grinned.

When she reached the top landing, she heard Benson ask Samuel, "What's a Magica?"

Maggie sighed. Strange things were brewing.

CHAPTER 7

Minerva's anger sat in her gut like a hot rock. Her mother casually admitted to two strangers she was a witch and then acted as if it was no big deal. She and her siblings endured years of spellings and discussions about never revealing their truth. Mom was getting careless, and Minerva chalked it up to being pregnant.

Her mother was cooped up in the house all day and oblivious to the perilous times they lived in. A whole swath of America had devolved into conspiratorial and superstitious beliefs. People were burning books and passing laws blatantly discriminating people. The internet made it so easy to create one's own personal reality based on misinformation, and even the media were willing to spin fabrications to capitalize on these fantasies. It made the whole world unsafe. These nutjobs were brazen about their attacks as well. The rock had been kicked over and all the hate in the country had slithered out from under it.

Minerva stalked back and forth across her bedroom floor too upset for bed. Everything felt crazy. Everyone for the most part acted nonchalant about all the lying and bad behavior. Where was the outrage? People dying, starving, hurting. Who cares? She cared. Even at college where people should've paid attention, she saw too many turn a blind eye. They were more concerned with their social media accounts than standing up for what was right in this world. In that respect, Minerva felt old-fashioned and disconnected.

As she turned to stalk in the other direction, she stubbed her toe on the trundle bed. She wanted to howl, but everyone was asleep. Stubbed toes and papercuts always seemed ready to injure when a person was already down. She didn't even know why the trundle bed was there. No one had ever slept on it, even though as a tween she daydreamed about slumber parties. Girls applying eye shadow on one another, practicing kissing imaginary boyfriends with a pillow as surrogates, and telling ghost stories at the end of the night. The slumber parties never happened. Maggie homeschooled Minerva, but to be honest, it had been Minerva's choice not to attend school. Sure there were get-togethers and outings with other children for social interaction, but she'd never made any real friends. It wasn't until she went off to college that she found friendship, even her first best friend. And in her junior year, she met Carey, her first and only boyfriend.

She held up her hands before her, palms facing away, and uttered a short spell to shove the trundle bed back in place. She felt calmer and plopped down on the edge of her own bed, finally able to sit still. Her mom just didn't understand how dark the world was becoming. First, it was religious persecution, then it was racial hatred out in the open. Next came book bans and limitations on free speech. Now it was an attack on women, restricting their rights. Minerva knew what was coming next.

She feared this final step. It was always on the heels of other hate, the need to control feminine power. That was when they would come for the witches. The crazies who wanted to imprison women and burn them at the stake. It was imperative that the existence of witches remain a secret.

Easy, Minerva, you're extrapolating here. Yes, it's a couple of strangers. The man less worrisome than that girl, who was especially worrisome, showing up in the middle of a thunderstorm claiming to be an Abecedarian and asking for the Magica by name. Minerva knew she was reaching but still she worried her mother was too forthcoming with the witch revelation. Maybe her mom knew something about Benson that Minerva didn't know. Her mom was the Magica and with it came the supreme powers of witchcraft. No witch possessed more power than the Magica. It was impossible.

Minerva grabbed her own pillow and hugged it to her. Holding something solid anchored her and brought Carey to mind. Even after years together, she still couldn't reveal to him that she was a witch. The idea frightened her. He could reject her, or worse, attack her. Maybe he would send others after her family. She had planned to tell him, but after the death of her father she felt it too risky to expose her family to unnecessary trouble.

She knew he was going to propose, and she couldn't allow him to before telling him the truth. She needed to steel herself and just do it, have the talk. Telling him after the proposal frightened her even more. What if the idea of her being a witch scared him? What if it disgusted him? What if he thought she was crazy?

What if. What if. What if. Minerva could conjure a million what-ifs.

Either tell him or break up with him, Min. End it before anyone gets hurt. Of course, her heart would be broken but that was mendable. Something bad happening to her family wasn't a thing she would risk, and right now, she wanted to protect her family from all the forces threatening them. Which reminded her, she needed to ward the doors. Her mom couldn't do it in her condition.

The hallway was dark, and from below she could hear the man snoring. She started with Luka's door, then Becca & Betsy's, Samuel's, and then her mom's. Minerva creeped downstairs to throw an extra layer of protection on the front and back ones, not that they needed it because her mom renewed the wards every year until each door was more spell than wood. Minerva felt a little more protection never hurt. She tiptoed into the living room, trying not to wake Benson, but this room didn't have a door, so she gave it a general protection spell.

Then she went down the hallway to the guest room. The door was ajar. A nightlight revealed the young woman beneath the comforter sleeping. Minerva saved her strongest warding spell for this door. Just as she was about to close it, Minerva's eyes landed upon the open eyes of their unexpected guest and shuddered. She hurried back to the safety of her room.

Minerva didn't know what Heather was about, and it worried her. She crawled into bed and pulled the comforter up to her chin. She hoped everything would be better in the morning.

She had her doubts though.

CHAPTER 8

Maggie fluffed up her pillows and then pulled the billowy comforter over her. She ran a hand across Richard's pillow. Two years later and it was still there and would always remain there. She hadn't washed the pillowcase, or even the laundry left in his hamper, after his death. It was a weird thing to do, but Richard's scent lingered in their bedroom, comforting her through her grief. It wasn't enough though, and she'd ended up using that pain to conjure him back from the dead. She knew better, but she was the Magica after all. It was within her power.

The baby somersaulted, over-stimulated by the night's events. "Take it easy, little one. Mommy's not going to do anything crazy. I just need to think this through."

She reached for her phone and remembered she left it plugged in on the kitchen counter. Her bedtime novel was languishing on her nightstand, and she picked that up instead. But her mind wandered. After a minute of struggling to read, she set the book aside. She lay there looking up at the ceiling thinking about the strange events that had descended on the house, and if she counted meeting Benson, the whole day. Two strangers were in her house, but she felt safe. It wasn't the calamity Minerva was making it out to be. She also knew her eldest was probably going about warding every door and double warding all exterior doors. As for Benson, she had complete trust in him because the baby approved. Heather didn't exactly trouble her either, but the cult she ran away from did. What kind of woman would take her child to live in a cult?

Maggie sat up.

Not just a woman but a witch. Why hadn't she thought of that earlier? She should have asked the girl for her mother's name. Heather said she was a lineage witch, which made her mother one too, meaning that Maggie knew the woman. With this information, they could then figure out the best way to help Heather. The biggest point troubling Maggie was whether the Abecedarians would come for the girl. She didn't want that group anywhere near her family. With the death of their father and youngest sibling, the children had endured enough in the last two years.

Maggie hadn't made her children's lives any easier since. The death of a parent and a sibling should have been enough pain for her kids. There was also the debacle with the Magica searching for the murderers. Then she became pregnant, and she didn't know how to explain that situation to her kids. They were confused by her announcement that their deceased father was the baby's father. Maggie's grief combined with her power of the Magica had brought Richard back to her, not corporeal or spectral, something in between. The children couldn't experience him and were angry with her for a long time.

And then her pregnancy became even more complicated.

A contingent of the Mothers of Hecate visited one afternoon to check on Maggie. As the three Mothers performed the magical ceremony to ascertain the health of the fetus, they made a startling discovery. Maggie had been alarmed when they interrupted the spell and went off to another room to confer. Left alone, Maggie imagined horrible scenarios relating to the baby: It was a specter like its father and lacked real substance. Or she wasn't pregnant, the baby a product of her imagination. Or the baby was ill or malformed. She didn't expect what the Mothers eventually revealed.

Her new baby was a Magica as well. A Magica born of a Magica was an Arch-Magica, and such an occurrence had happened only three other times in witch history, each time heralding in a new age of Magic. Some witches were angered by how Maggie had conceived, and then further angered to learn such an unusual child would also be a Magica. While she was responsible for the former, she had no part in the latter.

The power of the Magica was egalitarian—not hereditary, nor democratic. The Magica could be bestowed upon any lineage witch carrying a female child, whether she was highborn or a commoner, educated or illiterate, living in a palace or a hovel, like Maggie's own mother who found it convenient to ignore the fact that her own daughter was the Magica. She didn't forget the money though.

This mysterious force would gift the unborn baby with the Magica, all powers of Magic. She only led the witches until a new one was able to take over. Sometimes a Magica ruled for decades, sometimes only a few years. She might be young when she assumed the position or elderly. It was an elegant way to acquire a new leader. No one could seize power. No one could design to possess the power. The gift of the Magica was just that, a gift given to one worthy to lead.

Minerva had the strongest reaction to the revelation that her mother was pregnant and that the baby was the Arch-Magica. She was angry with her mom, felt deceived, called her selfish. It had been a terrible argument between mother and daughter. Minerva loved her father dearly, and as the eldest felt his absence more keenly than the other children. But Minerva felt everything to the extreme. Even before Minerva was born, Maggie had to monitor her own emotions. Incidents and emotions that affected Maggie also affected Minerva in utero. The baby's responses frightened Maggie, and she took great care to remain calm and happy for the duration of her first pregnancy.

Minerva's empathy became her dominant trait as a child and adult. To avoid feeling others' emotions she distanced herself not just from those outside their home, but also from each new sibling who came along. She loved her brothers and sisters, but Min needed more alone time. Maggie now regretted some of her decisions like homeschooling Min and allowing her to choose how and when to interact with others. She thought she was being a good mother, but her daughter was now too cautious and suspicious. Relationships drained Minerva. That she had remained with Carey for the past two years thrilled Maggie, but she wished Minerva would integrate him into their family.

After the argument about Maggie's pregnancy, Minerva made a surprising turnaround and became overprotective of her mom and the new baby. So much so that after graduating from college the previous spring, Minerva postponed an internship to return home and help her mom. Nothing Maggie said would deter her daughter from staying, and Maggie didn't want a replay of their previous fight.

She knew that Benson and the young stranger upset Minerva. Her eldest's words of warning weren't lost on Maggie, and she understood her daughter's fears. A witch lost all her powers when pregnant. So to have a nonmagical man and a runaway witch, one claiming protection and duty--bound no less, in her home was problematic. Maggie had no powers to protect Heather, or even her own family.

Maggie stroked her stomach, and the baby's tiny fist pushed up to meet her mother's hand. "Oh, yes. You're the strong one, aren't you?" Maggie cooed. It was well past midnight, and she would be a mess if she didn't get some sleep. She switched off the lamp and snuggled down into the blankets.

Everything would work itself out in the morning. An intrusive thought made Maggie sit up and stare out into the darkness of her room.

Or things could become more complicated.

Chapter 9

When Maggie woke, a low hanging fog, thick and foreboding, enveloped the house. She felt cut off from the world. With strangers sleeping within her walls, an awkward silence pervaded the space as its occupants tried not to disturb one another in the early morning hours. The wards still protected the bedroom doors, meaning no one could leave their room until Minerva lifted them, and as Maggie dressed, she heard her own door lock click open, followed by the others on the second floor.

She checked on the younger children first and found them asleep. She then went downstairs to start a pot of coffee for her guests and put the kettle on for her tea. Well, one guest and the other essentially an intruder, she told herself tiptoeing to the guestroom. She listened, catching the light breathing of the sleeping girl. A long talk in the light of day would hopefully right everything.

Maggie made her mug of decaf tea, laced with milk and a bit of sugar to make up for the lack of caffeine, and headed for her office. The space sat adjacent to the kitchen so she could be near the family. Its windows faced the backyard allowing her to keep an eye on the children when they were outside. Maggie retrieved her tarot deck and plopped into her office chair. She blew on the surface of the tea, taking a careful first sip. Getting up early before the children was one of her joys. Nothing in life was as decadent as that quiet stillness before the rush of the day's business.

She pulled a card. *The Star*. This was the symbol for rebirth and hope. The baby kicked, reminding Maggie someone new was coming into their lives. But other things were also ready to be reborn.

She swiveled the chair around to face the windows. Beyond the backyard sat a two-story schoolhouse some fifty yards from the house. It was a former barn that had become a repository for three centuries of antiques and odds and ends. She turned it into classrooms, a small library, and a study area. The boarders' bedrooms and a large living space with a kitchen were located upstairs. Two years after Richard's and Michael's deaths and Maggie wondered if it wasn't time to open the witch school, to turn the lights back on literally and figuratively.

After the murders, Maggie closed the school. Grief sent her in search of her husband's and son's killers. For months, she chased elusive leads which took her from the Hudson River Valley to New Mexico and finally London. Every day, no matter where she was, she worried the children with a plague of admonishments—be careful, don't talk to strangers, come straight home. The intensity of her emotions frightened her, and when the leads ran dry, she returned home where she tried to confine the children to the house. They refused. She realized she had a problem and sought professional help from a trusted doctor in their community. Once she felt herself righted, she brought the children with her to therapy, and they began the healing process as a family. Their grief softened, but didn't vanish, because that kind of grief she and the children experienced would linger all their lives. All Maggie hoped for was that the pain grew a little less sharp each day.

Reopening the school required energy and attention, even a small one like hers. It served twenty-five students a season. She admitted only two teenagers, those exhibiting the highest degree of witchcraft skill. All the rest were in their twenties or thirties, but a few were in their later years as they realized their true nature for the first time. Lineage witches were as rare as black opals, but every woman carried within her at least one gene for magic, which came in various forms: healing, cooking, gardening, mothering, even hexing. Some women possessed magical strengths in science, engineering, art, business, leadership. A woman could turn even the slightest bit of magic into a powerful ability, and Maggie wished more women would understand that. The world would be a different place if they did.

From the kitchen, she heard ceramic cups clinking, the fridge door opening and shutting, drawers pulling out and sliding back in, and knew Samuel was setting up a breakfast bar. The hosting gene proved strong in her eldest son, and she loved that about him. He cared about aesthetics and the well-being of others. He was growing into a fine man. Maggie waddled to the kitchen.

"Good morning, eldest son." She kissed his shoulder. "This is beautiful."

He grinned. "Morning, Mom. Thanks." He placed a pan of cinnamon rolls in the oven and then started whipping eggs.

She inhaled the yeasty, cinnamon scent and sighed. "I am definitely going to have some of those this morning." Maggie took her tea to the banquette overlooking the backyard.

Benson knocked on the doorframe before entering the kitchen. "Good morning."

The sound of his voice made the baby kick, and Maggie felt the same flutter in her chest. He was definitely handsome, and she imagined what it would be like to wake up next to him. She grinned. "Grab some coffee and join me. Samuel is baking his award-winning cinnamon rolls. You just wait until you taste them."

Samuel stopped whipping eggs. "I'm also making scrambled eggs, so we get some protein in our diets."

"Sounds like my lucky day." Benson poured his coffee adding a splash of half-and-half. He took the chair next to her, sipped his coffee, and stared out the window. He didn't say a word, just took in the November fog and the soggy autumn leaves downed by last night's storm. They patchworked the lawn in squares of red and orange and yellow. Maggie appreciated his silence. Mornings were for quiet.

It only lasted for four minutes. The chattering of her teenage daughters entering the kitchen broke the calm, but Maggie didn't mind. They brought with them an infectious energy, full of joy and potential.

Maggie went to them. "Good morning, girls." She hugged them to her sides, her protruding belly separating the two girls. Becca & Betsy placed their hands on Maggie's belly. Feeling the presence of her sisters' magics, the baby perked up.

"Oh, did you feel that?" Becca asked.

"Good morning, little sister," Betsy cooed into Maggie's belly. "Can we have coffee this morning, Mom?"

Maggie kissed each girl on the forehead. "Yes, because it's Saturday morning and if you make it au lait." Becca went to get the pan, and Betsy the milk. Samuel warned his sisters not to get in his way, and Betsy hip checked him in fun. Maggie looked about the kitchen feeling satisfied at the scene of domestic tranquility. Her son cooking, the girls preparing their coffee, Benson enjoying the view. For right now she could ignore all the other stuff.

The backdoor flew open, making Maggie spill her tea. "Mom," Luka screamed. "Mom!"

Luka coming from outside surprised Maggie. "Good grief. What are you doing out there? It's still drizzling." She noticed the paleness of his face. This wasn't excitement, fear dilating his pupils. His slight frame trembled. Maggie didn't wait. She rushed for her slicker and boots. "Show me." On her way out, she grabbed her mobile phone off the counter. "Becca & Betsy, stay here and watch over things."

"Mom." Luka tugged her hand and led her outside. "This way, Mom."

He pulled Maggie around the back of the house, heading for the driveway. Maggie's boots sunk into the grass, pushing water up from the ground that puddled around her feet. With the heaviness of her belly, progress was slow. "Hurry up, Mom," Luka called back at her.

Maggie panted. With her diaphragm pressing into her lungs, she couldn't inhale deeply. Halfway down the driveway, she heard the Land Rover start. The car pulled alongside her, Samuel behind the wheel. Benson hopped out of the passenger side to allow Maggie the roomier front seat. Minerva popped the back door, and Luka crawled in, Benson following him.

Luka stood between the two front seats, leaning over the center console. "Down by the road." He pointed toward the driveway's gate. "There. There."

Samuel stepped on the brakes too hard, and everyone heaved forward. While the others got out, Maggie sat and stared. It couldn't be what she was seeing, but she knew the shape all too well.

A pyre. The kind they used to burn witches.

In the middle of the night, or maybe even early morning, a group had parked here and set up the pole and the logs. They were both partially charred, but the rain and damp fog must have put the fire out before it could take hold.

Benson opened her door. Maggie hesitated but needed to see the pyre up close. Samuel, Luka, and Minerva stood around it. Her children knew what this meant. She had raised them to understand the pyre's history and symbolism.

"There's a plastic bag nailed near the base," Minerva said.

Samuel moved to pull it off. "Wait," Benson said. "Does anyone have gloves?"

"There might be a pair in one of the compartments in the back," Maggie said. Samuel went to retrieve them.

Gloved up, Benson removed the bag and took it back to the Land Rover where he placed it on the front seat. He pulled the bag open and took out its contents. He moved the plastic bag out of the way, taking care not to discard it or rumple it. Water drops speckled the car's seat, and he wiped them off with his sleeve. He set the plain white envelope on the dry seat. "Maggie, do you want me to open this?"

Though its exterior appeared harmless, there would be nothing but malice in its contents. "Go ahead."

The envelope had not been sealed. Instead, the flap was tucked into its opening. Benson removed the single sheet of paper. Handling the page by a top and bottom corner, he unfolded it. He held it to Maggie to read first.

We are coming for the woman, the book, and you.

Maggie read the message to herself first. She didn't want to frighten the children, but they demanded to know what it said. She read the single sentence aloud.

"Heather," Samuel said.

"Mother, I told you that girl was no good." Minerva crossed her arms and frowned.

"Mom couldn't just throw the girl back into the storm," Samuel said, and Minerva frowned at him directly.

Her daughter's presence surprised her. Minerva hadn't been in the kitchen with them.

"Maggie," Benson said, "what's this about? Should I call this in?"

Minerva didn't wait. "It's about scaring us. It's about bullying us."

Maggie looked around. "Becca & Betsy are up at the house with Heather."

Benson put the letter back into the envelope and then into the plastic bag. A sick feeling was overwhelming Maggie. The baby twisted within her, the pain forcing Maggie to rest her bulk against the side of the Land Rover.

"What book?" Luka asked. His clear voice overrode all the noise the adults were making.

They looked at him and then at one another.

Luka was right. What book? "I don't remember seeing a book last night."

"She had that backpack with her," Benson said.

"We need to get back to the house." Maggie looked over at the pyre. "We should take pictures, and then dismantle it before anyone sees it."

"I'll do it, Mom," Samuel volunteered.

Benson turned to Maggie. "I'm going to help Samuel." Maggie nodded.

"Mom, let's get back," Minerva said. Maggie and Luka climbed into the Land Rover, and Minerva drove them back to the house.

In the kitchen, Becca & Betsy were sitting at the table eating cinnamon rolls. "Did Luka want to show everyone another dead snake or some fox tracks?" The girls rolled their eyes. "Anyway, while all of you were gallivanting about we saved the cinnamon rolls from burning," Becca said.

"And cooked the scrambled eggs," Betsy finished.

"Something bad happened," Luka said. "There's a—"

"Luka, wait," Maggie said as Minerva helped her settle in at the kitchen table. The pain had relaxed its hold on her, and Maggie found it easier to breathe. "Where's Heather?"

"She asked if she could shower. We told her to go ahead," Becca & Betsy said.

"Can I tell now, Mom?" Maggie gave Luka permission, but he made sure to whisper. "I found a pyre down by the road this morning with a warning from some bad people."

"What?" both girls exclaimed. They ran into the laundry room and pulled on boots and jackets over their pajamas. The backdoor slammed, and the girls flew by the kitchen windows, heading down to the scene of the excitement. Luka followed them. For a moment, Maggie worried all this was too much for children, but she also knew what could happen if they weren't all prepared.

"Is it safe for them to be outside?" Minerva asked.

"Benson's down there. And I don't think the cult's hanging around."

"You're putting a lot of faith in him, Mom. You know he could be in on this."

Her daughter had a point. "Is that the feeling you get from him?"

Minerva scrutinized the ceiling as if the answer lay up there. She shook her head. "No, I'm not picking up anything negative."

"But from Heather you are?"

Minerva stood. "No. I'm not getting anything from her. I'm going to be in my room." Minerva needed some alone time after all the excitement.

Benson came through the backdoor. "We're done. Where do you keep your plastic bags? I want to preserve this evidence." She pointed to the pantry.

After he finished, he took a seat across from Maggie. "First, do you want me to call the police about the pyre?" Maggie shook her head no. "Are you afraid? Do you need police protection from this cult group?"

"Afraid, yes." She picked up her teacup and found it empty. "Police? I need to speak to Heather, and then I'll call my people. We have an internal system for situations like this."

"Okay. Good." Benson nodded. "Another thing, we've only known one another less than twenty-four hours and a lot's happened. I don't want to intrude or over-step, which I think I've done a lot of but not intentionally. If you want me to leave, I will."

"Do you want to leave?"

He folded his hands upon the table and stared out the window. Maggie liked this about him, that he used silence to figure things out. Most people talked too much.

He turned back and met her eyes. "Actually, if it's okay with you, I would like to stay."

"Yeah, me too," she said. She found herself overjoyed by the prospect of him staying more than she expected. She wanted to slide her chair closer to him.

"I know you've got a lot going on, but I think we should take a few minutes to talk about some stuff."

"Fine. Let's talk. But first, I need to eat." She started to get up.

Benson stopped her. "I'll do it." He warmed up a plate of eggs and a cinnamon roll for her. Then fixed one for himself. Before he sat down, he filled the tea kettle and placed it on the stove. "Can I get you anything else?"

His actions softened her heart. "No, thank you. But you should just bring the whole pan of cinnamon rolls over." He set it in front of her and gave her time to eat, refilling her cup with herbal tea.

When she finished, she leaned back feeling full and satisfied. "Thank you so much for that." She nested her teacup into its saucer. Before he could ask, she answered him. "Yes, we are witches, the females, not the males." She knew what he would say next. "No, not wiccans. Real witches."

"Maggie."

She recognized the look he was giving her. It was disbelief, which wasn't surprising. He would require evidence. "No, I can't show you any magic right now because I'm pregnant. Both magic and creating a new human require a lot of energy. Evolution made it so we can't do both at the same time. Becca & Betsy would enjoy showing you their abilities, but they're young and learning. Minerva is more experienced."

"Minerva hates me."

"No, she doesn't hate you. She just doesn't like you right now." They both laughed. "Not having magic makes me vulnerable. It's why Minerva is so protective. Her anger is also with me. I know she disapproves of what I've done." Maggie held up her hand and ticked off points. "1) Inviting a strange man to the house 2) then allowing a strange girl to stay over and 3) revealing our family secret."

"Who can blame her," he said. "Creepy guy hits on your pregnant mom and then comes to dinner, discovering 'all of them witches.'"

"Nice *Rosemary's Baby* reference. We don't worship Satan."

Benson cleared his throat, worry clouding his eyes. "Is that a real thing?"

"Satan?" Maggie shrugged. "'I know nothing of God, or the Devil.'"

"Touché. Excellent line. *Interview With the Vampire*?"

Maggie smiled. "I love horror movies."

"Me too," he said. "So why tell me? My guess is that it isn't something you readily do."

"That pyre—" She waved her hand toward the windows. "—is symbolic of hundreds of years of persecution. Yes, we're cautious." Maggie placed her hand on her belly. "As to why, the baby likes you."

"Thank goodness." He put his hands over his heart. "I'm not a total outcast around here. Can I ask you another question?" He put his hands on the table palms up.

"Since you know most of our secrets, go ahead."

"What's a Magica?"

She finished her tea and found tea leaves in a random pattern at the bottom. How much should she reveal? The leaves didn't have an answer for her, trusting her intuition was the next best thing. "I'm the Magica, the most powerful witch of all the witches. All magic is centralized within me. But I'm not queen of the witches or even their leader. I'm more of a the-buck-stops-here figurehead. I was born the Magica, but it isn't hereditary. The power of the Magica can settle upon any unborn witch child. But," here Maggie paused, "this baby has also received the power of the Magica, making her even more powerful than I am. She is the Arch-Magica." She left out the part about how within the witch community her baby had become controversial.

"Wow."

Maggie laughed. "That's all you've got to say is 'wow'?"

"Well," Benson grinned, "I know how to pick'em. Beautiful, cool, and a superstar."

Maggie couldn't believe this man. Nothing fazed him. "You're too much."

"You haven't seen anything yet." He took her hand and held it. "Last question, I promise. What's that building out back?"

"A school," Maggie said. "Since there's no witch government, every witch is trained in the responsibility of her powers. A witch without training is dangerous. But I don't teach children. I like teaching adults. I especially love teaching older women who discover they have a talent for garden magic or science magic. Yes, that's a thing. It's like they get a new lease on life."

It was a good time to end the lesson. "I've droned on and on while your breakfast's grown cold."

He looked into her eyes, causing her to become unaccustomedly bashful and avert her face. "Have you ever met someone and just wanted to know everything about them?" Benson asked. "This is like that. I believe that it happens because we need it to happen. I want to know about you."

"Thank you for being so understanding and supportive." Maggie stopped speaking. Someone was coming.

"Good morning," Heather whispered.

Maggie smiled at the girl, wanting to put her at ease. But the moment Heather showed up at her door last night, life had stopped being easy. The hard stuff was just beginning. And Maggie needed to start by having some questions answered.

CHAPTER 10

The young woman stood at the entrance to the kitchen, too timid to advance any further. Her hair was wet, and the oversized sweatshirt and pants made her look childlike. Minerva appeared behind her like a shadowy sentinel.

"Do you take coffee?" Maggie asked. The girl asked for it black, and Minerva poured her a mug. She also set a cold cinnamon roll in front of Heather, who took a chair at the far end of the banquette. Minerva pulled out a seat at the counter.

"We have a lot to talk about, Heather." Maggie tried to sound motherly but stern. "I know you're frightened. We got our own surprise this morning, but we need to know who you are and where you come from."

The girl wrapped her hands around the hot mug as if comforting herself. "You know then. You found out." She cast her eyes to the table and drew her shoulders together. "I know they do bad things. They have certain beliefs, but I don't believe in what they believe in." She spoke forcefully, trying to emphasize her position. "I didn't have anything to do with them burning down that library or killing the librarian. They made me watch."

"Someone was killed?" Benson exclaimed.

Minerva stood. "What are you talking about?"

Maggie was confused and she held up her hands to stop everyone from chattering. "Hold on, everyone. Heather?"

The girl sniffled. "The library—" The confused look on Maggie's face caused Heather to falter. "You d-don't know?"

Maggie reached for her phone, but it wasn't on the table. She struggled to stand, but Benson stopped her. "I need my phone. It's in my raincoat." He got up and retrieved it himself.

Benson came back and handed it to her. She pressed the power button. As the phone came on, it buzzed like angry hornets. Dozens of phone calls were queued, along with a string of text messages. She read the texts first: *Check your voicemail. Something horrible has happened.*

The first caller was one of her former teachers. As Maggie listened to her description of events, the colors of the world drained away until she had to shut her eyes against the black image.

The next call came from her sister-in-law Sylvie Mills, letting Maggie know the Sisters of Minerva would be there by the afternoon. There were more calls, but Maggie had heard enough. She returned to her teacher's message. "You need to listen to this." She handed the phone to Benson.

He winced.

"I want to listen." Minerva took the phone after Benson finished. Her hands shook as she handed the phone back to her mother.

Benson cast a hard look at Heather. "You were there? And you didn't tell us all this last night. These are heinous crimes, arson and murder, and you had information the police could use. You're an accessory."

"You would've kicked me out," Heather wailed. "I didn't do anything. It wasn't me." Heather's cup slipped from her hands. Coffee sloshed across the table. "I had nowhere to go, and the Magica is duty-bound to protect me." Heather crossed her arms on the table and buried her head in the space between her elbows. "I don't want my mother to go to jail."

Maggie's heart sank hearing the girl confess to witnessing the murder of Maggie's dear friend. "Heather, my family is now in serious danger."

"I'm s-s-sorry. It wasn't me. I didn't mean to cause t-trouble." The girl was so distraught her teeth chattered. "I had nowhere to go. She's my mother even if—" Heather couldn't finish her sentence. "I was taught the Magica was duty-bound to all witches. She had to take me."

"No, Mom. She's got to leave. Benson can take her to the police station," Minerva said.

She was right. After Maggie failed to protect Richard and Michael, she had to prioritize her family's safety. The note said they were coming for her, the girl, and the book, but she needed more information from the girl.

"I want the book," Maggie said.

Heather didn't offer up a lie. "It's in my backpack."

Minerva headed for the guest room. "I'll get it."

"It's my stuff," Heather growled.

Minerva paused in the hallway and looked back.

The girl's hostile tone surprised Maggie. Up to then, Heather exhibited a meek persona, a young woman coping with an abusive family. What leaped out of the girl was animalistic and defensive.

"No, Heather. Minerva will get it."

"I'm sorry, Magica."

Minerva returned with the backpack.

"If it's okay, can I open it?" Benson asked. Maggie looked at Heather who shrugged. Minerva was all too happy to hand over the grimy bag.

He still had the gloves in his back pocket which he put on once again. Benson unzipped the bag and pulled out an oversized book. Across the cover, the title stamped in gold leaf read *LIBRUM HECATE*.

"Oh no," Minerva said.

Maggie agreed. This was no ordinary book but one of the most sacred of all witch texts. And whatever the Abecedarians wanted with it could only mean trouble for almost every lineage witch alive.

Maggie knew then that handing Heather over to police wasn't going to help them. They were all being dragged into something vicious and evil. Something only the Magica could handle.

Chapter 11

"This book barely fits in this backpack," Benson said. "How did you schlep it through the woods in that hellish storm we had last night?" Heather answered with a shrug. "So what is this?"

Minerva glared at her mother which didn't deter Maggie from explaining. "*The Librum Hecate* is *The Book of Hecate*. It's a sacred text that contains the names and lineage of every full-blooded witch for the last thousand years."

Benson's eyes grew wide. "Like a phone book of witches. That puts all of you at risk of what, being hunted down?"

Maggie nodded. She couldn't believe what was happening. Last night, she thought the whole ordeal with Heather would resolve itself in the light of day, and either the girl went back to the Abecedarians, or Benson would find a woman's shelter for her. Instead, everything had become complicated and dangerous. "Heather, I need to know your full name as well as your mother's name," Maggie said.

Heather shook her head. "I can't. They'll find me and hurt me."

Maggie bristled, her patience wearing to a nub. Just breathe, Maggie. Remember sugar and flies. Speaking to the girl with concern and understanding would win her over. "Look, we can't help you unless we know what's going on."

"I only want your protection, Magica," Heather said.

"Stop, I'm Maggie right now. The Magica is not here."

Heather looked at her confused. "I don't understand."

"Never mind. I need to know who we're dealing with. Please, Heather."

"No," Heather exclaimed. "They'll find me. They'll take me back. I can't go back there." She paused. "Not after what I've seen."

"I'm going to have to insist that you tell us what's going on." The girl's obstinance was forcing Maggie to take a firmer approach. "If you don't, you can't stay here. I won't put my family in danger."

Heather's eyes grew wide. She must have realized Maggie was serious because she started talking. "I don't want to get my mother in trouble. I'll tell you other things but not about my mom."

"Okay, that's a start," Maggie said.

Heather stared into her coffee for so long Maggie thought she wasn't going to speak at all, but the girl cleared her throat and started. "Our leader believes the time is right to bring about a big change, kind of like the rapture. Or at least a reckoning. He wants to start by exposing the witches. The burning of the magic books was first."

"And you were there?" Benson said.

Heather wrapped her arms around her middle. "Yes." Her voice was laced with fear and shame. Tears fell on her arms. Maggie handed her a tissue. "I saw all of it. They poured gasoline on everything. They tied up the librarian in her chair and piled logs around her. The leader told me to get that book." She pointed to the *Librum Hecate* on the table. "It's the only one he wanted. And then—" Heather shuddered, goosebumps prickling her skin. "—they set the librarian on fire. They burned her."

"Like they did in the old days," Minerva said. "Burn the witches." Maggie frowned at her daughter. Minerva sat on the other side of the room, as far as she could get from Heather and still be in the same space. Maggie would have to ask Minerva later what emotions she was picking up from the young woman.

"Why this book?" Maggie asked.

Heather wiped tears off her cheeks. "He wants to release the names of all the lineage witches, so people go after them."

Bringing the book to Maggie was both a good decision and a bad one. She had the book in her possession, and they didn't, which meant they would be coming after it. "I have to ask, who's leading the Abecedarians these days?" Heather's shoulders sank, and she tucked her chin into her chest. "You've got to give me something."

Heather fidgeted with the wad of tissues. She shook her head.

Maggie touched Heather's arm. "If you want us to protect you, we need as much information as we can get. Okay?"

Heather swallowed, closed her eyes, and whispered the name: "Noah Corwin."

This was the suspicion she couldn't entertain last night, but Heather confirmed what she feared. After that confrontation four years ago, Noah Corwin was believed to be dead because Maggie had been there when it happened. "Give us a minute. Benson, Minerva, could you come with me please." Maggie led them to the living room.

"Mom," Minerva started.

Maggie held up her hand. She needed to speak first. "Noah Corwin is a delusional psychotic. He thinks he's a prophet, not the Messiah himself, but pretty close. He's ruthless. He kills anyone who gets in his way. We thought we had taken care of him some years back." Maggie didn't go into detail about what happened, maybe later. "If he gets his hands on Heather, he'll kill her. We have no choice but to protect her."

Minerva didn't hold back her protest. "Mom, that girl is a danger to all of us. Get rid of her. Send her to one of the Sisterhoods who takes care of these kinds of things."

Maggie understood the concern and fear of her eldest. "I know. Min, I need to ask you, what are you feeling from her?"

"Nothing."

Maggie gave her daughter a confused look. "What do you mean?"

"Nothing is emanating from her, not fear or sadness, nothing. Completely blocked," Minerva said. "She's hiding something."

Benson cleared his throat. "I know I'm new to this and an outsider, but could that be a way of hiding herself from this cult?"

"That's very plausible," Maggie said.

"I could take Heather someplace safe, and you could let the police handle this."

Maggie saw the concern in his eyes. More than concern, it had been less than twenty-four hours since they had met, but the connection between the two of them was real. Still, she had to do what she knew was right. "Thank you, Benson. But it's not going to stop what's in motion."

"Just let him do this," Minerva said.

"You know I have to try, but I also feel the police should be involved as well. Can that be concession enough for now?" Maggie said.

"Okay." Benson smiled in relief.

"You just don't get it, Mom." Minerva walked away.

"Min."

She stopped at the foot of the stairs. "I can't be around her."

"You said you didn't feel anything from her."

"That's the problem." Minerva went up to her room.

Maggie wondered what Minerva meant. She would ask her later. Right then she had Heather to contend with. Maggie and Benson returned to the kitchen. "Heather, I will help you, but you are obligated to help me as well. No more secrets. I need to know everything, which means your mother's name too. Promise?"

Heather nodded.

Samuel, Becca, Betsy, and Luka streamed into the kitchen, interrupting the conversation. "It's done, Mom," Samuel said. "Everything's documented. All the pyre pieces are at the road behind some trees. Benson said he might need it for evidence."

"Thank you, Samuel."

Becca & Betsy flanked Maggie, each linking an arm into their mother's. "What's wrong?"

"Children, we know a lot more about what's going on. It's not good. It's dangerous. But we won't be alone." She withheld the information about the library and Lavinia. "Your aunties will be here this afternoon. Right now I need your help opening the school and getting the rooms ready for all our guests. We'll need groceries. A schedule. Can we do this?" The children rallied around their mother. Benson stood just outside the circle and watched.

Maggie's phone buzzed with an incoming text. "Well, seems like we're going to have two more guests. The Mothers of Hecate will be arriving too."

"What?" Heather exclaimed. "No one said anything about Coven members being here. No police and no Coven members."

Again, Heather's tone surprised Maggie. The girl wasn't going to make any of this easy. Maggie wondered if she was making a terrible mistake not listening to Benson and Minerva.

CHAPTER 12

By noon, seven rooms in the living quarters of the witch school were prepped. They pulled down cobwebs and wiped dust away. Beds were made up with clean sheets and comforters. The men took the trash to the dumpster, Luka in their wake lugging a bag too large for him. Benson offered to stay even though Maggie felt the imposition too great, but he insisted. Now watching the children interact with him, she was glad he was there. It did the children good. It did her good too.

She stood in the school's hallway and remembered what it felt like to teach. Small schools like hers were common in the community. Witch mothers either home-schooled their youngest or sent them to special day schools, or even to boarding schools, all in preparation for the magical life in the unmagical world. Even the sons of witches attended specialty classes because Magic was a family affair. Everyone needed to understand the workings of Magic and how to deal with it. Once they reached the age of ten, they attended public or private schools.

Maggie had homeschooled all her children in their early years. Samuel, Becca & Betsy insisted on attending middle and high school. After Michael was born, Luka, claiming he was no longer the family's baby, rebelled and demanded to be placed in a "normal" school and be a "normal" kid.

Only Minerva had been homeschooled up through high school, which she chose to do. College was her first long foray into the unmagical world. Even then, she chose to attend Maggie's alma mater Vassar, allowing Minerva to live at home since the college was less than twenty miles away. Maggie now thought it all a mistake. Minerva never felt comfortable in the world of humans, and when she chose a boyfriend who had no connections to the

Witch World, Maggie worried. When witches partnered for life, they either paired with another witch or a male from a family of witches. Though a lovely young man, Minerva's choice perplexed Maggie.

"Mom, they're here," Luka yelled interrupting Maggie's reverie. "They're here." Maggie hadn't seen Luka this excited for a long time. Maybe she had kept the kids too isolated from their witch families. She gathered the children to her. "I know you're excited, but remember we suffered a tragedy last night. Your Aunt Sylvie was close to Lavinia. Okay?" Becca & Betsy completely understood.

Three women came up the path from the back of the house to the school.

"Aunt Sylvie!" Not realizing he had grown considerably since he'd last seen her, Luka launched himself into Sylvie's arms. Sylvie Mills caught her nephew easily, smothering his face with kisses.

Maggie shook her head. So much for containing his excitement, but she couldn't fault Luka. It had been a long time.

Behind Sylvie stood the other members of the Sisters of Minerva, June Nguyen and Shondra Denny. They had all been friends since college. After discovering their magics complemented one another's, they formed their own Sisterhood, taking the goddess Minerva as their symbol. It was no coincidence Minerva bore the same name.

The embrace between Sylvie and Maggie felt as awkward as it looked. "Wow, you've gotten round since I last saw you." Maggie couldn't tell if her sister--in-law's words were sincere or accusatory. Five months had passed since Sylvie last visited. She had tough words for Maggie then about grief, the spectral visitations of a dead husband, and the conceiving of a new Magica. The two hadn't really spoken since that day, other than out of family necessity.

"I'm sorry about Lavinia," Maggie whispered. Sylvie winced.

"Look at you!" Shondra hugged her friend. "You aren't the easiest to hug."

"You look radiant, Maggie," June said.

"I want to know what's in the box," Luka said pointing to the one Shondra held. Everyone laughed at his childlike honesty.

"Let's go inside the school, and I'll show you," Shondra said.

The others were inside finishing the last of the tasks. When they saw the Sisters, they dropped everything and rushed to hug the women. They considered Shondra and June to be aunts as much as Sylvie, since Sylvie was married to June's sister Lucy. Blood didn't make family. Sometimes shared genetics could even create the worst of enemies.

Shondra placed the box on a table. "Presents."

Luka dived in, pulling out item after item.

"Presents for everyone, Luka," Shondra playfully admonished. "Sorry, there wasn't time to wrap them."

As the kids went through the box, the women stood back to watch and talk. Heather came downstairs. The children quieted and drifted away with their gifts. Minerva took a chair and crossed her arms.

Maggie went to Heather and put an arm around the girl's shoulders. "Sisters, this is Heather. Heather, I would like you to meet Sylvie, June, and Shondra. They're here to help us." Heather mumbled hello and thank you. She then excused herself and hurried back upstairs to her new room. Minerva had suggested she be put in the school, away from the house.

"We need to have a private place to talk," Sylvie said.

As they exited the school, Benson appeared, drill in hand, and Maggie introduced him. June and Shondra gave him suspicious eyes but shook hands out of politeness. Sylvie, however, ignored Benson's outstretched hand. "I'll see you in the house, Maggie." June and Shondra didn't know whether to stay or follow, eventually trailing after their friend.

"Well, that wasn't warm," Benson said.

"I'll have a lot to answer for."

Benson returned the drill to a maintenance closet in the school. "You know, Maggie, now that your troops are here, I should go. You'll be okay?"

While she wanted his company, further angering Sylvie didn't seem wise. "I can't thank you enough for staying and helping. Are you sure you're okay with everything going on here?"

"Oddly enough, I am. I don't know why. I should've been shocked and running away, but here I am," he said. "And don't worry. I understand the need for secrecy."

She thanked him for his consideration. The idea of Benson telling anyone never even crossed her mind. That's how much she instinctively trusted him.

"Well, I should get going." He hugged Maggie, holding her to him for a little longer than expected. And she had to admit, it felt good.

Out of the corner of her eye, she caught movement. When she glanced over, Richard stood near the boarding school, watching her. He turned and disappeared into the forest. Maggie felt her heart pulled in that direction.

"Something wrong? You look surprised."

She composed herself. "No nothing. I— I'm just tired." The baby kicked, and Maggie rested her hands on her belly. "Oh, she doesn't want you to go. He'll be back," she said to her daughter. She looked up at Benson. "You'll be back, right?"

"If you want me to."

"I do. I mean," she laughed, "we want you to come back and visit us."

Benson grinned at her and then yelled goodbye to the kids. The deep rumble of his car let everyone know he was leaving.

Maggie wanted to head into the woods after Richard, but that would have to wait. Minerva came out of the school right then. "We're meeting in my office," she said to her daughter. Maggie knew Minerva wanted nothing to do with Heather, but her eldest wasn't a child. She was an adult woman and a witch who needed to participate when matters like this arose. That was another worrisome aspect of Minerva's life. She'd never formed her own Sisterhood, having few friends, witches or nonmagicals. Maggie considered bringing her into the Sisters of Minerva, at least until her daughter found her own, and she made a mental note to bring it up with her friends.

～

June and Shondra were settled on the couch, while Sylvie chose one of the two armchairs. Maggie went to her chair behind her desk, feeling conspicuous, as if the position declared her the leader. Minerva chose the window seat, placing herself behind all the women. Maggie noted the tense lines around Sylvie's mouth.

"What's going on?" Sylvie said. Maggie was right. Sylvie's anger ran deep and hard like a mineral vein through granite.

"Last night Heather showed up—"

"Not the girl," Sylvie interrupted. "The man." She spit the word out as if it were a bug crawling around in her mouth.

"Benson is a friend who came to dinner and was here when Heather showed up. Because of the weather, he couldn't drive home."

"And he knows about us?"

Maggie understood Sylvie's concerns, but the intensity of her anger suggested something deeper. "What's wrong?"

"What's wrong?" Her sister-in-law slid forward, sitting on the edge of the armchair, her hands on her knees. "You're asking me? Well, for starters, you've got a strange man here while you're pregnant with my deceased brother's child which you conceived by conjuring him into this world with your grief. And you've got a run-away staying here who was a member of that group that burned our library down and murdered Lavinia. Lavinia!"

Sylvie and Lavinia dated for nearly two years, many believed they would marry. There was nothing in her sister-in-law's argument that Maggie could dispute. "I'm sorry about Lavinia. But I'm not sorry about this baby. As for my grief, my husband and child were murdered. And though they were your brother and nephew, for me their loss felt as if a chunk of me had been hacked off. I hope you never suffer that kind of pain. If you don't want to be here, I can understand. The Mothers can get someone else to help."

When Maggie stopped talking, no one said a word. Shondra sniffled, obviously bothered by the tension between Maggie and Sylvie. June focused on looking at a painting. Maggie and Sylvie eyed one another like gunslingers.

"You trust this man? And what about this girl?" Sylvie said first.

Everyone in the room exhaled as the crisis between the two women passed. Maggie knew they could all go forward with what needed to be done. She just needed to allow Sylvie the space to express herself, which was usually gruffly. Her sister-in-law spoke her mind, no matter how ineloquently, and wouldn't bring up the issue again.

"The man, yes. As for the young woman, I'm duty-bound to see what I can do for her," Maggie said. "She exhibits all the characteristics of someone suffering abuse. When you speak with her, you'll see that she's clearly frightened. She witnessed Lavinia's death."

Sylvie looked shocked. "Damn."

"But that's not everything," Maggie said, overlooking Sylvie's profanity. Maggie held up the plastic bag with the note, reading it aloud for everyone.

"What book?" Shondra asked.

"*The Librum Hecate*. I have it locked in my safe."

June whistled. "The plot thickens."

Shondra's left eyebrow arched upwards as she bit her lower lip. She was never one to shy away from visible signs of her emotions, which also made her the most honest member of the Sisters of Minerva. "Why that particular book and not one of the others that actually holds magic in its pages?"

Maggie told her friends everything Heather had revealed.

"Mother f—" Sylvie caught herself before the word erupted from her mouth. "Sorry."

Maggie hated profanity as most of it was either misogynistic or sexist in origin. Damn, hell, and a few Shakespearean expletives were the only curses that came from Maggie's mouth. Words possessed power and were not to be wielded lightly.

"So we need to prepare for a confrontation," Sylvie stated. "Any ideas about when this is going to happen?"

A soft knock interrupted their conversation. Becca poked her head in. "Mom, the Mothers of Hecate are here." Becca pushed the door wide, and the older women entered the room. As Becca closed the door, Maggie saw the awe in her daughter's face. Becca wanted to start her adult witch training so she could participate in important witch business, but Maggie wanted her daughter to wait at least another year.

The armchairs were offered to the elder witches. The two Mothers were distinct contrasts. Esme Pineda dressed in her preferred uniform of neon pantsuits; her gray hair piled upon her head in a confection of billowy white cloud curls. Before she took a seat, she placed a bag of Amaranth on Maggie's desk. "For the Magica, an offering from the witches of Guatemala," Mother Esme said.

The second Mother, Dr. Nina Simone Bearstone Williams, towered a good foot above her co-hort. Dr. Williams was also a decade younger. Her clothing style leaned to the conventional and professional—slacks, silk blouses, and jackets. Jewelry had become her signature: chunky necklaces and drop earrings of natural materials. Dr. Williams placed a basket woven from brown ash and sweetgrass beside the bag of seed. "For the Magica, from the witches of the Wabanaki people. Maggie, neither of us expected to be here for another couple of weeks." She was Maggie's obstetrician, while Mother Esme served as midwife. When Maggie was younger, she had relied only on the services of a midwife, but since her pregnancy was considered geriatric, Dr. Williams had been included. The term geriatric seemed ridiculous. Maggie felt young and healthy at forty-four.

Maggie thanked and hugged the two women. "I'm sorry we all must be here under these circumstances. Mothers, as I was telling my Sisters, Heather is not responsible for the burning of the Witches Library or the death of Lavinia. She was a child when her mother joined the Abecedarians. Heather came to me for help and wants to free herself of them."

Mother Esme held her hand up to pause Maggie. "Who is her mother? That might give us a better understanding of what we're up against."

"Heather refuses to give us that information. She doesn't want her hurt in all of this."

Shondra broke in, "But her mother is involved. Heather said she was there during the fire and murder."

"That doesn't mean that her mother wasn't coerced in participating," Maggie said.

"You know how men can be," Sylvie sneered.

Maggie was taken aback. She'd never seen her sister-in-law so antagonistic toward men.

Dr. Williams spoke up, "Maggie, I know you're feeling protective, but we need to talk to this girl."

Maggie did feel protective. As a child raised in a cult, Heather bore no responsibility for her mother's actions or the cult's. Heather was trying to do the right thing, seek assistance from the only person she knew could help her. But Mother wasn't wrong. They needed more from Heather.

"Minerva, could you please get her?"

Begrudgingly, Minerva did as her mother asked.

"What's up with Min?" June asked.

"She's going through something," Maggie explained. "I don't know what. She's not happy about my new friend. And she definitely doesn't want

Heather here. When we get the opportunity, I would like to discuss bringing Min into the Sisters of Minerva, just for a little while. She's smart and personable, but I don't know why she never found her own in college." The women agreed to discuss the matter later.

"Ladies, we should hold a vigil for Lavinia tonight," Mother Esme said, and everyone agreed.

Minerva appeared with Heather in tow but returned to the window seat, leaving Heather stranded in the doorway. The girl looked surprised by how many women occupied the room. Maggie motioned for her to come inside. Sylvie vacated her chair for Heather, not out of altruism, but because standing, Sylvie was intimidating. The girl's fear left her pale and shivering.

The Mothers introduced themselves. "We're not here to harm you," Mother Esme said. "We need to know what is going on and who your mother is."

"I don't want my mom to get hurt." Each word was an effort for the girl to speak. Maggie wondered if maybe she had been spelled.

"It's okay, Heather," Maggie said. "You can trust me. That's why you came here." The girl's head was tucked so deep between her shoulders it looked like she was turning herself inside out. Was the room full of women intimidating her, or was it something else?

"Heather, I don't mean to frighten you," Dr. Williams said. "We could compel you to tell us, but it would be best if you gave the information willingly."

Heather sat up straight, a shadow passed over her face, the same darkness Maggie witnessed earlier. Heather's eyes narrowed as if declaring no one would be compelling her. "That won't be necessary." Her previous meekness now replaced by a slap of truth. "My mother is Esther Goode."

The room full of women sat in stunned silence, getting much more than they bargained for.

"Your mother had been pregnant with the next Magica," Maggie said. "There hasn't been another one conceived since that happened a decade or so ago. Until now." She placed her hand over her belly.

"That baby was stillborn," Mother Esme said. "I was there. The entire witch community had been shocked that a Magica could die in utero.

"Esther's husband died a month before the baby did. That would be your father, Heather. Losing her husband and daughter broke Esther, and she renounced the Coven. I was also a member of the tribunal that accepted her separation. That was the last the Magic world heard of her."

"What was her reason for separating?" June asked.

Mother Esme pursed her lips and shook her head. "She said she hated magic, it had failed her, and she wanted nothing more to do with it."

"Is she out for revenge?" June asked. They all looked at Heather.

"I don't know anything. I'm not part of their planning meetings."

"No one's heard of her for over a decade," June said.

"We all thought Noah Corwin dead until today," Maggie said.

"I don't get it," Sylvie said. "The Abecedarians abhor technology and witches, and you're telling us Corwin welcomed a witch into the cult?"

Everyone in the room looked at one another, but no one had an answer. Heather offered no explanation.

Shondra softened the tension. "Your father was my father's cousin. This means we're cousins, Heather."

"What?" the girl said, looking confused and suspicious.

Maggie found Heather's reaction off. Anyone else would have been happy to learn she had family. Shondra went to console her, but Heather went stiff, refusing her newly discovered cousin's support.

"I want to go back to my room. If that's okay?"

"I'll help her back." Shondra offered, unwilling to be put off by Heather's rebuff.

The group waited for the door to close. "So what about the book?" June asked.

Maggie stood, needing to work out the coils of pain pulsing up her spine. "I believe their plan is to target the witches listed in the book, maybe even go public with that information."

"Why now?" June said.

Minerva spoke up. "The social climate is ripe for a little witch burning."

They all turned to Minerva. "Yeah," said June. "A whole segment of the population believes that the other side is in league with the devil. Proving the existence of witches would vindicate their position."

"That's not true. We don't have anything to do with the devil or evil," Mother Esme said.

"Truth is irrelevant. They don't care," Minerva said. "We're not dealing with truth or logic here. People will believe in anything that supports their world view."

"Minerva," Maggie said, "that's so pessimistic."

Minerva shrugged and resumed looking out the window.

Sylvie shook her head. "She's not wrong, Maggie. First, Corwin steals the *Librum* planning on releasing all our names, and then the masses go witch hunting. Think about the bounty laws that have been placed on women. Or the vigilante groups attacking segments of the population. And you gotta understand, witch hunting and killings still occur across this planet."

The women simultaneously expressed their horror of such a thing getting started here.

Dr. Williams stood, holding her hands up like a referee separating two sides. "Focus on the matter at hand. The note said they'll be coming for Heather and the book. We can only assume the *you* refers to the Magica. This means we need to be prepared."

Sylvie leaned forward. "Well, Maggie, what's the plan?"

Her plan had been to resolve the matter with Heather and then transition her to a situation where she would be safe. But each new revelation dragged them all deeper into a quagmire of— Well, she didn't know of what. And Maggie realized there lay the real problem.

What was really going on?

CHAPTER 13

The meeting resulted in a plan that upset Minerva so much she had to go to her room to calm down. She couldn't believe the nerve of her mother volunteering her to go with June on an exploration mission to the Abecedarian compound, the location the Mothers finally coaxed out of Heather. Sure, her Mom was in no condition to go herself, but Minerva wasn't a daredevil. She preferred to stay home, even though they all promised she would be safe. They were going to have a look only, not engage. Minerva offered her own suggestions again: Throw Heather out or turn her over to Benson. All her ideas had been discounted by the group of women. Right now, Minerva needed to be alone, away from everyone, and just spend time mulling over the whole situation.

Benson. There was another problem she didn't want to deal with. What was her mother even thinking letting some strange man into their home? If dad was still around, this wouldn't be happening. But even that had created problems. Minerva didn't want to think about that either. There were a lot of things she didn't want to deal with right then.

Two sets of raps at her door interrupted her thoughts. What could the Olsen Twins want? She opened the door to two beaming faces. "What?"

"Your boyfriend is here," they sing-songed. "Samuel just buzzed the gate for him."

Great. And there was one more thing she didn't want to deal with. Carey should have called before showing up. She grabbed her phone and realized he'd sent dozens of texts and placed six phone calls. She skirted her sisters and flew down the stairs. She pulled open the front door to find Carey about to push the doorbell. No wonder her teen sisters were giddy. Carey

Marshall Adams was Prince Charming, everything a girl could want. Tall, rich, and handsome. He was both chivalrous and a feminist, seeing no contradiction in the two. Her sisters called him swoon-worthy. They met at a college football game when she was an undergrad. He was in law school, planning on continuing in the family firm where he had worked since turning sixteen. The first time he asked her on a date she said no, intimidated by his looks and pedigree. On the third ask, she consented.

After two dates, Minerva floated through that first November on a cloud of love and happiness, not realizing her friends didn't ask her to study dates or parties anymore, while other undergrads whispered behind cupped hands. Minerva found herself isolated. She had no idea that Carey was in a long-term relationship with his high school girlfriend, a debutant from a family equal to Carey's in terms of money and prestige, their courtship leading to marriage a given. Once Min realized the drama surrounding her, it was too late. She felt stranded on the island that was Carey. At least she loved him. But their bond was also the reason she had no friends. It didn't matter that Carey broke off his previous relationship before asking her out. As far as everyone was concerned, Minerva was a home wrecker.

She stepped out onto the porch, forcing her boyfriend to take several steps back.

"Min, why haven't you answered a single text or call? I've been worried sick about you. We were going to make big plans for this weekend. What happened? Did you at least listen to my voicemail?"

She looked over her shoulder before closing the door. "Carey, I'm so sorry. It's family stuff. You didn't need to drive up from the city. I would have called." She led him to a bench away from the front windows and any curious eyes. She wasn't about to let him meet all those strange women. What would he think? A short Guatemalan woman, a very tall Native American, a Vietnamese woman, a Black woman, and her angry lesbian aunt. And then there was her pregnant mother whose husband had been dead two years. And don't forget the fugitive residing in the boarding school. Minerva just didn't want to explain any of what was going on.

Carey's family descended from old New England stock, and while her family had inhabited the same geographical stretch of place for just as long, maybe longer, his ancestors and hers existed on opposite ends of the social spectrum. After two years of dating, she hadn't told her boyfriend she was a witch.

He reached out to hug her, and she pulled back. "What's going on?"

"My family."

"Seriously? You're worried about your family seeing us hug. We're adults, not teenagers."

He was right. "I'm sorry."

Carey pulled her to him and kissed her forehead. "How's that for chaste?"

"Stop it." He had made her laugh. For a few minutes the unease she felt since Heather's arrival melted away. She remained pressed against his chest. With her arms around his waist, she felt the outline of a box, one holding a large engagement ring, the diamond putting off an intense heat. Several weeks earlier, her witch's intuition had alerted her to the imminent proposal, the reason for the big weekend plans. She hoped he wasn't bringing the proposal here. Her anxiety returned like a sledgehammer. The last thing she wanted or needed was for Carey to propose. She pushed away from him.

"I'm sorry. There's a lot of family here and we're kind of in crisis mode. We have a lot of stuff to do."

"Good. I want to do family stuff with you."

The look on Minerva's face stopped him.

"Stupid me," he said. "You don't want me to do family stuff with you. You never do."

She wasn't ready to tell him about her family. Just like she wasn't ready for him to propose. "It's not that, Carey. It's complicated right now. Some bad stuff is happening."

"It's always complicated, Minerva."

Laughter filtered out onto the porch from inside.

"Doesn't sound like trouble. Two years and I've met your family twice. Are you embarrassed by me? Have I done something wrong?"

"No, it's not you. You're perfect," Minerva said.

He waited for her to continue with some explanation. When she didn't, he stood. "Since you don't want me here, I'm going. Call when you think you want me to be a part of your family."

"Carey." She didn't chase after him. He slid into his Porsche. Before shutting the door, he looked at her, waiting for her to change her mind and go after him. Min walked to the front door. As she closed it behind her, she heard his tires squeal on the asphalt.

Minerva leaned against the doorframe and cried. Samuel came out from the kitchen, flour dusting his hands. "Where's Carey?"

Sylvie appeared behind him, took one look at Minerva, and redirected Samuel back to the kitchen. "Sir, your biscuits are waiting for you. I got this." Once he was gone, her aunt held her arms open, and Minerva rushed into them. "Tell your aunty all about it."

"Oh, I'm so awful. I don't know how to tell Carey about being a witch. Mom didn't seem to have any problem spilling everything to a man she just met. A total stranger. How did she make that decision to trust Benson? And now that he knows everything, including this crisis, he probably won't come back." Sylvie guided her niece to the empty living room.

"I know. It's hard to figure out who's safe." Sylvie offered Minerva a tissue box.

"Carey and I have been together for two years, and he's perfect. They call him Prince Charming. He even gave up a princess to be with me." Minerva blew her nose. "He's going to ask me to marry him. That's why he wanted to make weekend plans. He had the ring with him just now, but how can I think about any of that with all this going on." Minerva waved her hands toward the back of the house. "How do I explain all of this?"

"What do you think keeps you from telling him?"

Minerva curled into the corner of the sofa and laid her head on the armrest. She wiped tears off her cheeks. "You never know what the nonmagicals are going to do. Look, someone built a pyre at the end of our driveway."

"Yes, but the Abecedarians aren't like regular nons. They're radical," Sylvie said.

"It doesn't take much to turn level-headed people into crazies," Minerva said. She just wanted to close her eyes and sleep.

"So that's it? You're just afraid of the burn-the-witches reaction? I know I talked about Burning Times being just around the corner, but we can't live fearing that. We have to trust the ones we love, even if it's scary. So that's it then? No other reason for not telling him?"

Minerva sniffled. She thought about it for a minute. "No, it's more personal. Dad died because of all this, his connection to magic. What if I tell Carey and then something bad happens to him?"

Sylvie took Min's hand and massaged each finger. "Men married to witches don't die at higher rates than nonmagical men married to nonmagical women. Bad things happen. It was a tragedy, but your father grew up in the Witch World. He was no stranger to the antagonism and persecution."

The women in her father's family were lineage witches as well, her Aunt Sylvie and Granmommie. Her father marrying her mother had been a big deal, and Minerva always detected a tension between her mom and grandmother.

Sylvie chuckled. "Oh, it was a big deal for my mom. Sorry to eavesdrop. Your emotions are so potent right now I can hear some of what you're thinking. Anyway, when my mom found out her son was going to marry the Magica, she wasn't happy. She loves you kids, but she didn't think your mom good enough for her son. You know how snooty your grandmother can be."

Minerva sat up. She didn't know this about her parents and grandparents, and it made her more sympathetic to her mom. She was learning new stuff about her family. "I didn't know you're an empath?" She had never asked her aunt where her talent lay.

"I'm not. Not like you. The situation has to be charged for me to pick up on anything. It's probably what makes me good at security. People committing crimes tend to be in a volatile state. So got any more arguments about why you can't tell your boyfriend you're a witch?"

"What if he rejects me? What if he finds me repugnant?"

"No one could ever find you repugnant. You're smart, talented, beautiful, and my niece. You're Princess Charming."

Minerva laughed. It hurt her ribs.

Sylvie smacked her niece with a pillow. "Don't you go and get all snooty with that comment. Look, Min. You said he has a ring, so he believes you're the one for him. I don't think revealing you're a witch is going to be his deal breaker. Not saying it's going to be perfect, but all relationships have something that needs more understanding, more support, more forgiveness."

When Minerva thought of the perfect marriage, Sylvie and her wife came to mind. They couldn't have problems. Could they? "Do you and Aunt Lucy have issues? You seem so perfect."

Her aunt rolled her eyes and shook her head. "No one's perfect. Every relationship is a test of yourself, not the other person. So, what are you going to do, tell him or not tell him?"

Minerva sat up and wiped her nose. "I don't know. It's not something I can decide right now. We've got bigger issues on our plates." She sighed. "We should be preparing for tonight."

Sylvie stood and offered a hand to Minerva. "Okay, but we'll be circling back to this topic. Let's see if Samuel has dinner ready. I'm dying to try his biscuits. Go get cleaned up."

Minerva saw a glint pass by the living room window. She recognized the silver Corvette. "It's Benson."

"Well, look at that. He came back. I guess we didn't scare him off," Sylvie said, giving Minerva's arm a little squeeze.

Chapter 14

Benson had been surprised when Maggie called asking for his help that very same night. Her ask was direct, without hesitancy or equivocation. He didn't even have the details before he said yes. Her sister-in-law's hostility did give him pause, but Maggie reassured him Sylvie had cooled. Maggie explained she didn't want to wait for the Abecedarians to come for the book or Heather. She had a plan and needed his help.

When Benson arrived for dinner, he headed for Maggie, but two interesting women he didn't know intercepted him at the door, introducing themselves as Mother Esme Pineda and Dr. Mother Nina Simone Blackstone Williams. "Like the singer?"

"One and the same. My mother was a big fan."

Mother Esme explained that Dr. Williams was Maggie's obstetrician and she Maggie's midwife.

"Isn't it too early for the baby?" he asked.

"When we heard about everything—the fire, the murder, the stranger, and then that hideous pyre—we decided we should come now. That's a lot of stress on mother and child. Maggie's due November 19. Plus, she doesn't have any magic right now because of the pregnancy," Dr. Williams said.

"We heard you're a police officer." Each woman had taken an arm and led him into the dining room, where they plunked him into a chair and took the ones on either side of his, sandwiching him in.

"I should go see Maggie," he said.

"Oh, she's busy in the kitchen, dear," Mother Esme said.

Everyone streamed into the dining room and took their seats. The kids greeted him cheerfully. Benson was surprised to see Heather. Maggie entered the room and hugged Benson from behind. He touched her arm, finding her skin warm and silky. She released him and went to her chair. He felt an emptiness when she let go.

"Before we share this meal, let us remember Lavinia Hamon and what she meant to us," Maggie said.

They stood and took hands. Benson didn't know if he should participate, and he looked to Maggie for guidance. She nodded. Mother Esme and Dr. Williams gave his hands a hard squeeze. Maggie started the blessing, passing the next part to the woman beside her, even Becca & Betsy participated. When they finished, they waved their hands lighting all the candles placed around the room. It was beautiful.

Benson thought he would've felt uncomfortable at the display of such intimacy, but he wasn't. It felt good to be amongst this family and this group of special women.

Even though it was a somber moment, the children's energy changed the focus to something livelier. As the food was passed around, the chatter picked up. He could only wave to Maggie across the table. Her children assailed him once again with questions and comments. Maggie formally reintroduced him to Shondra, June, and Sylvie. Shondra was a dentist, and June an attorney. Sylvie's occupation interested him the most. He discovered she was a security specialist, working for the wealthy, and running her own business. He wanted to discuss her career, but Sylvie continued to snub him. A sullen Heather was hunkered down at the far end of the table next to the loquacious Becca & Betsy. With all his time spent with her family, he didn't know if he was dating Maggie or her clan. Dating wasn't the right word at this point. He'd only known her since...yesterday. He couldn't believe it had only been a day. So this was how it was.

At the end of dinner, he was swept up by the group and deposited into the living room to face off against two cats. Benson tried not to trip as the cats weaved about his ankles. "All of you don't see an orange cat and a tabby?" The others in the room shook their heads, holding in their laughter.

Luka giggled out loud, cupping his mouth with both hands as if trying to contain his amusement. "Nope," he said. "I see June and Min."

"Okay, enough teasing of the new guy," Maggie said. "Benson, you aren't seeing cats. You're seeing a projection of cats. Minerva and June are standing in front of you, and they're making you see cats."

The cats continued to circle him, and he tried to reconcile Maggie's explanation with what he was experiencing. "So they didn't actually shape shift into cats?"

"No, that's nearly impossible for most witches," Maggie explained. "Matter doesn't work that way, at least most of the time it doesn't. Sure, maybe our magic could transform a person into an animal, but the energy it would take could harm or even kill a witch. I've heard of it happening, but it's too dangerous. Or that would be one super witch. That's a rare ability. The Magica might be able to do it. Instead, what's easier, and safer, is mind manipulation. They're projecting the idea of a cat onto everyone."

"That's still pretty magical," Benson said.

"Indeed it is." She was impressed that he was quick to catch on.

Benson clapped his hands. "Well, we should get going." Maggie fetched the keys to the Land Rover. "Guess I should think of getting a practical car if I'm going to be spending time here." He gave Maggie a mischievous smirk. She reached up and kissed his cheek. The orange cat howled as if she had been stepped on. "Minerva?" he asked. Luka nodded vigorously.

Benson walked out to the Land Rover, both the orange cat, Minerva, and the tabby, June, trailing behind him. He opened a back door and the cats jumped onto the seats and settled in. "If I hadn't volunteered to drive, who was going to take them?"

"Sylvie or I would have," Shondra said. "But it's best we stay here in case the Abecedarians show up because Maggie has no magic."

He wondered if they might need more than magic against the cult who proved they were willing to kill.

"We've got all kinds of fire power between us, magical and nonmagical." Sylvie pulled back her jacket. She was carrying a gun. "Magic isn't always enough," she said.

He was taken aback when Sylvie answered the question he was thinking. So mind reading was one of her talents?

"Sort of."

He needed to be careful around her and try hard not to think about his deepest, darkest secrets.

She cocked her head at him. "Oh, good one." He'd made Sylvie smirk.

"Be careful, Benson," Maggie said. "I don't have to tell you how dangerous these people are. No unnecessary risks. Okay?"

"We'll be cautious. A quick look and then we'll come back," he promised. He wanted to give her a deep kiss, but everyone was watching. A hug would have to suffice for now. It felt so good to touch her. "I'll take good care of them, especially Minerva. I promise."

As he drove, he reflected on what Maggie had told him. Extracting the location of the Abecedarian compound out of Heather had proven to be difficult, only the threat of being truth-spelled forced Heather to give up the location. In the end she told them about an abandoned resort in the Catskill Mountains. Maggie said that was twice now Heather had given up information only on the threat of being truth-spelled. His conjecture was the girl was hiding something. Maggie, on the other hand, believed Heather's mother had placed a spell on her, and that not wanting to be truth-spelled didn't make Heather guilty of anything. While he respected Maggie's idea, as a police detective he was a little more skeptical.

The drive to the compound would take about two hours. Benson had seen a documentary on the resorts that once riddled the area known as the Borscht Belt, getaways for New Yorkers and surrounds who wanted to swim, dance, and partake of croquet. When airline travel promised exotic locales like Hawaii and Paris, the popularity of the resorts waned. Their doors closed, and buildings, including multi-story luxury hotels, were left to rot, some with chandeliers and furniture in place. Urban explorers, the homeless, and teens made use of the places. The Abecedarians had taken advantage of one of these neglected properties.

The plan was simple. Benson would take Minerva and June to the compound, and they would scope out the situation. In cat form, the two women could move freely. Maggie wanted some idea as to what the ABCs were doing so she could figure out what her next step would be.

Within forty-five minutes of leaving Maggie's house, Benson turned off the highway and onto a road leading further into the mountains. For the entire drive he kept up a steady one-way conversation with the cats sitting behind him. He talked about his fondness for Maggie and how he was intrigued to discover that witches were real, which didn't surprise him at all because as a police officer he'd seen some strange things. He asked the cats if his feelings for Maggie were real, or if she'd put a spell on him. Neither cat answered. Of course, he thought, they wouldn't be talking cats. That would be too much, pushing the boundary of the illusion. Minerva did yowl whenever he said Maggie's name.

Heather advised them to use the service entrance located on a backroad, and he kept a lookout for it. He tried to imagine life as a child growing up in a cult—moving from one derelict place to the next and never attending public school or going to the movies. Benson's childhood had been filled with summer camps and family vacations. Was Heather's childhood just one long indoctrination into the group's radical beliefs? He couldn't imagine living without electricity and modern appliances. The left turn was just ahead. Trees arched over the dirt road and in the dark it looked like a tunnel leading to nowhere. Even if they didn't believe in technology, they had to drive cars. He couldn't see them using horses and wagons to move around up here in the mountains. He should've asked Heather how they were getting around.

A gate appeared on his right. He stopped in front of it and turned off the Land Rover's headlights. A shiny new padlock barred intruders, and a no trespassing sign detailed what would happen to those who dared ignore the locked gate. This was it. He drove past the gate until he found a clearing to park. Keeping tight to the tree line would conceal them, but he also made sure to have the vehicle primed for a quick retreat.

Benson turned off the engine. The sudden silence spooked him. He wasn't the kind of man who wasn't afraid to be scared. Being scared saved lives. He'd seen too many fellow officers charge into situations that required a little more caution. That was one of the purposes of fear; it made you stop and think, or run. He was worried for the two women about to go off on their own. The cult had demonstrated they didn't have qualms about committing murder.

"Well, ladies, are you ready?" He glanced over his shoulder, and for a tenth of a second, he saw Minerva and June in human form. He blinked, and the two cats reappeared. He shrugged it off as an anomaly and exited the vehicle.

Screeching and flapping descended on him. Startled, his head smacked against the door frame. "Damn it. Good jump scare, Universe. That got me."

He looked into the backseat. The cats were sitting on their haunches giving him a look. "I'm going to trust you two aren't going to tell anyone about that. Okay?" June purred while Minerva hissed.

"Well, time to get started." He opened a back door for them. "So you two are going in, snooping around for a bit, listen to what they have to say, and then head straight back here. Good plan?" Both cats blinked. "Let's do this."

Minerva and June leaped to the ground.

He watched as the two cats, tails held high, bounded across the road and into the woods. Now he just had to stay awake. He cracked the window a few inches so he could pay attention to any suspicious sounds. He checked his phone and found only two bars. Maybe he should delete his match. com account. That's presumptuous. What if Maggie doesn't want him like that. Maybe she thought of him as just a friend. He whiled away the time thinking about Maggie and where they might be heading. In his mind, he relived the first time he saw her in the produce section. She glowed, that halo of auburn hair, those green eyes. Her skin enticed him, and he wanted to run his hands across her. He had to admit he had it bad for her.

A small creature scrambled out of the ditch and headed for the vehicle.

Something was wrong. Benson shook off his fantasy and sat up. The shape switched from cat to human. It was June. He scrambled out of the Land Rover. "Where's Minerva? What's wrong?"

"She's hurt."

Damn, he promised Maggie no harm would come to Minerva. "Did you get attacked?"

"There's no one there. Come on. We need to hurry."

They jogged across the road. "Heather lied?"

June shrugged. "I don't know. They set traps though. Minerva's caught in one."

They hauled themselves over the seven-foot barricade. Benson headed for the trees bordering the road trying to stay out of sight. Unseen sentries could be hiding, watching them. He touched his gun in the holster under his jacket. Better always to be safe and cautious was a philosophy he got behind. The rain made the fallen oak leaves soggy, masking their footsteps. A faster runner, June dashed ahead. Dressed in head-to-toe black made seeing her in the dark difficult, but he spotted a moving shape and followed. He kept his senses alert to others who might be hiding nearby.

The woods ended, and a multistory structure appeared, incongruous to the forest landscape. In the dark it gave the impression of some giant monster lying in wait. He crouched at the edge of what would have been a lawn in the past, now just a field of weeds. The hotel had six stories and hundreds of rooms to accommodate all the resort's guests in its heyday, meaning hundreds of cult members could be holed up in there now. How many Abecedarians were there?

Even though June said she hadn't seen anyone, it didn't mean that no one was in there. He waited, watched. He expected the glow of candles or kerosene lamps, but the building was dark. Either the cult members weren't inside like June said, or they were being stealthy. He relied on his gut to tell him no one was home.

"This way." June disappeared around the corner of the building. More structures lay beyond the hotel, but no one appeared to be occupying those either. June waited for him, standing beside a shape lying on the ground. Minerva, no longer a cat, wasn't moving.

A trap like a hungry mouth was clamped shut around her ankle. Benson winced imagining it snapping closed. Fortunately, it wasn't a big bear trap, but instead one used for smaller animals. And it didn't have teeth. Minerva was unconscious. The trap needed to be gingerly opened, and Minerva's leg pulled from it. "I need your help."

June crouched beside him.

"So this is the plan. I'm going to open the trap's jaws by pressing on these levers, which are springs." He pointed out the trap's parts. "You pull her leg free. Ready?" He placed his hands on the levers.

June gave him a thumbs up.

He took a deep breath.

"Wait."

He froze, his hands already applying pressure to the springs.

"You're not going to slip up and crush my hands. Right?"

He hoped not but reassured June she would be safe. "No, I've got this." His biceps stung maintaining the tension on the springs. "Ready?"

She nodded.

Don't think about slipping, Benson. Don't think about the jaws clamping onto June's hands. "Let's go on 3." She nodded. "1, 2, 3, now."

He pressed down on the levers. June reached in and pulled Minerva free. When they had cleared the area, he released the trap with a metallic clang, allowing it to close so no animal would fall victim to it. Benson examined Minerva's ankle. A deep groove braceleted the flesh.

"I can't tell how badly she's hurt," he said.

"What's on her forehead?"

He touched the streak of black. "It's blood. She must have hit her head when she fell."

He would have to carry her. At least she was light, but the seven-foot fence was a problem. The only way to get Minerva on the other side of the gate was to walk the fence line until he found a break. They tramped through the grass, having to pass the Land Rover.

A twig snapped in the woods. He stopped and watched the trees for movement. Minerva started to feel heavy. He continued after June. Bushes behind him rustled. This time he kept walking. He had the impression eyes were on him.

"I found it," June said. The newer fence met up with another fence whose owner wasn't quite as diligent about keeping his side in good shape. There was a gap big enough for them to crawl through. They backtracked to the Land Rover. He laid Minerva on the backseat, and then he and June hopped into the front.

"Benson, I got the feeling something was trying to cut us off."

"I felt it too, like there were eyes on us."

June looked over the seat at Minerva. "I'm going to call and let Dr. Williams know about Min. I don't want her injuries to be a surprise."

Benson started the vehicle. "Good thinking." Something nagged at him. The compound was too empty. Had they been caught off guard? "June, do you think the Abecedarians might have chosen tonight to get Heather and the book back?"

"I'll talk to Sylvie too. Let her know what we found. And see if anything's happened there at the house. It's going to take us almost two hours to get back."

He imagined cult members storming Maggie's house. "We need to get back fast then." He stepped on the gas, dirt and gravel spraying up on either side, the heavy vehicle slow to respond. He reminded himself it wasn't his Corvette.

"Benson, let's get there alive," June said. "They can handle whatever comes their way. Even though Maggie doesn't have any magic right now, she has a lot of magic at her disposal. Sylvie, Shondra, the Mothers. You don't have to be the knight in shining armor. Okay?"

He felt the sting of her comment. She wasn't being reproachful or unkind, but as an officer of the law, riding to the rescue came as second nature for him. Maybe a little masculine pride spiked his mindset as well, but he never saw himself as sexist, working with women officers taught him everyone brought something to the table. That wasn't true for all his male colleagues who saw women as a threat, or worse, diminishing law enforcement. He didn't have those hang-ups and didn't want anyone to think he did.

"Sure. Of course," he said. Still, he wanted to get back to Maggie. A sense of urgency dogged him, making him press down on the gas pedal a little harder as they flew down the mountain. Then June said something that made him drive faster.

"Do you think Heather told her people we were coming out here tonight?"

Chapter 15

"They're back," Samuel yelled as he hurried outside to help.

Dr. Williams waited by the kitchen door, Mother Esme at her side. Benson carried Minerva into the house, and the Mothers instructed him to take her upstairs to her room.

Maggie felt guilt for insisting Minerva go on the mission. Maggie told her it would do her some good, teach her some of the responsibilities that came with being a witch. She had overprotected Minerva for too long, but maybe trial by fire wasn't a good way to get her daughter involved. A twinge of pain stabbed the lower part of Maggie's back, and she grabbed the edge of the counter with both hands waiting for the agony to dissipate. Not now, little one. Minerva needs to be cared for.

June ran from room to room, as if searching for something.

Sylvie watched her sister-in-law. "What are you doing?"

"Samuel, turn on the outside flood lights," June called out. The lights snapped on, and she went from window to window.

All the commotion made Maggie dizzy. The pain in her back felt as if someone were wringing her spine like a dishtowel.

Sylvie followed her. "Talk to me, June."

June returned to the kitchen. "Are all of you safe? Did you detect anyone trying to get in?"

"I told you two hours ago when you called that we were fine," Sylvie said. "That status hasn't changed."

Maggie needed to sit. As she moved away from the sink, her back spasmed, forcing her to her knees.

"Oh, shit." Sylvie caught her, softening the fall. Luka started crying. "Girls, get Mother Esme." Becca & Betsy bounded up the stairs, returning seconds later with help.

Mother Esme took Maggie's wrist and pressed two fingers to the bluish veins. "Benson, bring Maggie into the family room."

"Minerva," Maggie said as Benson guided her onto the couch. Shondra and June hovered over her.

"Don't worry, Maggie. I'll go upstairs and help Dr. Williams," Shondra said.

Chaos filled the house as people rushed upstairs or into the family room.

"Becca & Betsy, please take your little brother to his room. Luka, don't cry. We've got this under control. Go upstairs with your sisters," Sylvie said.

Mother Esme turned to Samuel. "Please fetch my black satchel from my room. You three need to wait over there while I care for my patient."

Sylvie, June, and Benson reluctantly complied with the order and took seats near the fireplace.

"And you, Maggie, are going to lie here quietly. Your blood pressure is high. Benson, get Maggie a glass of water." He shot up, hurried to the kitchen, and quickly returned. Mother Esme took the glass, holding it to Maggie's lips. "Drink this."

Maggie pushed the glass away. "I have to help my daughter." She tried getting up from the couch.

Mother Esme pressed lightly on Maggie's shoulder. "I understand that, dear, but you need to help yourself first and the daughter within you. Drink." Maggie took the glass and surprised herself by drinking it in one gulp. Samuel returned with the bag and after handing it over, joined the adults on the other side of the room. He didn't need to be told. Mother Esme brought out a stethoscope and a blood pressure cuff. "How have you been feeling, Maggie? You've been having pain?"

"I feel helpless in this condition. I have no magic. I'm not a help to anyone."

"The pain?" Mother Esme repeated.

Maggie confessed. "Since yesterday, and now I had a terrible stabbing along my lower back."

Mother Esme palpitated Maggie's belly and sides. She slid her hand under Maggie's back, who flinched.

"Okay, you need to stay off your feet. I would also add reduce your stress, but since that isn't possible you are going to have to run this operation from right here on the couch or your bed."

"There's something wrong with the baby?" She put Minerva in harm's way and now her unborn child as well.

"I think you're in labor," Mother Esme said.

"Couldn't it be Braxton Hicks?"

"You're due in a couple of weeks so I wouldn't be surprised if you're in real labor. What you need to do now is rest."

Maggie protested. "How can I? Minerva's hurt. The Abecedarians are after witches. They've got some notion about getting that book back and exposing all of us. They've vowed to come for Heather. And we don't know when they're going to attempt that."

"We'll help." Becca & Betsy stood at the entrance to the kitchen.

"Girls, you should be in bed," Maggie said. "This is a matter for adults, not children."

Both her daughters kneeled beside her. Mother Esme didn't stop them. Becca took her mother's hand, and Betsy stroked her hair. Maggie felt the baby respond to her sisters. The frantic edge consuming Maggie softened.

"Your daughters are healers," Mother Esme said. "Let them."

"Mom, we're not little children," Becca said.

"And we know we're not grownup," Betsy said.

"But we can help. And let Luka help too," both girls said.

Luka. With so many things going on she had forgotten about her little guy. He was just eight and still needed his mother.

"Luka's fine, Mom," the girls said. "He feels dismissed when you send him to bed."

"Listen to your daughters. They're wise for their ages. Now, I'm going to check on Minerva, and then after that we'll give you a thorough going over. Until then, you stay on this couch, Maggie, and let the girls tend to you. Girls, you let me know if anyone bothers her."

"Yes, ma'am."

On her way out, Mother Esme glared at the group near the fireplace.

Maggie relented.

She did have to consider the baby's welfare. While she desperately wanted to get off that couch and take an active role in helping Minerva, Maggie also knew she carried the responsibility that no harm came to the little Arch-Magica. Maggie settled back into the sofa cushions. Becca brought her a glass of orange juice, and Betsy massaged lemongrass oil onto her swollen ankles.

"I'm going to brew some red raspberry leaf tea," Samuel said and left for the kitchen.

With Mother Esme out of the room, Sylvie felt safe to start the conversation but kept it whisper level. "So what happened out there?" she asked Benson and June.

Maggie couldn't believe it. They acted as if she wasn't even there. "I can hear you. I'm only ten feet away."

"We're not excluding you, Maggie. We're just not engaging you per Mother Esme's directive," Sylvie said.

"Oh," Maggie whispered. "Go on then."

"Everything was going as planned," June explained. "When Minerva and I got to their compound, we found it vacant. We looked around but didn't find anything meaningful. That's when Min stepped on a trap."

"A trap with jaws that snap shut?" Alarmed, Maggie spoke too loudly, and the others hushed her. She tried not to see the trap's teeth digging into Min's flesh.

Benson craned his neck to get a look at the staircase. "No teeth. One designed for small animals. We freed Minerva. That's when we realized that the Abecedarians might be coming here."

"And they must know Maggie doesn't have her powers," June said.

"But no one attacked us here," Sylvie said. "I put a shield around the house that would keep just about anyone out."

"What about another witch?" he asked.

June groaned. "Heather's mother. We keep forgetting that factor."

"And we shouldn't," he said.

Sylvie leaned forward, her hands on her knees, directing her statement to Benson. "What's this we business? Why are you even involved in any of this?"

"Sylvie," Maggie said.

"No, it's okay. I'll answer." He also leaned forward and looked Sylvie in the eyes. "I don't know. My involvement doesn't make sense to me. I just feel," here he paused, "compelled to stay and help."

"How do we know we can trust you? You might be in on all this, which is why you made a move on Maggie yesterday." An iciness edged Sylvie's voice.

Maggie struggled to lift herself from the couch. "Sylvie, that's enough." The girls tried to keep their mother from getting up.

"You're not helping." June admonished Sylvie for agitating Maggie.

Sylvie stood and addressed everyone. "Do I need to remind you what I do for a living? I'm a security specialist. I need to know why he's here. Who are you?"

Instead of feeding into the hostility, Benson smirked. "You know who I am because you did the background check."

The room went silent. Sylvie nodded. "Yes, I did. I needed to see your reaction to my questions. I'm not completely happy you're here. But you are. Maggie and the baby seem to want you. So I guess I have to live with that."

June cleared her throat, trying to get their attention. "We need to get back to the matter at hand. As to the question of how the Abecedarians knew we'd be at the compound tonight—"

"Heather told them." Samuel came back with a cup of tea for his mother.

"That's exactly what I was thinking," June said.

They looked at the quiet young man. "It only makes sense."

June nodded. "So where is Heather right now?"

"She's in her room out in the school," Becca said.

"I need to talk to her."

Maggie didn't like the harshness in Sylvie's tone. The tension Maggie was trying to control shot through her like mercury in a thermometer. "She's a child and a victim, Sylvie. Remember that. And you question her here, in my presence."

"I'll go get her." Samuel left the room to return within minutes with Heather.

"Are you okay, Maggie?" Heather asked. She sounded sincere.

"She's in labor," Sylvie said. "Sit down."

The force in her voice troubled Maggie. She would have to find a way to temper Sylvie's anger. Heather slinked over to a straight back chair located as far as she could get from everyone in the room.

"Minerva was hurt tonight," Sylvie said.

"Oh."

"So the Abecedarian compound was empty. Your information was incorrect. June said it looked abandoned. How'd they know we were coming? They set traps, and Minerva got caught in one. She's in her room right now unconscious. Why was no one at the compound? Were they expecting us? And where would they get an idea like that?"

Heather burst into tears. The onslaught of questions too much. She covered her eyes with her palms and bent forward until her forehead touched her knees.

"Jeez," Benson said aloud.

Sylvie didn't look at Maggie, but she felt her sister-in-law's anger, laying the blame on her for trusting a stranger. Duty gave Maggie no choice but to help the young woman. She still believed Heather was a victim. It was hard to believe that just last night she and the children were gathered around the dinner table getting to know Benson. Then Heather appeared from nowhere, and now Minerva was lying in her room unconscious and bleeding. Maggie wondered what she had allowed into her home.

"I only told my mother," Heather said through her tears. "I didn't want my mom to get hurt."

"You didn't think your mother was going to tell the leader of the cult she belongs to?" Sylvie asked.

"No." Heather hesitated as if she wanted to say more. "I was protecting my mom." Her nose dripped, and Samuel handed her a box of tissue.

"Heather, we weren't going to hurt anyone. This wasn't an attack. We just needed to see what they were doing. We have no idea when they plan to come for the book or you," Maggie explained.

"I didn't know that." Heather wiped her nose and eyes.

"Seriously, you're just going to accept that story?" Sylvie asked. "So how did you contact your mother?"

"I called her using the house phone," she said.

Sylvie blew out a sigh of exasperation. "Your mother has access to a phone? I thought the Abecedarians were against technology."

Heather shrugged.

"Damn it! Don't shrug at me."

Maggie couldn't believe the intensity of Sylvie's anger. Of course, the situation building around them was dire, but something else seemed to be affecting her sister-in-law, something personal. Both Minerva and Sylvie put out signals that an issue beyond the immediate was troubling them. "Sylvie, please don't do this."

Sylvie turned to Maggie. "Lavinia is dead. Remember that. This isn't just some runaway teen from a bad homelife situation. Minerva got hurt tonight. They set traps. This is serious."

Her sister-in-law wasn't wrong. Maggie shook her head. Was her sympathy for Heather blinding her to what was actually going on? With the baby due in weeks, her maternal instincts felt overwhelming. Was this affecting her judgment?

The Mothers appeared. They looked about the room taking stock of the situation but made no comment. "Minerva is awake," Mother Esme said.

Maggie felt relief hearing her daughter was okay. She struggled to stand, and Becca & Betsy helped their mother to her feet.

"Wait." Sylvie inhaled deeply and went to Maggie. "I'm sorry. I didn't mean to take it out on you."

While she acknowledged Sylvie's apology, aggravation prickled Maggie. "I don't know what's going on, but we need to talk, just the two of us."

"Yeah, sure, but before you go upstairs, what are we going to do about Heather? We can't trust her."

Maggie didn't hesitate. "Bind any magic in her and then lock her in her room. Let's go check on Minerva, children." Becca & Betsy and Samuel guided her up the stairs. Maggie made sure not to look at Heather, ashamed of seeing her reaction to Maggie's harshness. The Magica served the witch community to bring hope and peace, and Maggie felt she was failing in her mission. Moments like this made her think she didn't deserve to be the Magica.

PART 2

<h1 style="text-align:center">CHAPTER 16</h1>

THE FARMHOUSE LAY NESTLED BETWEEN A BRIGHT RED BARN AND A stand of black gum trees whose scarlet foliage stood out against a dreary afternoon. Inside, a fire danced and crackled in a woodstove, warming Jinny Long's sewing room, a quilting frame at its center. Though the weather was stormy and bleak, Jinny along with Lucy Nguyen and Susan Levie had gathered around the frame to enjoy an afternoon of working on a love quilt for Jinny's daughter's upcoming wedding. Both the women and the quilt imbued the room with color on that overcast day.

Like all quilting bees, no matter the size, this one turned into a celebration of food, catching up, and laughter. Jinny had made an autumn quinoa salad with apples and maple roasted butternut squash. Susan brought her much adored, and rumored to be spelled, cucumber and herb aioli sandwiches. She swore none of the ingredients were magical. Lucy brought homemade short bread cookies and petit fours because a party wasn't a party without cake.

"Who said that, ladies?" Lucy asked.

Jinny put down her needle to sip her tea. "Who said what, dear? You didn't say anything out loud, and you know neither of us reads minds."

"Sorry," Lucy laughed, as a telepath she often forgot to speak out loud. "Who said that a party without cake is just a meeting?"

"Julia Child," Jinny said.

"That's it."

Susan cleared her throat. "I don't want to bring negativity to the quilt, but let's take a few minutes to discuss Lavinia and the library. Is that okay?" The women set down their needles and moved away from the quilt.

"I considered canceling today," Jinny said. "I feel terrible, but I also felt we needed to gather." Both June and Susan nodded in understanding.

"It's horrific," June said. "Poor Lavinia. And what are we going to do without our cherished library?"

"Does anyone know who did it?" Susan asked.

Lucy debated whether to reveal what she knew. Sylvie had called her that morning and related the previous night's events—the runaway and her connection to the Abecedarians; Maggie's new boyfriend Detective Benson Scott; the mission to the ABC's compound; Minerva getting hurt; and Maggie's problems with her pregnancy. Lucy felt overwhelmed and worried by everything Sylvie told her. Lucy wanted to know if her wife was safe, and Sylvie reassured her that she was. At no time during their phone conversation did Sylvie give her any restrictions on the information. The witches deserved to know the evil that had committed the attacks.

"The Abecedarians," Lucy said.

Both women grew quiet. "But—" Jinny said.

"The Magica dealt with them years ago, but here they are again," Lucy said.

"This is more serious than I thought. Let's discuss this outside," Jinny said. "I don't want any of these words to poison the quilt or house." She led them onto the lawn where the November wind could blow away the negative energies.

Lucy hugged herself against the chill. "Sylvie and the Sisters of Minerva are at Maggie's house right now. And that's not all." Lucy paused. How much should she reveal? Vagueness seemed the best route. "There are some things going on at Maggie's that are connected to what happened at the library."

Susan shivered. "Is this the start of something?" The three women looked at one another but no one had answers.

"At lease the Magica's dealing with it," Jinny said. "Since there's nothing we can do, let's get back to the quilt and out of this cold." Susan and Lucy agreed.

They settled back into their spots around the quilt frame. There would be no more talk of the library or the cult. To do so in the presence of the love quilt would ruin it. So each woman picked up her needle and put away negative thoughts.

"The design of this love quilt is breathtaking," Susan said. "Your daughter is going to love it." At the center of the quilt was the goddess with her consort, magical sigils surrounded the pair. No magic imbued the quilt just yet. The bride spelled the sigils herself according to her wishes.

"The pattern's been handed down for generations in my family," Jinny said. "My mother gave me a quilt with this very design, but my wedding ceremony colors were silver and gold."

"The red and silver is striking," Lucy said.

"My daughter's colors."

Lucy grinned. "Our colors were aubergine and black. They were the only colors Sylvie would agree to."

Jinny and Susan gave one another a look and raised their eyebrows. "That was an incredible wedding, Lucy," Susan said with a smirk.

Lucy set down her needle. "Come on, friends. It wasn't that crazy. So Sylvie drank a little too much champagne. A few of you did too as I recall. Wasn't there some flying around on a broomstick going on?" Lucy teased Jinny, who blushed at the memory.

Lucy resumed sewing. "Anyway, Sylvie drank because she was a little upset her sister-in-law didn't show. At least Maggie had the decency to send all of Sylvie's nieces and nephews."

Jinny and Susan grew quiet, but Lucy heard them clearly as their thoughts turned to the deaths of Maggie's husband and youngest child. Sylvie had been so angry. She found it difficult to understand how the Magica could have let such a thing happen to her family. Some felt Maggie not up to the position, and now there was the new controversy with the child she was carrying. Lucy went to rub her own abdomen but didn't want to draw her friends' attention. She and Sylvie decided to keep their pregnancy secret for now.

Jinny steered the conversation in another direction. "It would've been so nice if I could've invited my daughter's future mother-in-law to participate in this quilt making tradition, but I couldn't explain the magical components to the design. We're still hiding from nonmagicals. Aren't we? Nothing's gotten better," Jinny said.

Susan put down her needle. "Well, I thought things were improving. The world was making such incredible progress, but things seemed to have regressed."

Lucy picked up a petit fours. "Thank the goddess, we witches never revealed ourselves."

"How does Lily's fiancé feel about her being a witch?"

Before Jinny could answer, a crash from the front of the house startled the three women. Lucy dropped her cake. The door cracked in half as it burst open. Figures in white robes poured into the house.

Lucy instinctively threw up a protective shield to stop the intruders but then remembered she possessed no powers. The three women ran for the kitchen and the backdoor, but more figures barred the way.

"Here," Jinny said, leading them to the cellar door. Once on the other side, she locked and spelled it. On the wall furthest from the stairs stood a cupboard. "Help me move this." The three grabbed a side and worked it away from the wall revealing a door.

The cellar door rattled.

Susan grabbed the knob to the hidden door, but it wouldn't turn. "It's locked."

A voice from upstairs caused the three women to pause. The words of an incantation drifted through the cracks in the wood floor above their heads. "Is that a witch?" Lucy asked. Maybe there was more to the story than Sylvie had divulged.

"Those are Abecedarians. They don't tolerate witches," Susan said.

The woman's voice grew louder, and the cellar walls trembled.

"That's a witch," Jinny said. "Let's get out of here." She spoke a spell, and the door unlocked. She led them through a tunnel. "It goes to the barn," she whispered. "I've got my lab there and enough chemicals to stop them in their tracks. Here it is." She scurried up a ladder and lifted a hatch that opened into a horse stall. After Lucy cleared the opening, Jinny spelled the hatch too. "Come on. The lab's on the other side."

As they exited the stall, a man stood waiting for them in the middle of the barn. With their path blocked, the three women joined hands and spoke a binding spell to keep him at bay. Lucy wondered if the others noticed she possessed no magic, but if they did, no one had time to say anything. Instead of being stopped, the man kept walking toward them.

"That's not possible," Susan said. More Abecedarians appeared, trying to corral the women.

"This way." Running headlong toward a wall, Jinny lifted her hands and made three slashes. An opening appeared. Lifeless winter fields stretched out before them.

Susan screamed.

Lucy looked back. Three Abecedarians held Susan. Lucy backed away from them. The witch appeared, a hood pulled over her face, hiding her features. Lucy recognized the man next to her, Noah Corwin. Lucy wanted to rush to Susan and drag her away, but more Abecedarians were closing in. Without any powers, she was helpless. She ran after Jinny across the field. They would find a way to free Susan.

Not yet plowed under, cornstalk stubble slowed Lucy's progress, her feet tangling in them. Her foot hit one of the stalks and she tripped, going down hard on her hands and knees. She looked over her shoulder to find the Abecedarians advancing on them. Lucy got up and ran until she caught up with Jinny.

"Where's Susan?" A winter wind cut across the field and carried Jinny's voice away.

Lucy pointed back the way they had come. A line of Abecedarians plodded toward them, the witch in the middle of the pack. Two white-robed figures gripped Susan's arms, dragging her along. Lucy regretted leaving her friend behind.

"The only way to help her is to get out of this field. This way." When Jinny turned, she found a line of cult members coming at them from the other direction. "Damn."

"Who's that witch?" Lucy asked. She shivered as the biting cold pushed at her back.

"I don't recognize her. Sylvie didn't say anything to you about this?"

"What I told you earlier," Lucy yelled.

Jinny watched the Abecedarian acolytes closed in on them. "We need to combine our powers to get out of this. Brick defense?"

Lucy shook her head. She felt responsible for their predicament. If she'd told her friends, they could've been prepared. "I can't. I'm pregnant."

Joy and concern flashed across Jinny's face. "I'll see if I can do it solo but go through the motions with me." Jinny held out her hands, and Lucy took them. They walked in a clockwise circle chanting the incantation to produce a fortified brick enclosure. If it worked, they could shelter within until their pursuers gave up and left.

Each brick Jinny created disappeared as quickly as she made them. "That bitch." Jinny said the spell faster, hoping to keep ahead of the witch thwarting her magic. Jinny stopped, exhausted. "I can't keep this up." The remaining magical bricks dissolved into the ether.

Lucy grabbed Jinny's arm. "Look."

A pickup truck hurtled toward them. Panic hammered in Lucy's chest. Escape wasn't just about her. She turned to run, but a ring of Abecedarians surrounded them. The truck stopped twenty feet from where she and Jinny stood. All routes of escape were blocked. Not conceding, Jinny threw spells at the ring of white-robed figures and at the truck. Nothing worked.

The witch stood in the bed of the truck and beside her was Noah Corwin. June couldn't believe what she was seeing, an Abecedarian and a witch side by side. She tried to probe their minds but was blocked. The witch threw her arms skyward as if beseeching a higher power. Clouds gathered and moved in a counterclockwise motion.

"What is she doing?" Lucy asked.

Above their heads, the wind picked up speed, rotating faster. Two cult members dragged Susan over to Jinny and Lucy, pushing the woman at them. Jinny caught her. Susan's pale face broke into a grin of relief when she realized she was back with her friends. Lucy untied her hands.

"Let's combine our powers and put an end to this," Susan said.

"Lucy's pregnant."

Susan hugged Lucy. "Me and you then, Jin."

"Let's protect Lucy and the baby." She and Susan hugged with Lucy sandwiched between them. The three protected the unborn child. "Let's try going up."

The women managed to levitate ten feet before the traitor witch's rotating winds took on tornado viciousness, forcing them to the ground. The women sprawled in the dirt. Susan pulled Lucy to her, covering her body with her own.

Lucy thought of Sylvie. Starting their own family thrilled them, and they had big dreams for a happy future. The Abecedarians would regret crossing Sylvie.

Jinny wasn't giving up. She directed a push powerful enough to knock the witch off her feet. Instead, the witch absorbed the magic. "She can't do that."

The witch raised her arms again, and the rotating winds she'd conjured dropped from the sky forming thin, white filaments. These attached themselves to the witch's fingertips. She cast them in the direction of the three women. The threads burned and twisted into their flesh. Lucy screamed and thrashed on the ground. Despite the filaments boring into her own flesh, Susan held Lucy. Jinny tried pulling the filaments from Lucy's skin, but burn marks lashed her palms. The filaments pulsed and sucked like umbilical cords, feeding the rogue witch their magic.

Susan felt Lucy's body convulse. "Stop this," Susan screamed at the witch attacking them.

"Let Lucy go," Jinny yelled. "She's pregnant."

The witch's arms dropped, and the hooded face looked down at them. For a second, Lucy believed they would set her and the baby free.

"Don't stop, woman," Noah Corwin screamed.

"So what?" the witch said, directing her comments at Jinny. "More magic for us then." The witch lifted her arms, the filaments shooting out at the three witches on the ground.

Jinny and Susan formed a protective knot around Lucy, and Jinny covered the bodies of the younger women with her own. Lucy wanted her last thoughts to be of Sylvie and the baby, and she pictured Sylvie holding the infant in her arms. Atop her, Jinny and Susan jerked and moaned. Lucy, still semi-conscious, was forced to watch her friends die.

The filaments withdrew, disappearing into the witch's hands. She reeled backwards from the sudden force, one of the cult members catching her. Her arms and hands blackened from the magic she'd consumed. They lowered the witch onto the truck bed.

Corwin kneeled beside his witch. "Now heal me!" He grabbed the witch's hands and brought them to the dead, white orbs of his eyes.

Lucy, still alive, watched as the witch grasped Corwin's head and mumbled a spell. He went rigid and then convulsed for nearly a minute. The witch released him.

"I can see! Take me to those witches. I want to see their bodies."

Lucy tried to quiet her breathing, but every inhalation burned from her nostrils to her lungs. She could hear herself wheeze and feared the others could too.

Corwin laughed. "They look like scorched cornhusk dolls–brittle and dead." He signaled for his followers to come to him.

"Let's go, Noah,"

"Yes, let's do that. Everyone, we are leaving," Corwin announced.

Thank the goddess. Lucy wanted to cry but knew she had to stay quiet. If she could get to a hospital, the baby had a chance. The truck started rolling forward. She would call Sylvie—

The truck stopped. Lucy held her breath. *Just go, please just go.*

The reverse lights came on. *No, no.* She needed them to leave so she could crawl out from under Jinny and Susan and get help.

"We're going to take the bodies."

Lucy wanted to scream.

The acolytes hopped out of the truck bed. One of the men grabbed Ginny's hand too roughly, and it crumbled. Lucy kept still.

"You idiot, gently," Corwin screamed. "I need them to stay intact. Do you understand?" The man nodded.

"What are you going to do with them?" the witch asked.

"We're going to gift them," Corwin said.

The men loaded Ginny and Susan into the back of the truck. They picked up Lucy, and she groaned. She didn't mean to, but the pain felt like knives fileting her skin from muscle.

The men dropped her, startled. "Prophet Corwin, this one's alive.

Corwin turned to his witch. "Well..."

And that's when Lucy finally screamed.

Chapter 17

Something nudged Minerva awake, and she sat up. Mother Esme, asleep in a rocking chair placed beside the bed, snored softly. Minerva wondered why the woman was there. Lying back down, she tried to piece together events. She along with June and Benson had been in a car. They were going—

Minerva tried to remember.

Right. The Abecedarian compound, that's where they'd gone. Minerva closed her eyes as pain pierced her right temple. It felt as if someone was driving a spike into her skull with a mallet. The house felt abandoned. She picked up her phone on the nightstand. It was six in the morning. At the top of her phone it read Monday. That couldn't be right. They'd gone to the compound on Saturday, but the phone said it was now Monday, which meant she'd missed an entire day of her life.

She breathed deeply, hoping the pain would subside. When it lessened, she let her mind go back to the fuzzy events. The three of them went to the compound to see what the cult was up to, but no one was there. Minerva tried to remember what happened next. After several minutes she gave up. She allowed herself to drift back to sleep.

A scream jolted Minerva out of her doze. The spike returned to her head. Someone needed help, and she pushed back the covers. Her ankle stung when she tried to stand, and she fell back into bed.

"Stay. I'll go." Mother Esme helped her back into bed and then left the room. On the other side of her bedroom door, feet pounded down the stairs. Minerva tracked the movement through the foyer and out the front door.

An incredible shock of agony rolled across the landscape and crashed into Minerva. It was like the nudge but ten-fold.

Another scream, sounding like June, made Minerva go rigid with fear. The pain out there summoned her. She left her room. The walls slid from side to side, and Minerva put her arms out to right herself as if she were on a boat. She reached the first floor and found the front door open, Mother Esme standing on the porch. Samuel came around from the back of the house, drawn by the screams. Dr. Williams sprinted after him.

The other children appeared, and Mother Esme kept them from running toward the screaming. Only her mother was missing. Minerva went back to the stairs and called out to her mom. There was no answer.

"What's happening?" Luka asked. When he stepped toward the commotion, Mother Esme snagged him.

The pain called again. She started across the damp lawn. Groggy and unsure of what to do next, she knew only that she needed to follow the pain calling to her.

"Are you okay, Min?" Betsy asked. Her sisters didn't wait for an answer. They ran across the wet grass and guided Minerva back, making her sit on the brick wall edging the garden. Why was everyone trying to stop her from getting to the source of the pain? Becca & Betsy disappeared but returned with shoes and jackets. They handed her a pair of muck boots. She pulled them on and started down the drive.

Minerva turned around. "Why aren't you in school?"

"It's too early," Becca & Betsy answered.

"Oh."

"Minerva, come back here, please," Mother Esme said. "Dr. Williams is there."

Minerva couldn't stay. She didn't want to go down the driveway but she needed to. Whatever was happening remained out of sight, blocked by the knoll.

Another scream, a different one like the braying of a donkey. Scream. Pause. Scream. Pause.

Wailing replaced the screaming. Sylvie and June staggered back up the driveway, arms wrapped around one another. June had her hand across her mouth. Shondra and Samuel flanked the women, hands on their shoulders and elbows, guiding them back to the house.

Minerva gasped for breath. She felt their agony like punches to her gut. They reeked of horror and anger and fear. Something more than terrible had happened. This was catastrophic.

Shondra looked over at Minerva. "Turn around. Don't go down there."

Sylvie stopped and howled.

June collapsed, kneeling on the asphalt, sobbing.

Minerva had heard this type of crying once before. When her father and little brother died. The sound was of absolute, soul crushing heartache. She drew her arms around herself. She couldn't go through an experience like that again. The anguish had been intense on that day, and it wasn't just her own. Her empathic ability made her endure her mother's and siblings' as well. When Minerva vanished for hours to her room, people thought her cold and unfeeling, but no one could imagine how much she suffered as the emotions of so many bombarded her day and night. The only anguish she couldn't escape was her own. Minerva cleared her head of the past and continued down the driveway. She ignored the warnings.

She shivered, from both the damp November breeze and the thought of whatever was down there. The driveway gate came into view. Dr. Williams stood at the foot of a mound of something. In the distance, sirens shrieked. Minerva moved closer. What was on the ground?

When she got to the mound, she tried to make sense of what she was looking at. Things piled atop one another. Jumbled parts…

Minerva's hands flew up to her mouth like startled birds. A groan slipped between her fingers. Dr. Williams turned around. "No, Minerva, you shouldn't be here." She tried to redirect her toward the house, but Minerva went around.

She stood at the edge of the pile.

Twisted. Knotted. Blackened husks.

Pain had folded these bodies in half. Their faces warped by emotion. Arms, legs, torsos broken. Heads bent toward one another, foreheads touching as if sharing some terrible, dark secret.

"Those are…"

"Minerva, stop. Go to the house now," Dr. Williams ordered, her voice stern and made to be obeyed.

Minerva couldn't stop looking at the pile. Someone came here in the night and dumped them at the foot of their driveway. Like trash.

"These are people." Minerva fell to her knees before the corpses. Before she could stop herself, she reached out and touched what looked like an arm. Agony, fear, and heartache flashed through her mind. Minerva turned away as her stomach disgorged spontaneously, its contents splattering the driveway.

A fire engine and two police cars pulled up to the end of the driveway, slapping blue and red across the scene. An unmarked car slid in behind the other vehicles. Its driver-side door flung open, and Benson stepped out.

Dr. Williams took hold of Minerva and guided her away.

Minerva didn't look back. She didn't need to. She felt the pain pressing at her, trying to communicate with her. And she knew then that touching the dead changed everything in her life.

Chapter 18

The crime scene kept Benson busy. He was thankful he'd asked the 911 dispatcher to keep the murders off police and fire radios, as not to alert the media. Keeping the circus at bay made things, if not easier, a lot less complicated. He called his boss immediately and explained his involvement. Benson wanted to do more but he didn't want to compromise the investigation.

Police officers took statements from everyone, including him. Benson informed them that a cult had been threatening Maggie's family. He didn't tell them that the murders of these poor women and the librarian were connected. That would entail telling them of Heather's presence. If they knew there was a young woman locked up in the schoolhouse, it would bend the investigation in the wrong direction. The police would focus on Maggie and her family, and Benson knew that would just be wasting time. No, he was going to take care of Heather himself. He needed for law enforcement and emergency services to leave first.

Finally, the Medical Examiner's team took the three bodies away. Since the corpses were as dry as October leaves, no blood or bodily fluids stained the asphalt. And Benson was at least grateful that Maggie and her family didn't have to relive the nightmare coming and going from the house. Despite the horror of seeing their people dead, June and Sylvie identified the body of Lucy Nguyen, June's sister and Sylvie's wife, while Shondra recognized Jinny Long and Susan Levie.

The atmosphere of grief alternated between mausoleum quiet and sorrow-stricken exclamation. The Mothers confined Maggie to her room, afraid the stress would speed up labor. Benson asked Dr. Williams's permission to check on Maggie but was denied. So he stayed in the kitchen with the children who were home from school. All of them huddled together at the banquette. Becca & Betsy were clinched in an embrace that only a pry bar could separate. Minerva sat silently off to the side. Benson worried she was in shock after what she'd seen. Luka chose to stay next to him, his head resting on the man's arm. Though never one much for children, Benson didn't mind and in fact felt honored to be found safe.

Mother Esme tended an inconsolable June, whose sobs put her at risk of choking. After a strong tea and a sedative, June lay curled on the bed in the guest room. Samuel stayed with his aunt who occupied a chair next to the bay window in the living room. Sylvie stared at the driveway, her eyes following the path down to the gate, as if she were waiting for her wife Lucy to arrive, everything a horrible joke or misunderstanding. Benson knew that feeling. In the hallway, the grandfather clock ticked like a deathwatch beetle. Dr. Williams and Shondra were with Maggie.

The only person not among them was Heather, who was still locked up in her room out at the school. Benson needed to question her.

Samuel entered the kitchen and headed for the fridge. He set out eggs, half and half, butter, bread, and jam. "It's almost dinner time. No one's eaten a thing all day. I'm making plain omelets and toast for everyone." He donned his apron and turned to the stove.

Becca & Betsy separated. "We can't forget Heather. She's probably wondering why we haven't brought her breakfast." Both girls then pitched in to help their big brother.

"I'm tired," Luka said. Minerva fetched him a pillow and lap blanket, making up a cot on the bench.

Benson saw this as a good opportunity to talk to Heather and he headed for the back door. When he entered the laundry room, he found Minerva tugging on her shoes.

"I'm going with you," she said.

Benson nodded. Maybe he could use this to get right by her. He felt like bad luck for Minerva. He failed her that night at the Abecedarian compound. It was stupid going in all nonchalantly without considering that the cult would have something planned for intruders. Then this morning Minerva had seen the bodies. He needed to be more vigilant, more protective, and more prepared. He leaned in and looked at her eyes. "How's your head?"

"Okay," she mumbled.

"Any concussion symptoms?"

She paused before speaking. "Just a headache."

"How about your foot?"

"It hurts a little less right now."

He sensed there was something else troubling her. "I'm sorry, Minerva, about the other night. Being a police officer, I should've been prepared. And I'm sorry about what you saw this morning."

Minerva studied him. The effect made him want to squirm and look away.

"We should've all been better prepared. We knew things were serious," she said. "And, Benson, we're not helpless women. If you're going to continue seeing my mother, I want you to understand that. In fact, there are no helpless women, just women not empowered or disempowered to help themselves. We don't need a hero."

Hearing the sentiment for the second time cold-cocked him. He didn't see it until now. Maybe it took June and now Minerva to make him realize that. As a police officer and a man, hero was a role he assumed and thought others would appreciate. "Okay, I understand. I'm still sorry."

She shrugged, her lips stretched into something resembling a smile, letting him know things were okay between them.

Samuel entered the laundry room, read the temperature of the room, and said nothing. He handed Minerva a basket.

"Let's go talk to Heather. See what her story is now," Benson said.

The girl was standing at the window of her room. She snapped a compact mirror shut and shoved it into a back pocket of her jeans. "What's been happening? I saw lights, heard sirens."

Minerva placed the basket on the desk.

Heather didn't wait for an answer or invitation. She slid into the chair and dug into the food. "I'm starved. I thought you guys had forgotten about me."

Benson took Minerva's words to heart and didn't assume he should start the conversation. After she nodded to him, he launched into a description of the morning's events. He detailed the scene graphically, sparing Heather no horrific detail about the condition of the bodies. She stopped eating. He described June's and Sylvie's anguish over the murder of a beloved sister and wife. He wanted to see Heather's reaction.

The girl blanched and slid so low in her chair she seemed to be melting off the edge. Her behavior read as ignorant of the lengths the Abecedarians would go. The girl may have told her mother about them going to the compound, but she didn't seem to have any knowledge of the cult's actual plans. He asked the question anyway just to gage her involvement. "So you didn't know about their plans to do this heinous act?"

She shook her head so fast he thought she looked like one of those images in movies where they turn a character into a blur of movement, a little spooky.

"I told you. I just didn't want my mom to get hurt."

The bedroom door burst open, the doorknob striking the wall behind it with a bang, punching a hole in the wall.

Caught off guard, Benson and Minerva instinctively moved away from the door.

Sylvie stormed into the room and grabbed Heather by the shoulders, yanking the girl to her feet. Benson lunged for Sylvie, driving her arms up and off Heather. The girl fell back on the bed and crab crawled away.

"Murderer," Sylvie yelled. Her teeth pulled back like a feral dog wanting to sink its teeth into anything that got close.

Heather started to cry. She threw an arm up covering her eyes.

"Easy, Sylvie. Easy. Come over to this chair." Benson needed to diffuse the situation. He tried guiding the angry woman to a neutral corner of the room, but she pushed him away.

Mother Esme and Shondra came into the room, choosing to stay in the hallway just outside the room. Both women looked alarmed by what was happening.

"I don't want to sit down. She and her people killed my wife."

"Sylvie, stop." Shondra reached out to her friend. "You should sit down."

"I don't want to!"

Benson was prepared to intervene. Sylvie's volatile attitude was frightening.

"Don't yell at me," Shondra said.

Sylvie clenched her fists and fumed. "You don't understand."

Mother Esme bravely stepped forward and placed a hand on Sylvie's arm. "What is it?"

Sylvie paused. Her next words stuck in her mouth. "They killed my wife...and my baby."

"What?" Shondra said. "Oh, honey."

"You didn't tell us," Mother Esme said.

"We didn't tell anyone," Sylvie said. "We were waiting. And you—" She stuck her finger in Heather's face. "—you and those monsters killed my wife and my baby."

"I didn't know. I don't know anything," Heather howled.

"You keep saying that. But I think you know a lot." Sylvie lunged for Heather, but Benson restrained her. "Tell me who had the power to suck the magic out of those three witches."

"I don't know anything," Heather wailed.

"Is your mother the only witch, other than you, in the Abecedarians?"

Benson was surprised by her question, but Sylvie was right. Only a witch could've killed the women in that manner, but he never thought of asking Heather a question like that. Why would he? It wasn't part of his process. In three days, a whole new world became real to him. He couldn't approach this as if it were just another case. They waited for Heather to answer.

"Yes," the young woman said.

Sylvie continued. "So your mother killed them."

"He must have made her," Heather sobbed. "He was always telling her he would kill me and the other children if she didn't do what he said." Heather dropped her face into the palm of her hands.

"We're done, Heather. I'm going to put you in a car and drop you off at the compound if you don't come clean with us."

Heather stopped crying. "No, they'll kill me."

"There are now four dead women and a dead baby. My baby! Do you think I give a shit about one more dead person?"

Benson saw a hard cast appear in Heather's eyes, the look of being a helpless victim replaced with something suggesting Heather could be dangerous if cornered.

"So what's their plan, Heather? What do they want out of all this?" Sylvie asked.

"I don't know."

"Try. Or I'm driving you out of here."

Heather wiped her nose. "He preaches that he wants to expose witches. Show the world they're real. He thinks this will upset the status quo and start a war between humans and supernaturals. Maybe another Burning Times. Then he was going to connect witchcraft and science. He wants to let people know the truth," Heather said.

"Which is what?" Minerva asked.

"That only God's Word in the Bible is truth."

"What's the purpose behind that?" Benson asked.

Heather shrugged. "I don't know."

"For no purpose. Right?" Sylvie said. "Zealotry needs no end game other than these terrorists thinking they're doing their god's work, creating the world they believe their god wants. There's nothing to understand beyond that. My family died for nothing."

"But I ran away," Heather said trying to dissociate herself from the Abecedarians.

Sylvie turned and kicked the desk chair, sending it crashing into a wall. Everyone in the room flinched. "She stays here. Got it?" Sylvie said. "No one visits her without me."

Sylvie stormed out, and Mother Esme and Shondra followed her. Heather lay on the bed crying. Benson couldn't believe that this girl's mother, a witch herself, would kill other witches, other women. And a baby, Benson reminded himself.

Minerva closed the door after he exited and spelled it. "I used a much more serious locking spell than I usually use," she explained. She leaned against the doorjamb.

"Hey, are you okay? Dizzy?"

"I'm tired." Minerva hesitated as if she were mulling over her next words. "I'm an empath and all this emotion..." She paused again, but he waited, giving her time. "I've never said those words to a nonmagical."

"Oh." He didn't know what to say. She'd been giving him the cold shoulder treatment, and now when she divulged this about herself, all he could give her was a one syllable response.

"I think I need a drink. Is that terrible to want right now?"

"No, I could use one too." Benson didn't really want one but he felt he needed to support Minerva in this moment.

"There's some whisky in dad's study."

Benson was surprised by Minerva's suggestion. He took it as a truce, or at least a ceasefire, between them. "Sure."

～

She led Benson through the living room and down a hallway with only one door at the end. She stopped. "No one's been in here for some time. Mom wants to leave the room as it is. It was my dad's space." She opened the door. This was no man cave. The room was a traditional study—rich mahogany paneling, patterned carpet, bookcases on two walls, several original landscape paintings, two wingback chairs fronting a large desk occupying the center of the room, a family portrait in a silver frame on the right side of the desk. Benson left the door open in case anyone needed to find them. Minerva opened an armoire turned liquor cabinet. Her hands shook as she took down two glasses.

"Sit down, Minerva. Let me do this." Benson spied *Lag* on a bottle toward the back. He pulled it out and whistled.

"Something wrong with it?"

He held the bottle as if it was a precious object. "This is the good stuff, Minerva. The very best. Very expensive. Take care of it." He started putting the bottle back.

"Leave it out."

"Are you sure? This is much too expensive for just soothing our nerves," Benson said.

"I think Grandad gave Dad the bottle when I was born. Pour me some, please. It's every bit mine as it was his."

Benson suddenly realized that he knew nothing about Maggie's husband, but this wasn't the time for those questions.

"Everything okay?"

"Oh yeah." He splashed the whisky into the cut crystal. "Hope neat works for you. I can get some ice."

She said no to the ice and took a sip. "Tastes like grass."

Benson swirled the velvet liquid. Cupped the glass to warm the contents. Smelled it. Let a single drop touch his tongue. "You're tasting peat."

"Can I have more please?" Minerva held her empty glass out to Benson.

He wanted to tell her to savor it, make it an experience, but she had been through so much. He poured out two fingers for her this time. He set the bottle down. "I'm very sorry about your aunt and her baby, and your friends."

"Thank you. Sylvie must be going crazy, losing her wife and baby. I can't believe she didn't tell us."

"Sometimes people wait to announce. Just in case." Benson cringed realizing that this time *just in case* was a much worse scenario.

"I need to check on Mom and the younger kids. See how they're all doing." Minerva took a small sip but didn't get up. "Funeral services will need to be planned. When do you think they'll release the bodies?"

After all the violence and confrontation, it felt odd to be sitting here in a dead man's office with Minerva talking of practical and mundane things. "I'll check for you," Benson said. He needed to return to work and his own life as well. It was a good thing he didn't have pets or even a houseplant.

"I don't trust Heather," Minerva said. "I get the wrong feeling from her. Actually, I get no feeling from her."

"Have you told your mom?"

"I brought it up. She says she has to adhere to the duty-bound code until there's proof otherwise. But the whole situation is escalating. What do you think?"

"I agree with you. I want to interview Heather again, and I don't want Sylvie around."

"Yeah, I—" Minerva swirled the amber liquid in her glass, looking pensive, her thoughts lost in the motion. "This—" Minerva's stop-starts worried Benson. Was the concussion worse than Dr. Williams diagnosed?

"You can talk to me, Minerva."

She nodded, but when she spoke, she kept her eyes on her glass. "You must think this is all crazy. Witches. Magic. Dead people."

Benson sat back in his chair. "Well, let's say this isn't what I expected when I became smitten with your mom."

"Smitten? You were smitten?"

"Bewitched. Infatuated. Hooked. Mesmerized. I made the biggest fool of myself in the grocery store. Is that weird to hear about your mom?"

"A little. Didn't it freak you out that she was pregnant?"

"Yes. And then I spit tea all over her white blouse when she told me she already had six kids and a seventh on the way."

Minerva cocked her head and looked hard at him. "But you still came to dinner. Why?"

He wondered if Minerva was testing him. "The heart wants what the heart wants. I know that's cliché but still true."

"And the witch stuff. You just believed it?" Minerva took another swallow of the whisky.

He got up to put a touch more into his glass. He held the bottle up, but she declined. "I think I was shocked for like one second, but then it just felt natural. Like it was something that's always been. Maybe some of us have learned to accept people for who they are."

She nodded, reflecting on those words. "Can I ask you something then?"

Benson stiffened, afraid that she was going to ask him to leave her mother alone. What she said next caught him off guard.

"I have a boyfriend." She took a sip. "I'm pretty sure he's going to ask me to marry him. But I haven't told him about the witch stuff."

He tried not to turn and gape at her. The conversation wasn't what he expected, but he would roll with it. Maybe she needed a male, and a nonmagical, perspective. "Why not? Your mom told me, and now you told me about your ability."

She sipped her drink. "Yeah, I did. An attempt at courage. I guess I'm afraid. What if he rejects me? Or what if he reveals us? Or what if he gets people to hurt us?"

"I understand. Your people have had millennia of persecution. If it's real, you'll feel it and tell him. If not..." He put up his hands and shrugged. He could tell she'd heard this all before. Maybe hearing it again would help with her decision. Something else was still troubling Minerva.

She nodded. "There is." His startled look made her explain. "Mild telepathy, emotion induced. No, I don't read minds, only emotions. This morning—" She stopped and looked away.

"Minerva?" He waited for her to explain.

"When my hand came in contact with Lucy's body, I saw it all happen."

"Holy shit. How?"

"I'll tell you everything, but not right now." She set her glass down on the side table and stood.

"Why?"

A door slammed, followed by running footsteps. "Shondra!"

"That's Samuel," Minerva said. "He sounds worried."

"Benson?"

He was surprised to hear his name. "Let's see what's going on." The last thing Maggie's family needed was one more crisis. He would have to wait for Minerva's explanation.

In the kitchen, Becca & Betsy stood off to the side, clinging to one another. Shondra was nowhere in sight, but Sylvie was there. On the floor between her and Samuel sat a bowling bag. A tense knot formed in Benson's gut. After having watched enough gangster movies, his imagination fed him some gruesome images.

"Becca & Betsy found this on the porch," Samuel said.

"We were taking out the trash."

Benson squatted next to Sylvie. "Hey, let me do it."

"As a security professional—" Her eyes were swollen and filled with an impenetrable sorrow.

"I know," he said. "I'm not usurping power. It's just that you don't need to deal with this if you don't have to. Not today."

She sank back on her heels and looked at him hard. He stayed quiet. After several beats, she stood and handed him the towel she was holding.

"Anyone who doesn't want to be here when I open this, leave now." Becca & Betsy scurried away. Samuel, Minerva, and Sylvie stayed. Using the towel, Benson gripped the zipper's pull, ready to open the bag.

A scream interrupted the moment. He shot up. "Shit, what was that?" From upstairs, another scream answered his question.

Benson threw the towel onto the bag. Now what?

"That's Maggie," Sylvie said. She led the charge up the stairs.

He followed Sylvie and the others. How many things could go south in one day for this family?

The bag remained unopened and forgotten on the kitchen floor.

Chapter 19

Sylvie burst into Maggie's bedroom. Dr. Williams threw up her hands. "Stop."

For a few seconds, Maggie forgot about the pain ripping through her. A group of bodies congregated at the room's entrance like cartoon characters all trying to get through a doorway at the same time. Maggie laughed, which was followed by a groan.

Shondra addressed the group, "Maggie's in labor."

"Does she need to be driven to the hospital?" Benson asked.

"Maggie's having the baby here, in the house. That's why the Mothers are here," Shondra explained.

"Should I go then?" Benson asked.

Dr. Williams pushed through the crowd to speak with him. "If you could stay, I would appreciate it. Maggie's only a little early, and I don't foresee any complications, but you never know. We might need a hospital transfer, and as a peace officer, you might prove yourself handy." He nodded and hung back out of the way.

Mother Esme started peeling the others away from the door, reassuring them everything was fine, no need for panic. Maggie was glad for the crowd control, especially for shooing Benson away. Giving birth in front of a man she just met was the last thing Maggie wanted.

"Minerva. Children," Maggie called out. "Sylvie, you too."

Maggie clenched her jaw as another labor pain hit her. "Minerva, you'll have to contact the hotel to change those reservations for today. Samuel, make sure the younger children pack their toothbrushes and underwear, and not just swimsuits and electronics." Minerva and Samuel promised they would take care of everything.

Becca & Betsy went to their mother's side, but Luka remained at the end of the bed.

"I don't want to go to a hotel," Luka announced. "I want to stay and watch my little sister be born."

Maggie had allowed him to be in the room when Michael was born. "Not this time, my love. Things are a little different with this one." She placed her hand on her belly. "Come and give your mother a kiss."

"It's not fair. I'm not going," Luka yelled.

Maggie wasn't prepared for his outburst. "We had a family meeting about your sister's birth. Remember we talked about how things might be dangerous and that it would be safer if all of you went to a hotel?"

"I don't care. I want to be here." Luka plopped down on the bedroom floor and crossed his arms over his chest.

"Luka, I promise your little sister will be fine, but it's not safe for you children to be here right now. Go to the hotel. Eat pancakes. Watch some movies," Maggie said.

Samuel stooped to talk to his little brother. "Come on, kid. Let's go."

Maggie threw her head back and groaned as a current ran through her. The lights in the bedroom flickered.

Luka rushed to her side. "Mom, are you okay?"

Outside the wind kicked up, forcing the oaks and maples into shaking off the last of their autumn leaves. Large raindrops smacked the windowpanes. This was just the beginning of much worse conditions to come. If the children didn't leave now, it would be too late. "Baby, it's not safe for you children. It could become dangerous, especially for you and Samuel."

Birds shot from their perches and rushed heavenward. A blackbird lost control and careened into the bedroom window with a bang. Becca & Betsy screeched. The kids had to leave before conditions became too severe and they couldn't leave. Magica births were not ordinary, and to add to that this was the birth of an Arch-Magica. When that much energy was brought into the world, it affected all the forces of the universe. One story told of a volcano erupting. Others described violent earthquakes and raging fires. And people caught in these forces were hurt, and even killed.

"No. I'm staying to protect her."

Maggie understood now. This was because of Michael. "Luka, look around. The Mothers are here. Your aunties are here. This baby has a lot of protection."

"I'm not going. And no one can make me!" Luka hunkered down, anchoring himself to the floor.

Lightning blitzed the sky, turning the room into a photo negative. Richard appeared in the corner of the bedroom, flashing in and out of sight. Not him, too. Maggie tried to shake him out of sight, but when she opened her eyes, he was still there. Thunder rocked the house, and the building shuddered to its roots. A piercing crack like the earth being rent open meant one of the nearby trees had been hit. Maggie worried an oak would come smashing through the roof. Her own pain struck suddenly, followed by a clash of more lightning and thunder. A tree branch flew by the second-floor window.

Maggie gasped around the pain. "It's too late. Everyone not needed here go to the basement." The house creaked like it was trying to lift itself from its foundation. Luka flinched, his face going white. "Now," Maggie demanded.

Samuel pulled Luka up, who wrapped his arms around his brother's neck. Becca & Betsy kissed Maggie. Shondra appeared with June and led the group to the storm shelter.

Luka looked back. "Be careful, Mom."

Benson broke through the ranks and planted a kiss on Maggie's forehead. He couldn't help himself. "I'll keep them safe."

Sylvie stood off to the side, hands clasped behind her back, eyes red and puffy. Maggie felt terrible. Her sister-in-law needed time to grieve for her wife and their child.

"Sylvie, I'm sorry this is happening right now." Maggie winced as a metallic pain rippled through her.

Sylvie shrugged and looked away. "It's not like you're doing this on purpose. Your baby is coming." Her voice broke on the word baby.

"Yes, but still." Maggie put her hands out, palms up. "I know this isn't fair to you or June. No one's had time to grieve."

"I said," Sylvie said tensely, "it's fine."

Maggie tried one last time to connect. "If anyone knows your pain, it's me."

Sylvie huffed. "So do you need anything from me right now?"

Nothing Maggie said would bring any peace to Sylvie. Only time could mend the woman's heartache. She didn't want to hear anything Maggie had to say, but she understood her sister-in-law's pain too well. Immediately after Richard's and Michael's death the hurt felt like someone stabbing her over and over, or sometimes it was a hole opening right in front of her, threatening to suck her into a world of oblivion. Two years later, the pain of loss popped up sporadically, like a jump scare, maybe while she was driving or doing laundry. No one can tell another person how to grieve, or even describe what heartbreaking grief feels like. Sylvie needed to go through it, but she didn't have to do it alone.

The Mothers had been keeping their distance from across the room, allowing Maggie and Sylvie space. As soon as she left and the room cleared, Mother Esme brushed Maggie's hair back into a ponytail. "Don't worry about her, dear. We'll keep an eye on Sylvie. Right now you have other concerns."

Dr. Williams checked Maggie's dilation, blood pressure, and oxygen levels. After a squirt of gel, she ran the probe over Maggie's abdomen picking up the strong beat of the baby's heart.

"Maggie, it's time," the doctor said. "She isn't in distress. She's just ready to be out here."

Hail pelted the roof, sounding like marbles being thrown by the handful. The wind slithered through invisible cracks, moaning and whistling. She looked over at Richard, now no more than a whisper of his solid self. He seemed troubled. "I hope everyone stays safe. This is going to be a long night," Maggie said.

The Mothers guided her to a modern birthing chair, comfortably upholstered, sporting hand grips and foot pedals. The chair acknowledged the fact that giving birth was never meant to be done in a helpless, reclining position.

"You need to focus on this," the doctor said.

Maggie couldn't help it. She was worried. Her family needed to be safe. Sylvie's family had not been protected, her wife and unborn child murdered. Maggie wouldn't be caught off guard again. She groaned, clutching the grips of the birthing chair.

"You need to be present," Dr. Williams chastised. "Stop thinking about other things."

"Aside from Magica, what will you be calling the baby?" Mother Esme asked.

The older woman was trying to distract her. Maggie appreciated the effort even if it didn't do much to lessen the powerful contractions squeezing new life from her body. "Becca & Betsy decided we should call her Gia."

"Oh good, I was afraid they would choose something like Archie or Gica." Maggie laughed. Thunder reverberated like a metal sheet being shaken.

"Don't push yet," the doctor said. "It's a bit too early."

Maggie tensed up and moaned.

"Or maybe not," Mother Esme said.

"I don't think she wants to wait another minute," Maggie said. She pictured the children huddled together in the basement and worried for their safety. The Magicas did not come easily into the world. Her mother never told Maggie the story of her birth, but her mother had also never brought up the fact that Maggie was the next Magica.

"Not yet, Maggie."

Rain continued to pour upon the house, blurring the world outside the bedroom window. Maggie lay her head back and breathed. She focused on the deluge, using it to mask the pain. Thunder rumbled overhead. They were prepared for hours of labor, but she wasn't sure if the house or neighborhood could sustain this prolonged attack of nature's energies.

A contraction seized Maggie, like fishhooks pulling her apart. An empty feeling in her abdomen alerted her that it was time.

"Mother Esme!"

"Oh, dear," Mother Esme said. The baby slipped from Maggie's body like a fish from one's hands. Mother Esme reached for the infant, and static electricity zapped her.

Maggie felt a rush of heat course through her. Mother Esme stood frozen with the baby clutched to her breast. Dr. Williams's knees buckled.

The world crackled and sparked. A white light exploded across the planet like a super nova.

Maggie threw back her head against the chair and exhaled. At that moment all witches in the Magic world experienced a surge of new power. A Magica born of a Magica ushered in a new era of magic. Maggie felt her own power start to fill her body, from her feet bubbling up to her head. The witches were all now more than they had previously been.

The baby wailed.

The surge ended releasing Dr. Williams and Mother Esme from their paralysis.

Maggie leaned back into the chair. Mother Esme wiped away only the blood and then handed Maggie the baby. Richard had vanished from the room.

"That happened so quickly. I was expecting a lot more destruction," Dr. Williams said, now able to stand.

"Look how thick the vernix caseosa is. This baby looks like a stick of butter," Mother Esme said. Maggie was too exhausted to laugh, but she grinned at the comparison. Unlike hospital practice, the vernix would remain on the newborn for two days.

The Mothers guided Maggie into bed. "Do you want us to stay or go?" the doctor asked.

"Thank you, Mothers," Maggie said. "You go ahead. Get a cup of tea. Check on the others. We're going to rest for a while."

The Mothers departed. Being alone with her newborn just after giving birth was Maggie's favorite time. "Welcome to the world, Gia. I'm your Mama and I'm here to love and protect you." Maggie kissed her baby's head.

At least one thing was going right.

CHAPTER 20

Flower bouquets and balloons filled Maggie's bedroom. It appeared at if everyone in the Witch World had sent a card or called to offer congratulations on the birth of the Arch-Magica. Downstairs, gift baskets covered every surface. Maggie was a little embarrassed by all the attention and presents.

She lay propped up in bed, cradling Gia, while Luka and Becca & Betsy cuddled at her sides. Luka ran the side of his index finger against the baby's downy cheek. "Kind of furry." They all laughed.

"Can she do anything magical yet?" Luka asked.

"Don't be silly," Becca & Betsy said. "She's just a baby."

Despite everything happening, the children missed only one day of school. Maggie wanted normalcy for them. She wanted to sit at their sides as they did homework. She wanted dinners at the big table. She wanted to tuck them in at night. "Luka, have you been brushing your teeth twice a day?"

Found out, a sheepish look crossed his face. "Sorry, Mom."

She pulled him to her and kissed his forehead. "It's okay, my love." Maybe this wasn't the time to fuss over such things. But when was it? There always seemed to be something interfering with their lives. Or maybe this was it. Maggie looked at her children. It was the first time she'd seen their lives from the perspective that trouble and danger couldn't be avoided. And now that Gia was the Arch-Magica, Maggie couldn't give up being the Magica. Its power would be with her for the rest of her life. This was a sobering thought.

"We'll help you remember, Luka," his sisters said. Maggie hugged the girls to her.

The plan had been to send the children away for a few days once Maggie went into labor, but now she was overjoyed to have them by her side. They were all safe, but things would've been different if her labor had been longer. Becca & Betsy confessed to being frightened when they couldn't move, even though they liked their new power of object divination. They demonstrated to everyone how they knew who the last person was to handle an object just by picking it up and concentrating. Kids had such resilience.

"Mom, when can we have her ceremony? Can we help plan it?" Becca & Betsy asked.

"Well, right now isn't the time for that kind of celebration. Remember your aunts just lost a wife, a sister, and a baby. Sylvie and June need time to grieve those losses. We all do."

"Oh, Mom, we're sorry. That was so insensitive of us." Becca started to cry, and Betsy hugged her sister. Then Luka teared up. His sisters drew him into their embrace.

Maggie felt terrible for hurting their feelings. She understood their enthusiasm. "That's okay, girls. I'm sorry. There will be plenty of time to consecrate the new Magica. And all of you can help plan the party."

"Mom," Luka said. "Things will get better." Now Maggie wanted to cry. Her children deserved better.

"Pizza's ready," Samuel yelled from the kitchen.

Luka scrambled out of the bed. "Bye, Mom. Bye, Gia."

"Pizza cures all," Maggie said.

The girls roused themselves, languidly stretching. Maggie was amazed at their litheness and remembered once being like her daughters. Now she was just a stiff-jointed old lady.

"Do you want us to bring you pizza?" Becca asked.

Samuel's five cheese specialty sounded wonderful. She thought about her figure for a minute but decided it was too soon to worry. "Sprinkle parmesan on it, please," Maggie said.

"And a salad," Betsy said.

"Of course, we would never forget to give you salad," Becca said. The girls drifted away, leaving Maggie with Gia.

Sylvie passed by her door. "Sylvie," Maggie called out.

Her sister-in-law came back and stood in the doorway. She wouldn't look at the baby. Maggie didn't push. "Have you heard from the police?"

The tendons in Sylvie's throat tightened. "Yeah, I've been in contact with them."

"What about the Abecedarians?"

Sylvie bristled. "Nothing."

Maggie nodded. She knew of the confrontation between her sister-in-law and Heather, but that subject was for another time. Maggie knew she needed to speak to Sylvie carefully. "How are you and June doing?"

"June is sleeping. I'm...I'm here. Sometimes I feel like I'm falling through a hole."

Maggie was surprised to hear Sylvie reveal the rawness of her grief. "I'm sorry, Sylvie." She pulled Gia closer to her breast. "I don't know how we got to this point."

Sylvie shifted her weight from one leg to the other. "Have you seen a bag, like a bowling ball bag?"

"No. Why?"

"About three days ago, a bowling ball bag was left on the back steps. I haven't seen it since," Sylvie said. "Can you call Benson. See if he knows anything about it?"

Maggie picked up her phone off the nightstand. His phone rang and rang. She prepared to leave a message, but he picked up.

After a few minutes of niceties, Sylvie cleared her throat. Maggie got the message and relayed Sylvie's question to him.

"Yes, I have the bag. Is Sylvie there? Can you put her on speaker, please."

"He wants me to put the phone on speaker," Maggie said. Sylvie shrugged.

"Sylvie, I took the bag, and it's safe," Benson reassured her. "But I didn't open it. I didn't think that was my place."

"Why did you take it?" Sylvie asked.

"I was afraid of what might be in it." He paused as if giving Sylvie time to fill in whatever frightening thing she could conjure in her mind. "So I brought it here to the station to have it scanned and checked over. There are no fingerprints on it either."

"And?"

Maggie felt embarrassed by Sylvie's terse replies. It wasn't Benson's fault all of this was happening. If anyone was responsible, it was Maggie herself.

"It doesn't contain a bomb. And it doesn't contain what I would call a severed head. But it does have something freaky in it. Do you want me to open it?"

Maggie jumped in. "Yes, Benson. Please open the bag."

The phone clinked as he set it down. For a minute, the two women heard items being moved around. A cabinet door squeaked open, followed by things falling with the soft pattering sound of tiny footsteps. "Damn," he muttered.

"Most likely he knocked over paperclips," Maggie said.

Sylvie sighed impatiently.

A clunk announced that he'd found the bag. "Are you ready?" Benson didn't wait for a reply. He pulled the zipper open. It sounded like a deck of cards being riffle shuffled.

"Well?" Sylvie asked.

"The scan showed me what was in it. So it's not a surprise, but I'm hoping it isn't real."

Now Maggie wanted to tell him to get on with it, but she waited.

"It's a skull. And there's a note." Maggie and Sylvie heard paper being unfolded.

"Okay, here it is. It says **FULL MOON**. Typed, not handwriting. What does it mean?"

Maggie explained, "The skull is a symbol for death. The note tells us when the Abecedarians are going to come for Heather and the book."

"Full moon? Isn't that kind of a cliché?"

"In magic it designates the end of a cycle," Maggie said.

"Well, not on my watch. And the only cycle that's going to end is theirs."

Sylvie snorted. "You joining us for the fight?"

"You bet I am," he said. "I'm on your side and nothing is going to keep me from being there that night."

Gia whimpered in her sleep. Maggie needed to cool the macho contest between the two. "We need everyone there to stop the Abecedarians."

Benson heard the message and switched topics. "I don't know what I'm going to do with this skull. It's not like I can send it to forensics."

"Just stow it some place for now," Sylvie said. "Turn it over later, after this settles."

He hesitated as if unsure about his own answer. "Sure. I can do that. About the note, do you want the police involved?"

Maggie leaned back into the pillows. "No. The police are working on the mur—" Maggie stopped herself.

"Murders," Sylvie said. Maggie winced.

"This other stuff is our business. The Abecedarians have a witch on their side. That kind of power can only be contained by other witches."

"Are you strong enough?" Benson said.

"My powers are coming back to me and stronger than ever," Maggie said. "The Full Moon happens in about eleven days. Today is Thursday. While both of you are fully capable, I don't think we can or should confront them on our own. We'll need help." Maggie looked at Sylvie.

"I know who to call."

As the Magica, Maggie could have easily called in reinforcements herself, but she knew her sister-in-law was one of those people who healed through purpose. It would help Sylvie if she kept busy.

"I'm here for whatever you need," Benson said.

Sylvie rolled her eyes and her head.

Maggie ignored her. "Since the police are already involved, having you with us would seem natural."

"You know this can get super dangerous," Sylvie interjected trying to dissuade Benson. "The Abecedarians have proven they're willing to kill."

"That's why I want to help. Maybe together we can stop any more deaths," he said. "Sylvie, do we start planning tomorrow?" Without answering, Sylvie turned and went downstairs. "Sylvie?"

"She left to make the phone call."

"So who are you contacting for additional help?"

"I think you need to see for yourself," she said.

"I miss you. Both Mother Esme and Dr. Williams said to give you some time."

"Yeah, they told me." She closed her eyes and allowed Benson's feelings to envelop her. "I miss you too."

"After all this, I'm going to ask you out on a real date."

She feigned outrage. "What? All this isn't enough for you?"

The phone went silent on his end. "I'm sorry, Maggie. Things went from bad to worse quickly. Even though I'm talking about missing you and going on dates, I feel your hurt and the hurt your whole family is going through."

"Benson, I was just teasing. I'm sorry. I didn't mean to make you feel bad." Maggie felt mortified.

"I know you were. I just wanted you to know how much I care."

"Okay, thank you. I'll talk to you later." She set the phone down.

Sylvie and Shondra reappeared in the doorway. "They're coming. They'll be here next week. Is that okay?" Shondra said.

"I hope so. Hopefully—"

"We have something to discuss," Sylvie interrupted.

"Come in and sit down." The women entered the room and settled on the love seat under the window looking out over the Hudson River, Maggie's beloved view.

"Now that we know when that cult is going to confront us, I'm going home for a few days to take care of things," Sylvie said. "I'll be back on Monday."

"I'm staying," Shondra said.

Gia stirred at the sound of the women's voices so close. Maggie tucked the blankets around her, giving her a sense of security. "What about your family, Shondra?"

"The girls are adults like Minerva. Can you believe that? Anyway, Rosemary is spending Thanksgiving with her fiancé."

"Thanksgiving?" Maggie said. "Is it Thanksgiving already?" Both women nodded. "What about your husband and Penelope?"

"Henri will be taking his parents and my mom and Penelope to a Thanksgiving dinner at Tavern on the Green, my mother's favorite restaurant."

Maggie thought how lovely that would be, getting dressed up, having an elegant meal, and then a postprandial walk about Central Park. Right now everything felt chaotic, and a life like that out of reach. When they moved past this crisis, things would be different. She would make sure of that. "What about June?"

"She wants to stay here. Everyone here knows what happened, and she says she can't face questions or even condolences. Her twins are with their dad, who gets visitation during Thanksgiving."

"What can we do for her?" Maggie asked. Sylvie just shrugged. "What if Minerva talks to her?"

"Oh, she has," Shondra said. "Min offered to take some of the pain from her."

"She asked me too," Sylvie said.

"What do you mean by take away the pain?" Maggie asked.

"It's her new magic," Shondra said. "We all have something new, but I haven't discovered what mine is yet."

This news surprised Maggie. She had no idea her daughter who protected herself from the emotions of others would offer to lessen their distress even if it was her newly acquired power.

"Maybe she's finding her path now," Shondra said reading a few of Maggie's thoughts. "That's why I chose dentistry to focus my empathic powers through."

"And that's why you're freaking rich," Sylvie said. "Everyone wants a pain-free dental experience."

Shondra, who should have been addressed as Dr. Denny, chuckled. "I've got something a lot of people want, but I also had to find a way to dispose of all that hurt, pain, and even anger so it wouldn't infect other things in my life. That's the hard part. Minerva's going to have to learn what works for her."

Rocks were Shondra's answer to that problem. She'd discovered that large boulders could absorb negative emotions without any repercussions to the world, and because of that she took up the sport of bouldering.

"What's your new power, Sylvie?" Maggie said.

Sylvie shrugged. "I don't know. I'm going back downstairs." Shondra excused herself as well.

Her sister-in-law didn't make things easy. Maggie considered all the preparations to be undertaken in less than two weeks, and now Sylvie would be away for three days. Maggie didn't know what kind of confrontation they were up against, but she trusted her sister-in-law's expertise in these matters. If Sylvie thought it safe to leave for a few days, it must be. Maggie worried for her children though. She needed Minerva with her, and even though her heart ached just thinking of it, Samuel would have to take Becca & Betsy and Luka to their grandparents in Florida. The children wouldn't be happy about having to leave, but their safety was more important than their preferences. Luka could not pout his way out of this. Maggie cringed thinking of calling her in-laws. It didn't matter if she was the Magica. Her mother-in-law hadn't spoken to her since Richard's murder. It took months before Sylvie took her phone calls. Both women never forgave her for the death of their son and brother. At least, they never took their anger out on Maggie's children. They loved their grandchildren.

There was also the issue with school. The kids might even miss a few days in the week after Thanksgiving. She would have to call in with a good explanation and make arrangements for their schoolwork.

She had no idea what would happen on the full moon but hoped the event would quickly and peacefully resolve itself. The skull didn't give her much comfort, though. Heather didn't want to go back to the cult, and there was no way the Abecedarians were getting the book. If that failed, Benson reassured her that the police could round them up and arrest them. That would put an end to the cult's nefarious plans.

The baby would stay with her. Gia needed her mother. No infant should have to come into the world amidst violence—or death. But she had. Gia had been born on the day that Lucy, Ginny, and Susan were found dead in her driveway. What kind of mother was she to expose her children to all these dangers? Was she any better a mother than her own?

Samuel appeared at her door bearing a tray with pizza and salad. He'd provided a little bowl of grated Parmigiano Reggiano and plated two of the delicious truffles sent as a gift. There was small vase of flowers and a cloth napkin. He peered over at Gia sleeping next to Maggie and whispered. "I repurposed some of the flowers from one of the bouquets sent to you."

She told him it looked beautiful, and she started with the salad. When she took her first bite, she realized she was ravenous.

"Mom, Thanksgiving is seven days away. What do you want to do?"

She was happy for the distraction. "I was just reminded of it. What do you think?"

"I want us to celebrate the holiday and I'm going to take care of everything. I'm in charge." He had only one request. "Can you let the younger kids know this? They never want to listen to me."

Maggie assured him she would. "Samuel, thanks for being a great person." He grinned.

A man's voice drifted upstairs. Maggie tensed. "Who is that, Samuel?"

"It's the repairman for the dryer."

Maggie laughed, and Samuel looked at her quizzically.

Here they were surrounded by death and destruction and still the mundane things of life needed attending to. Well, if nothing else they would have clean clothes.

Chapter 21

Maggie knew she had a lot to be thankful for, but she asked the Goddess for one more favor. It was Thanksgiving day, and she wanted another day of peace. For nearly a week, things had been quiet. The Abecedarians seemed to be sticking to their plan to come on the night of the full moon—unless it was a ruse.

She checked the baby in her crib. Gia had taken two feedings during the night, finally falling asleep at four a.m. She looked down at the little Arch-Magica, thinking about her future. All Maggie wanted was for her children to be safe. Before heading downstairs she looked in on Luka who was still sleeping, burrowed beneath a family quilt he loved. He was her little traditionalist. All her children were such different people.

Tomorrow, Samuel, Luka, and Becca & Betsy would fly to Florida to stay with their grandparents. And she would miss them terribly.

~

Last week she'd spoken to the children's grandfather Hermann Mills, Richard's father, about sending the children to stay with them, and he told her he would take care of the flight reservations for his four grandchildren. Angela, her mother-in-law, refused to join the call. In the background, she did hear her ask about the baby, and Maggie assured him, them, Gia was healthy and safe. The other children crowded around the computer to talk to their grandparents. Samuel explained he would be the one overseeing his siblings and would ensure their safety. Becca & Betsy chattered about how thrilled they were about the warmer weather in Florida. They could go swimming and hang out at the beach.

While his siblings talked with their grandparents, Luka chose to throw another tantrum. "I'm not talking to them because I'm not going!"

Maggie tried to draw him onto her lap, but he pushed away. "I'm not the baby anymore."

"I need for you and your brothers and sisters to be safe."

He kept himself five feet away from her, palms clenched at his sides. "What about Minerva? Don't you want her safe?"

She wanted to reach out to her little, angry guy but knew that wouldn't help. He wanted to have a serious discussion. So Maggie changed her tone. "If I could send your sister, I would. I don't want anything to happen to you children."

"But you did. Michael's dead."

The sting went deep, but she couldn't deny it. "That's why you have to go to your grandparents."

"No, I need to stay and protect my baby sister."

"There will be eleven women and Benson here. You know they'll let nothing happen to Gia. I'm sorry, but this discussion is over. You're going."

"I hate you!" Luka said before running off. His bedroom door slamming.

Maggie shuddered. It was the first time one of her children had uttered those words to her. She let him cool for thirty minutes before going to his room with a cup of ginger and honey tea. When Luka became upset, he always developed a stomachache. She knocked before entering. He was curled on his side but sat up when Maggie proffered the mug. He slurped half of it down, then handed it back to her.

He leaped up and flung himself into her arms. "I'm sorry, Mama. I don't hate you. Don't be mad at me."

The *Mama* melted her heart. "Baby, I'm not mad at you. I understand your feelings. I'm scared too." They calmly discussed the events and going to Florida. She promised to put Benson in charge of protecting the baby, and Luka agreed he was a good choice for that job. In the end she swore nothing would happen to Gia or any of them.

THAT WAS A WEEK AGO, AND LUKA HADN'T HAD ANY MORE TANTRUMS about going. She headed downstairs to help Samuel with the holiday preparations. In the kitchen, Samuel set a cup of coffee on the counter for her and the half & half. "Are you doing breakfast too?" she asked.

"Preventing a traffic jam in the kitchen." He had set up a breakfast bar near the banquette and out of his cooking path. The cauldron slow cooker was filled with oatmeal and all the toppings placed next to it in glass containers—brown sugar, honey, maple syrup, fruit. There were bowls, spoons, knives, along with the crystal glasses. Carafes were filled with juices and milk. Toast was also on the menu—wheat and gluten-free bread, along with the strawberry and blueberry jams Samuel canned himself in August. "Anything missing, Mom? I'll make some bacon too."

"It's beautiful and perfect." She squeezed his arm. "I'll be in my office. Come get me if you need help with the cooking," she said on her way out.

She set her coffee cup on her desk and retrieved her tarot cards. With the cards fanned out in front of her, she ran her hands over them, feeling the energy. Her index finger stopped and touched one. *The Moon.* She groaned, but it was apropos to what was heading their way. The card dealt with uncertainty and illusion. It advised to be careful with decisions as only half the information was being made available. The card also warned that fear from the past was being projected into the present.

Nope.

She wasn't having that today and set the card aside. It wasn't often she felt forced to redraw.

Three of Swords

Seriously? She would have nothing to do with that card either. She chose again and again.

Ten of Swords.

The Devil.

And again.

The Tower.

Maggie stopped. Her whole body trembled, and she wrapped her hands around the warm coffee mug to calm herself. No more. She was going to own the day and not allow it to be dictated by outside forces.

There was a knock, and then Mother Esme entered holding Gia. "Look who I found awake and hungry." She noticed the cards face up on Maggie's desk. "Oh dear." She met Maggie's eyes. "Don't worry. The cards aren't fated. We have the divine right to make our own destiny. Come on. Put the deck away. Let's all go and have breakfast, especially this sweet little one." Mother Esme burbled nonsense syllables at the baby. From the kitchen happy noises and the scent of bacon filled the house.

"Mom," she heard Becca & Betsy whine, and Maggie knew her energies were needed elsewhere.

∼

By afternoon the whole house smelled like Thanksgiving. Considering the cards she'd pulled that morning, she kept expecting some terrible event to happen at any minute. But the worst thing that occurred was the squabble between Becca & Betsy and Samuel. The girls wanted to make a crudités platter of carrots, radishes, celery, and hummus to tide them all over until dinner, defying their older brother's mandate that everyone stay out of the kitchen. Maggie had to play referee. Samuel relented and gave the girls a small slice of counter. He allowed the vegetable appetizer but told them to be quick and no bread. They agreed.

Sylvie hadn't returned yet, deciding to stay at her own home for the holiday. Maggie couldn't leave Heather locked up in the school. She brought her into the house, but out of respect for June's feelings, Maggie restricted the young woman to the children's playroom upstairs.

To combat the negativity of the cards, Maggie fluttered about the house making sure everyone was happy and comfortable. She headed upstairs to check on Luka and found him in the playroom working on a puzzle with Heather. Maggie stayed out of sight and watched. Luka, ever sociable, had Heather laughing. Maggie wondered what Heather's life was like in the cult. They probably didn't do Thanksgiving. A cult was a family, a hyperbolic and psychotic form of one but still a family in their minds. They probably had their own traditions. Without modern technology, she doubted Heather enjoyed carefree moments like this. Maggie decided to leave the two of them be.

With June still grieving, seating was going to be difficult. Maggie decided Heather had to stay in the kitchen. She hated doing this, but June was in a difficult place. Heather appeared crestfallen until Luka volunteered to have dinner with her. When Becca & Betsy heard of the arrangement, they wanted to be in the kitchen as well. Maggie had mixed feelings about the younger children not sitting at the dining room table for Thanksgiving, but to subject Heather to isolation on a holiday was something Maggie couldn't stomach. The mother in her just couldn't do it. Luka asked if they could have a tablecloth, flowers, and the good China. Maggie gave the kids the go ahead.

Benson arrived at 1:00 promptly bearing a pumpkin pie and a Dutch apple crumb with a half-gallon of vanilla bean ice cream. On the pretense of showing him her office, the two snuck off for ten minutes. She felt drunk on her feelings. All she wanted was to be close to him. Luka came knocking, and she quickly sobered up. On the way out, Benson stopped her and kissed her hand. That first date couldn't come soon enough for either of them.

Samuel announced dinner was ready. Maggie directed family and guests into the dining room. She headed the table with the baby's bassinet at her side. She declared the chair nearest the kitchen as Samuel's, but everyone else was free to sit wherever they liked. The table was laden with mashed potatoes, stuffing, roasted vegetables, gravy, cranberry sauce, biscuits, and ham. Once everyone found a place, Samuel entered the room with a golden turkey on a platter, which he set in the middle of the table. The group applauded.

Maggie stood. She lifted her glass of wine and looked at each person seated at her table: Dr. Williams, Minerva, Mother Esme, Shondra, Samuel, June, Minerva, and Benson. From her position, she could see Luka, Becca & Betsy, and even Heather in the kitchen.

"I want to thank everyone for their support for what has passed and what is to come. We remember those we have lost, and we are grateful for who we have and what we have. Happy Thanksgiving!"

"Happy Thanksgiving." They all clinked glasses.

They ate and talked. Samuel received numerous compliments. Becca & Betsy were showing Heather something on their phones, which made them all smile. Heather looked young and at ease. June nibbled at her food, but she smiled often. Shondra and Dr. Williams drank too much wine. And Benson proved to be a natural storyteller.

As they sat around in the late afternoon eating their desserts, Maggie was glad they had overcome the dark portents of the cards. The following days would be unknowns.

CHAPTER 22

As planned, on the Friday after Thanksgiving Shondra drove the four children to the airport. Maggie cried when they left, but she was glad not to have them to worry about. Only the baby had to be protected, and Benson and Mother Esme were tasked with that responsibility. He didn't have the magical power to fight a witch, but most of the Abecedarians were nonmagicals. All he needed was a gun to fend them off. Noah Corwin's focus would be on retrieving the book and Heather.

And Sylvie was back.

Maggie stood at the sink washing baby bottles. She would pump enough milk to feed the baby through whatever melee incurred. Something grazed the back of her arm. Maggie jerked away and took up a defensive posture, ready for an attack.

"Whoa. I'm sorry," Benson said, holding his hands up in surrender.

"You scared me."

"You're scared? You don't look scared. You look like you could've killed me."

"I'm a little on edge."

He nodded. "Got some time?" He pulled out a chair at the banquette for her. Gia was upstairs napping with both Mothers. It was wonderful to have people in the house who were devoted to helping her with a newborn. Not everyone had that luxury. Maggie sat down, and he took the seat across from her.

"Things have been happening so fast that you and I haven't had time to talk."

This is it. He's leaving. "I'm sorry. This isn't what you expected when we met. I understand if you want to go."

Benson leaned back in his chair. "Are you kidding? I'm not going anywhere. Listen, you're right about one thing: Things are crazy around here. You just gave birth. A wacko cult is threatening to attack you. Why?"

Maggie was bewildered and alarmed by his questioning. "What do you mean why? They want Heather and the book."

"But there's another why, like why are you letting this happen?"

He didn't understand. He couldn't. "I'm the Magica."

"Duty-bound. I get it. But you don't have to take on this cult. Let me take Heather away. Give the book to someone to hide. The police are already investigating the four murders. This problem stops being yours alone."

"Of course, as a police officer I know your primary goal is to make sure the murders get solved and the bad guys apprehended, not all this other stuff," she said. If he wanted to leave, he should just go.

"Maggie, you're not listening." He picked up her hand and kissed it. She wasn't expecting the gesture. "This has nothing to do with my job. I'm here because I'm completely smitten with you."

"I have no idea why. Four people have been murdered. I just gave birth to my seventh child. You know we're witches. I wouldn't blame you if you walked out that door and didn't come back."

"Let me take Heather from here. When your reinforcements arrive today, have them take the book far away. Be done with this."

Maggie closed her eyes. "I am the Magica. Just like you as a police officer have a duty to serve and protect. So do I. Corwin will never stop until someone stops him."

"Yeah, when you put it that way, I get it. I had to try." His hand brushed across her jawline up to her hair where he tucked a strand behind her ear. Her face flushed and her toes curled. "Can I kiss you again?"

She nodded.

He pressed his lips to hers. He then did a soft sweep as if tasting her. She moved closer to him. Benson wrapped his arms around her and drew her in tight. His kiss deepened, and Maggie met it with her lips slightly parted. They stayed like that for several minutes. She had forgotten how passionate kissing a new partner was. Kissing him was sexy but comfortable.

Maggie's eyes fluttered open.

Her dead husband was standing near the sink, just a few feet from her. Maggie pushed Benson away. She stood, her chair tipping backwards.

Richard.

Then he drifted away like mist.

"What's wrong? Did you see someone?" He looked around the room for an intruder.

"It was my husband."

Benson kept glancing about the kitchen. "I don't see anyone. Is he gone?"

Maggie put her fingers to her lips not wanting to lose Benson's warmth. "He's gone now. I opened my eyes, and Richard was right there. He startled me. I'm sorry, Benson."

"Sorry for what? For having a life? We've all got a past. Have you been seeing him recently?"

"Yes, this isn't the first time. He reappeared when you entered my life."

"Do ghosts get jealous?"

"They do."

His eyes grew wide, and he looked over his shoulder. Her answer wasn't what he expected.

"Maybe all this is too soon."

Benson moved to embrace her, but she stepped aside. "Maggie, he's passed on, and I'm here right now."

"No, he's physically dead, but he hasn't passed on. I haven't seen him since the night we conceived Gia." She waited for him to comment, but he only gave her what she was now calling his Benson-look—unsurprised and completely accepting of her life. Seeing that expression, she wanted to egg him on to get a reasonable reaction. "You don't find that's crazy? A spirit impregnating his wife?"

"Well, I kind of wondered how it happened, but that's not my business to meddle in. I figured you would tell me when you're ready."

"Benson, how are you so unfazed by all this?"

"Because I'm crazy about you."

"You've got to have something to think or say about my life."

He leaned back in his chair. "Okay, I'm trying to be supportive, but if you want to know what I'm thinking, here's something: Do you think you just might be manifesting guilt about us?"

She placed her hands on the edge of the counter where Richard had been leaning. She felt him, the warmth of his body, his smell. "Do I feel guilty? Of course, I do. Did I just see my subconscious acting up? No. His presence lingers." She released the counter. "I don't know what his appearance means. But, kissing you…"

Maggie blushed like a teenage girl. She was an adult woman, and she could tell this man how she felt. "Benson, kissing you was like something sweet and hot pouring through me."

He grinned as if proud he could rouse such emotions in her. "I hear a but."

"But I need to figure out what Richard's reappearance means before we take this any further—if either of us wants that after all this." It frightened her to say those things to him, but she needed to give him a way out of this if it was too much. And she knew they were already mired in too much.

Benson's crushed look snagged at her heart.

A van rumbled up the driveway, and Maggie was glad for the distraction. What was happening between them was too intense, and too fast. Richard's appearance after all these months complicated matters.

"I guess you've got company, but this conversation isn't over. It's just tabled."

She agreed. "Come on. Reinforcements have arrived. I want you to meet some amazing people."

~

Maggie and Benson went out to the front porch. Sylvie, Minerva, and Shondra joined them.

The black sprinter van came to a stop, and the doors popped open. Four women stepped out, but Maggie recognized only one, Kissa Hassan, the team's leader. The other three were new, and Maggie wondered what had happened. She would have to ask later. The team approached them, but she was also curious about Benson's reaction. The witches were dressed in military style black cargo pants, turtlenecks, and jackets. They all stood near or over six feet tall. They looked as if they should be walking in slow motion with explosions behind them.

Becca & Betsy would have thrilled over this moment, and Maggie was sad her younger children had to be sent away.

"Who are they?" Benson said.

"The Sisters of Bast," Shondra whispered in awe.

Maggie went to greet them, while everyone else remained on the porch. Kissa Hassan approached Maggie and bowed in acknowledgment of the Magica. Maggie was never comfortable with these displays. In her eyes she served as a figurehead, or at most her true reason for existing, as a fail-safe mechanism. She never saw herself as the leader of the witches. It went against the independence of women, but she wasn't going to argue with the Amazonian force standing before her. When in the presence of these women, Maggie was the Magica, and out of respect for tradition and the feelings of others, she had to keep that in mind. The other three women stayed behind their leader and bowed, slightly deeper, to the Magica.

"Kissa Hassan and the Sisters of Bast, thank you for coming," Maggie said.

"It's our honor to be of assistance to the Magica."

Maggie personally knew Kissa Hassan, having met on several occasions. Once at a Sabbat and one other time that ended very poorly for the people causing trouble to a family of witches living in a small town in Alabama. And there was the London tragedy. Kissa Hassan introduced her associates: Amanda Peters, Sarah Mercia, and Ellie Mercia. Maggie welcomed them into her home.

Everyone on the porch moved aside, creating a path for the warrior witches to pass through. Maggie made no introductions. These witches were here to protect them, not make friends. Clear boundaries had to be set. The familiarity between the Basts and Maggie's people would be determined by their leader. Kissa Hassan turned her attention in the direction of Benson for a scant second before she looked away. They followed the Magica into the formal dining room.

Maggie took the head of the table. Kissa Hassan sat to her right. Maggie directed Sylvie to take the seat to the left of her. The remaining three Basts took the other seats.

Shondra, who understood the protocol, spoke up, "Magica, we will return to our duties." Benson appeared confused, but Maggie met his eyes as Shondra dragged him from the room.

"Magica, forgive my impertinence but why is there a man here? Your husband died several years ago. Are you remated?" Maggie knew Kissa's formal language was a way to create distance and objectivity. The Basts were here on a mission.

"He's a friend and a police detective. His involvement helped a lot when the police came after the murders," Maggie explained. Sylvie flinched at the word. Maggie wanted to wrap a supportive arm around her sister-in-law.

Kissa Hassan reached out and took Sylvie's hand, surprising both Sylvie and Maggie. "I am and we all are very sorry for your loss. Nothing is worse than losing your partner and child. We are here to help. We will make those bastards pay." Sylvie thanked her for her compassion and support.

"Magica, you have a lovely home," Amanda said.

The comment shocked Maggie, but she masked it and thanked the young woman. The Sisters of Bast cast a different impression than what she previously experienced, a little more human. Maggie wondered what had happened to Kissa for the change in this team.

The Mothers came downstairs with the baby. Kissa Hassan stood and introduced her team members to both Mother Esme and Dr. Williams. The three women paid their respects to the Mothers. Then all four women of the Sisters of Bast kneeled before the little Arch-Magica, each pledging their lives and fidelity to the little witch. Baby Gia cooed and waved her arms around. Maggie saw Benson peaking from the kitchen, and he grinned at her.

Once the formalities were through, Amanda spoke to Kissa first. "Do I have your permission to ask?" Kissa granted the request.

"Magica, would you give us the honor of holding the Arch-Magica?" Amanda asked.

Again, Maggie couldn't have been more surprised than if they asked if they could have a slumber party and drink milkshakes. This was not the Sisters of Bast she was familiar with. Maggie told the women they could all hold the baby. They grinned at her and at one another.

Each woman held Gia for a few minutes, gazing at her in awe. Only Kissa demurred. The contrast of the warriors clad in black leather holding a baby dressed in a pink onesie in their callused hands was striking. When they passed Gia around, they took care with the newborn's delicate neck and head.

Gia gurgled; her big eyes focused on the newcomers. The baby's reactions delighted the women who laughed and baby-talked back to the infant.

"She seems so big for being so new," Sarah Mercia said.

"I get her next, Sister," Ellie, Sarah's actual sister, said. At six feet three inches, Ellie was the tallest of the Basts. Her dark brown hands swaddled all of Gia, making the baby look no bigger than a toy football. Ellie appeared to be the most enamored with Gia, cooing and kissing her forehead. "I could just eat you up. Yes, I can."

Kissa didn't admonish the warrior for expressing emotion so freely.

Gia smiled at Ellie.

"That's her first smile," Maggie said. She felt no jealousy, and in fact took it as an auspicious moment.

Ellie's eyes watered. "Thank you, Magica and Arch-Magica."

It made Maggie happy that Gia bestowed her first smile to a Bast. The four witches lived a rugged, nomadic life. Their Sisterhood had existed for thousands of years as the warriors and protectors of witches. There were few Sisterhoods like that of the Basts. New sisters were inducted when a Bast either retired or died, most never had the chance to do the former. Bast witches were both magically and physically powerful. They never married nor bore children.

Mother Esme cleared her throat. "Sorry to be a bother, but it's time for Gia to have her afternoon meal."

Ellie appeared sad as she handed the baby to Maggie. Sarah and Amanda expressed their gratefulness. Maggie let them know they were welcome at any time to interact with the baby. All three warriors smiled and nodded.

"That includes diaper changing," Maggie added.

The three warriors looked surprised and dismayed. Amanda blushed. They didn't know how to answer the Magica's terms.

"I'm just kidding," Maggie said. The Basts exhaled in relief.

"Sisters, see to our supplies and rooms. I have some business with the Magica," Kissa Hassan said.

Everyone excused themselves and left the two leaders alone. Maggie gestured for Kissa to follow her to Maggie's study. She didn't take her chair behind her desk. That would have been disrespectful to Kissa's position.

Instead, Maggie settled into a comfortable armchair. Gia burbled, knowing what was coming. Maggie undid the top buttons of her blouse and took out a breast. Gia latched on, humming as she suckled.

Kissa took the other armchair next to Maggie. "Do you have the book here?"

"I left the safe open. Help yourself."

Kissa fetched the book. Something else in the safe gave her pause. "Is this what I think it is?"

"It is." Maggie forgot her safe held artifacts precious to the Witch World. "Do you want to hold it?"

"I'm tempted." Kissa shut the safe with a sigh. "But the focus needs to be on the book. I would like to speak to this girl who came to you."

"Heather."

"May I?" Maggie nodded, and Kissa laid the book in the middle of the desk. She glanced at the safe.

Maggie understood Kissa's desire to handle the object. "Are you sure?"

"I'm fine." She turned her attention back to the book. "Do I need to wear gloves?"

"No, the pages are vellum."

Kissa pulled back the cover. She ran a hand over the first page. "Oh, it feels like velvet. I thought it would be dry and wrinkled, maybe sound like autumn leaves." She turned a few pages. "It's like the whispering of beautiful women."

Maggie turned the baby around and put her at the other teat. "I get so angry thinking of the Witches Library destroyed."

"The other Western and Eastern libraries have been put under extra protection."

"At least those books are safe. The Abecedarians want this book to prove the existence of witches since all the witch lines are recorded in it. Did you know Lavinia?"

Kissa shook her head. "We only frequent the library in London. I'm pained at the murders of our sisters."

Maggie waited. Kissa wanted to talk about something else, not books, or even the murders.

"The man who's here. Tell me more."

Everyone had the same question for Maggie. She explained everything that had occurred since Heather showed up at her door during a storm.

"No disrespect, Magica. The Sisters of Bast fight alongside no man. If you insist he stay, then we must go. I am very sorry to be so blunt. You know our history. These are our rules."

Maggie knew. As warriors the Sisters had joined with the forces of men to thwart evil, and on as many occasions the same men who sought their help betrayed them, murdered them, raped them, imprisoned them. After helping to destroy the great evil of Hitler and his Nazis, the Sisters of Bast no longer allied with men, even with men who seemed decent and virtuous.

The baby pulled away from her breast and drooled. Maggie set Gia against her shoulder, patting her back until she burped. Some witch queen she made, burping babies and changing diapers, but if she had to choose between being a mother and being the Magica, motherhood easily won. Being the Magica was dangerous and put everyone at risk. It wasn't like a regular job, which would have been more manageable, even with kids. She would have loved being a fulltime teacher at a community college. Well, there were a lot of witches in the Magic world who would agree that they would all be better off if Maggie did something else than being the Magica. But it wasn't like she asked for the job.

She didn't know how to respond to Kissa. It wasn't as if she needed a man when they went up against the Abecedarians, but there was something different about Benson. He had a quality about him that saw beyond gender or race or any label. He'd fallen for her despite her pregnancy. Her children adored him, even Minerva was getting there. Now Maggie would have to disinvite him from participating.

The baby's head felt heavy on her shoulder, and she knew Gia would sleep for several hours. She reached out to Mother Esme, lightly touching the woman's mind without being intrusive. Within minutes, the older woman arrived to take Gia off to her crib. It was strange to use magic after months of having gone dry.

Maggie tried to alleviate Kissa's hesitation without resorting to the position of the Magica. "Benson Scott is a good man. While we protect the book, he will be protecting Gia. I need the Mothers with me. Minerva's never been involved in anything like this. Shondra is reliable, but I worry about June. I don't think she can be of any help. Sylvie will be fighting with you. I need the help of the Sisters of Bast. We are in a serious position." Maggie was trying to argue her case.

Kissa flipped a few more pages, staying quiet. "Yes, losing one's sister or wife is very difficult. You think Sylvie's strong enough for this fight?"

Maggie knew Sylvie's pain was just as great, maybe even greater than June's, but a scab was forming over Sylvie's wound. Later, after all this was finished, that scab would rub off and Sylvie's hurt would bleed and pain her. For the moment, she'd hardened herself.

"Sylvie's more than capable. This leaves me with Minerva, Shondra, and the two Mothers," Maggie said. "Not much of a fighting team."

"And you, the Magica, and we, the Sisters of Bast. An ample army against a cult of nonmagicals and one rogue witch."

Kissa was right. They needed the magic and protection of the warrior sisterhood. Kissa remained quiet, turning the pages and giving Maggie time to think. She didn't know how she was going to tell Benson he would need to leave. It in fact embarrassed her. What choice did she have? "I'll let him know that we don't need his assistance."

"Thank you, Magica. We serve you faithfully."

"With that being settled, you must be hungry and tired. June and Shondra are in the kitchen to help." Maggie knew she was being harsh dismissing Kissa so abruptly but she wanted her annoyance registered. She might be granting Kissa this courtesy, but she didn't have to like it.

Kissa met Maggie's eyes, understood, and left the room.

In her ill humor, Maggie didn't want to leave her study. She picked up her cell phone and texted Benson who appeared within minutes. She explained Kissa's position to him.

"Are you sure?"

"I don't want to do this, but Kissa said they wouldn't stay with you here."

"First Minerva, then Sylvie, and now Kissa. I feel like persona non grata around here."

Maggie winced. "So why do you stay?" She knew she had asked him the question a dozen times, but she had to give him a graceful way out.

"I don't know, Maggie. It doesn't make sense." He paused and looked around her study. "My gut's telling me this is where I need to be. I know you don't need a hero, but I don't like leaving you to all this. Are you sure you're strong enough?"

She raised her hand, snapped her fingers, and whispered *incendio*. The papers in the trash can caught fire. She waved her hand and the fire died out.

"Impressive. Was that a special witch language?" Benson asked.

"Spanish." The surprised look on his face made her grin. "It doesn't matter what language you use. It's not the word that makes the magic. The power is already there. The gestures, the words, just ways to focus and harness the power."

"Can I hug you?" He put his arms around her and drew her in. "There has to be something I can do to help."

"You've done so much, and you hardly know us." His touch melted every tense muscle in her body. She rested her cheek against his chest feeling his heartbeat.

"I know it's a cliché, but I feel as if we've known one another a lifetime," he said.

Movement at the window caught her attention. A man, dark haired and wearing jeans and a t-shirt, walked into the woods. Richard. This time Maggie didn't push Benson away.

"Is he here again?" he asked.

"Yes. I'm sorry. You should go." She clung to him, not wanting him to leave her.

"I'll have my phone with me every moment, even in the shower. You call me if you need me. No matter what Kissa says. Okay? You are the Magica, right? No one should be able to boss around the Magica." He kissed her. Once again, her toes curled.

"You should be mad, Benson. Why aren't you upset? Fight back. Demand to stay."

He took her hands. "You have such beautiful eyes. The gold-flecks in them are sparking." He sighed. "Maggie, it's not my place to behave like that. You're in a serious situation and need real help. The kind of help only a bunch of badass warrior witches can provide. I'm just a mere man, a nonmagical. I'm not leaving you, just this particular situation."

A book fell off a shelf, and they both looked at it. He picked it up and read the cover: *Potions and Spells for Love & Relationships*. "I think this is a message." He put the book back in its place. "See you later, Maggie."

Benson left. She heard the front door open. Then the throaty sound of his car as he drove off. Once again, she experienced heartbreak. For the past two years that was the emotion that consumed her. Right now wasn't the time for love and relationships. She remembered her sobering thought that trouble and danger was her life. Maybe there never would be time in her life for anything romantic. She couldn't think about any of that right then.

Right then, they needed to prepare for the full moon—for Corwin, the rogue witch, and their cult.

Chapter 23

Maggie rose early hoping she could have time to herself.
First, she checked on Gia. Her deep and even breathing meant she would
sleep for a little while longer. Maggie tip-toed downstairs. When she entered the kitchen, evidence of the Basts having beaten her alarm clock could
be found on the counters and table, but the warriors themselves were not
present. Maggie assumed they were out doing a twenty-mile jog. Grateful to
have coffee back in her life, Maggie poured the biggest mug she could find
before heading for her office.

Richard's sudden appearance meant something. The dead didn't appear
unbidden or without reason. When Richard first came to her after his death, the power of love and grief created the opportunity for him to crossover.
But after Gia's conception, he stopped visiting her, and Maggie felt his death as reality for the first time. To keep seeing Richard appear only when she
was close to Benson bothered her. Her deceased husband was trying to send
her a message.

The altar was ready for Maggie to reach out to her husband. Starting a
fire in a trashcan was nothing compared to summoning the dead. She thought of little Michael and how much she would love to see him again, but
that was a path she would never go down. One thing to summon an adult,
but to do that to a child was unconscionable.

Minerva opened the door. "Mom, sorry to bother you, but can you
come out to the school please?"

The summoning would have to wait. Maggie closed and locked the
doors to her office before going out to see why she was needed. Whatever
Richard was trying to tell her would have to wait.

All four of the Bast Sisters along with Sylvie and Shondra had crowded into Heather's small room. They encircled the young woman who cowered on her bed. Maggie couldn't believe this was happening again. She squeezed in amongst the witches. Heather had buried her face in a pillow.

"She won't speak to us," Kissa said. "The girl insists she will speak only to you."

"Please, all of you. Come out to the living area." Maggie waited until the seven women assembled. "You're scaring her, Sisters. Look at yourselves, you are absolutely menacing in your black leather," Maggie chastised. "How about everyone leave, except for Kissa and Sylvie. And Minerva. The rest of you walk about the property perimeter and bind some sigils to trees and the walls surrounding the house. We need to secure the property and we only have today and tomorrow to do it." Maggie surprised herself at how easily she was falling into the role of leader.

The warrior sisters grumbled about having to do protection binds, which they saw as beneath them. Shondra led the way out, and the three warriors followed.

Maggie looked around the room and at the departing group. "Where's June?"

"Still not feeling well. I think she's sleeping," Sylvie said.

Maggie decided now was the time to discuss the change in plans. "We'll need June to watch over Gia and Heather on the night of the full moon."

"What about Benson?" Sylvie asked. "June's not up to this. I'm barely up to this."

Maggie didn't feel the need to explain his departure, surprising herself again. "I empathize with June. I understand her pain, but we need everyone right now."

"What was wrong with the original plan. Just let Benson do it. Then June can spend the time healing," Minerva said.

Before Maggie had to repeat herself, Kissa spoke up, "I asked the Magica to tell him to leave."

"Why?" Minerva and Sylvie asked.

"Minerva. Sylvie," Maggie warned.

"It's fine that they know." Kissa repeated the same explanation she gave Maggie.

"He's not like that," Minerva said when Kissa finished speaking.

The dynamic was changing. What had made Minerva and Sylvie change their minds about Benson?

"Maybe not but we can't risk it," Kissa said. "That is our way."

Minerva turned away from the group but immediately returned. "You know what? I don't understand any of this. Why do we even love men then? What good are they if we can't trust them?" Minerva's anger produced a swarm of welts on her arms and chest. She looked down at them and then ran from the room.

"I should go after her," Sylvie said.

"No," Maggie said. "I'll see to her later."

"Did you see her arms?" Sylvie asked.

"She's manifesting great anger," Kissa said.

Minerva's outburst was out of character for her. Maggie was convinced that something was troubling her daughter besides their immediate situation. She needed to find a few minutes to spend with her eldest and get to the real reason for her state of mind. It would have to wait though. "Let's take care of this now."

The smaller group returned to Heather's room. "This is Kissa Hassan, and she's here to help. She wants to ask you some questions about the Abecedarians so that we can prepare for the full moon."

"What's happening on the full moon?" Heather asked.

"You don't know?" Heather's blank look reaffirmed Maggie's belief that Heather was innocent of the cult's plans.

"You don't know that your people are coming here for you and the book?" Kissa asked.

Heather's eyes grew large, and she hugged her knees into her chest. "Don't let them take me. Please don't."

"She seems genuinely afraid, Magica." Kissa spoke as if Heather wasn't in the room.

"Heather's just a child. She was raised to despise and subvert her true nature as a witch. She was there when they killed Lavinia. It frightened her, and she ran away to the only place she knew would protect her."

"But her mother is helping the Abecedarians," Kissa added.

"Maybe she doesn't have a choice either. You know how cults manipulate people's minds and wills."

"Will you grant me permission to speak to Heather further? I'm sorry, Sylvie. I would like to do this alone." Sylvie shrugged and walked away.

"Are you going to interrogate her?"

"No, I will initiate a dialogue with her," Kissa explained. "I would like to know about her day-to-day homelife within the Abecedarian cult. I am hoping to get more facts about them, Noah Corwin, but especially about her mother. Everything we can find out now will help us when the full moon arrives."

"You have my permission." Maggie turned her attention to the girl. "What do you think, Heather? Willing to talk with Kissa about your life?"

The young woman nodded.

Maggie excused herself. Now maybe she could get back to the summoning spell.

A tendril of emotion reached out and prodded Maggie. Gia needed her mother. Richard would have to wait again. And she couldn't forget that she needed to talk to Minerva as well. Maggie felt pulled in too many directions.

Chapter 24

The day they dreaded arrived, but sunshine broke through the clouds that had haunted the skies for weeks. Maggie was grateful they wouldn't have to defend themselves in the rain. On the other hand, the irony wasn't lost on her that the day they feared was also turning into a beautiful one, the first in a long time.

Sylvie and Kissa had taken charge of preparing the house and property for whatever the Abecedarians had planned. The cult had demonstrated that violence and murder were on the menu, and the entire house was covered with a bubble of protection. Though their group was powerful, Maggie put out a call to the witch community asking other witches to lend a bit of their magic to help create the barrier. Nothing was breaking into her house. Outside, the Basts had laid a perimeter of binds and hexes.

Sarah and Ellie walked the property with Maggie, Kissa, and Sylvie. The two warriors pointed out their contributions. "These sigils are like landmines," Amanda explained. "Step on one and you'll regret it. I have advised everyone to stay near the house and not wander too close to any of the walls surrounding the property."

When they returned to the house, Minerva walked past Maggie without acknowledging her. Benson's dismissal from the campaign still angered her daughter. With all the preparations needing to be taken care of, Maggie hadn't found the time to speak with her. Benson's absence made Maggie feel awful, and she missed him more than she expected, more than she should have. Her attraction to Benson had been immediate and intense. She marveled at how such a thing could have happened to her. She always believed Richard would be her only and last love, but all of that had to wait.

Kissa asked everyone to join her in the dining room where a map lay spread out on the table. "I know we've walked the property, but it is helpful to see the plan on paper to reinforce our strategy."

The women nodded in agreement. Kissa continued. "Here is the house. As you can see the Hudson River protects it from the east. I doubt they'll be coming by boat, and the shoreline is difficult to traverse. On the westside is the neighbor's property. This is our weakest point." She put her finger on the property line. "Unfortunately, Maggie, your neighbors are very tidy and keep the trees and hedges trimmed, which means that side is easy to access."

Sarah raised her hand, and Kissa acknowledged her. "That's why you had us put so many of the magical protections there."

"That is correct. Now the back of the property is the most protected. After the schoolhouse, lie twenty-four hectares—"

"What's that in acres?" Sylvie asked.

"Sixty acres," Maggie answered.

"Yes, so there are sixty *acres* behind the school," Kissa sounded annoyed, "and then some public lands, which amounts to over two hundred acres of extremely forested land. I walked your property. Fallen trees, deep brush, unexpected ravines, and thorny blackberry brambles. This is a natural line of defense. The cult consists of nonmagicals, and they aren't getting through that forest." The group mumbled in agreement. "The cult's approach must be from the road. This is where the witch will be, and their main point of attack."

"That looks easy to defend then. So how do they expect to get Heather and the book?" Sylvie asked.

"The nonmagicals will rely on weapons, mostly guns, and Esther will use magic. Their strategy will be to tire us out, to wear us down," Kissa said.

"They might try a diversion or some way to separate our forces," Sylvie said.

"I agree. But we are eight witches on the ground against nonmagicals. We have the tactical advantage. Plus, within the house we have another three witches, and I think Heather would come to her own aid if the Abecedarians tried to take her," Kissa said. "Any questions?" No one spoke up. "Okay, rest, eat, and prepare yourselves for a long and grueling night of defending this place. The group broke up and went their own ways.

Once the major details were settled, Maggie made a video call to Samuel and the children. They and their grandfather begged to see Gia, and Maggie held her up for everyone to gush over. Once again Maggie's mother-in-law didn't join the call. Maggie spoke to each child individually, leaving Samuel for last. She filled her eldest son in on all the details of what was about to happen that evening. He promised to watch over his three younger siblings.

"Tell your grandparents not to worry."

Maggie's mother-in-law suddenly appeared in the frame next to Samuel who was forced to step aside. Encounters with Angela made Maggie cringe. Angela never wanted Richard to marry her, warning him of the complications of being in a relationship with a Magica. And if that hadn't been enough, she cautioned him about Maggie's background, considering her beneath Richard and his family. As far as her mother-in-law was concerned, all her dire predictions for Richard's union with Maggie proved true. And now with Lucy and the baby dead, Maggie couldn't blame her mother-in--law for hating her even more.

"Do you plan on having the ceremony?" No greeting or niceties.

Maggie didn't know how to respond. Was Angela in favor or against it? She would keep her response vague. "It's not something I can think about right now. We need to get past what's happening here. I filled Samuel in, and he has my permission to let you know what's going on."

Angela bristled and her face turned red. "I didn't know this was dangerous. What is going on? Is Sylvie there?" Angela's voice turned shrill. "I don't want my daughter there. Haven't you done enough damage. My son. My daughter--in-law. Two grandchildren. If you get another one of my children or grandchildren killed again, I will make it my mission to take them away from you."

Maggie started shaking. Her mother-in-law's threat was appalling. Before Maggie could answer, Sylvie came into the room.

"Is that my mom?"

Maggie wondered how much Sylvie had heard, but she took Maggie's place in front of the computer giving no indication that she had. Angela relaxed and beamed at her daughter. Standing on the other side of the room, out of view of the camera, Maggie watched a mother console her heartbroken daughter. Maggie left the room, needing to calm her own anger.

After Sylvie disconnected, Maggie returned to the kitchen. "We need to talk."

Sylvie grimaced. "My mom told me what she said to you. I'm sorry."

"No, she's right. You should go."

Sylvie leaned against a kitchen counter and shook her head. "I told my mom speaking to you like that was inappropriate."

"This has turned into a nightmare," Maggie said. "I—"

"Stop." Sylvie turned and looked out the kitchen window over the sink, her eyes fixed on a distant point. "I can't leave. This is about me and what I lost. I'm going to hunt down those fucking Abecedarians and the witch and make them pay."

Maggie didn't say anything about Sylvie's swearing. In this case, it was appropriate. What the cult was doing marked them as monstrous and deserving of hate.

"So I'm staying."

"Well, let's do this then."

"I was going to tell you earlier that I've locked and sealed the safe with a high-tech spell I created. The book will be safe," Sylvie said.

Maggie looked at the clock, five hours until nightfall. She was glad her younger children were far away, but Angela's anger troubled Maggie. It made her doubt herself.

Doubt going into a fight made mistakes inevitable. Tonight they couldn't afford any mistakes.

Chapter 25

As the sun set, Sarah and Ellie brought a trembling Heather into the house. Their original plan had hit a snag when Kissa insisted Benson be excluded. He and Mother Esme had been designated to care for Gia in the house, while Dr. Williams and June were to guard Heather in the boarding school. The loss of one person meant that the Mothers and June would watch over both the baby and Heather in the house. Gia started to cry when Heather entered the room, and Ellie picked up the infant, trying to soothe her.

Kissa produced her handcuffs, instructing Heather to put her arms around her back.

"Why am I being treated like the bad guy?" Heather cried. "I've been abused my whole life. I came here for help. I brought you the book, and I'm treated like the enemy."

Maggie placed an arm around the girl's shoulders to calm her. "Is that necessary, Kissa?"

"Her people will be attacking us tonight. This is a precaution."

"They're coming after me too for taking the book." Heather sat down, back against a wall, and drew her legs up into her chest, burying her face in her crossed arms.

"We'll take care of her," Mother Esme said.

Dr. Williams tugged at a window. "See. Secured. No one's getting in here."

Kissa looked at each person in the room and then reluctantly put away the handcuffs. "Fine. But in my experience, you can't take too many precautions."

"We should go," Maggie said.

Ellie took a minute to reassure baby Gia she would be well protected. The infant responded with gurgling and reaching for Ellie's face, and the

Bast dipped low for the infant's fingers to reach. A shower of silvery light descended over Ellie.

"Oh my," Mother Esme said. "I've never seen an infant do that ever."

"Thank you for your blessing, little Magica." Ellie kissed the baby's hand, bowed, and departed the room with a smile both proud and humble. Maggie thought the woman would have made a great mother.

"What do you make of that?" Dr. Williams asked.

Maggie cradled Gia to her. "I think we have someone exceptional here." She kissed the baby's head. "Mothers, I've left plenty of milk bottles in the fridge that's in the cabinet." Maggie turned to June. "Take care of her."

Dark half-moons hung beneath June's eyes. She didn't look well or up to caring for others. Maggie wished Benson were with them, not because he was a man but because he was an experienced law enforcement officer. Nothing could be done about that now. She kissed the baby once more and blessed them all with safety.

Maggie went downstairs and out to the front lawn where the witches had gathered. Keeping any magical or physical attacks outside the house was essential for everyone's safety. Ellie, Sarah, and Amanda split up to scout the area, while Shondra, Minerva, and Sylvie stood together. Kissa positioned herself next to Maggie.

"We don't even know how they're going to attack," Sylvie said. "Shit, we are at such a disadvantage here. Sorry, Maggie."

Kissa spoke up. "How can you say that? We have the Magica here and the Sisters of Bast. Plus, there are two Mothers of Hecate upstairs with the Arch-Magica. We have enough magic amongst us to stop armies. We can handle a small group of cultists and one rogue witch."

"Well, we haven't been handling them. Remember," Sylvie said. "So why don't we give that cult Heather and tell them we're keeping the book."

Maggie was horrified by Sylvie's suggestion. "They could hurt the girl, or worse."

"So?"

The anger emanating from her worried Maggie. It was justified. Losing the people you love was the hardest thing in the world to endure, but Sylvie's grief was soured with hatred and revenge. Sylvie and June needed time to mourn. Instead, this ordeal trapped them into helping Maggie deal with the Abecedarians. She should've sent Sylvie and June home to grieve.

"I won't be the Magica tonight, Kissa," Maggie said.

Kissa looked incredulous. "I don't understand. Why wouldn't you call on your greatest power in this situation?"

Kissa's pressure to call forth the Magica annoyed Maggie. No one understood how the presence of the Magica made her feel. She, the person Maggie, disappeared inside the entity. And while they shared a body, they were nothing alike. It served the higher purpose at any cost. When Richard and Michael were murdered, Maggie relied too heavily on the Magica as she tried to find the killers, and her own children had grown afraid of her.

"I won't because there's an infant in the house, and I need to be able to attend to her. I can't do that possessed by another entity," Maggie said with finality.

"Very well," Kissa said, clearly disappointed. "Let us—"

"Do you hear that?" Minerva said.

Beyond the gate, the rumble of several trucks announced the arrival of the cult. Minerva tapped the security app on her phone displaying what the cameras at the street were picking up.

"Look." She held the phone out.

Two box trucks and a pick-up were parked right in front of the gates, barring Maggie's people from escaping. Robed and hooded figures poured into the street and then disappeared out of range of the camera.

"We need to see where they're going," Sylvie said.

"Shall we?" Sarah asked Ellie. The two sisters handed their weapons to Shondra and Sylvie, then removed their boots and jewelry.

"We can't do this too often," Sarah said. The two sisters lay on the grass.

"What are you doing?" Minerva asked.

"They're going to check things out from the air while there is some sunlight on the horizon," Kissa said.

"I wasn't thinking. I should have brought a drone." Sylvie looked embarrassed at not having the proper security equipment with her.

"Drones are obvious," Kissa said. "This is why we use a more natural method."

Amanda motioned for them to move back. "Let's give them room."

The sisters whispered a spell as they lay on the ground. A haze emanated from their skin, enshrouding them in a mist. Maggie knew of this spell but had never seen it performed. The other women looked on perplexed.

Amanda breathed on the mist until it drifted away. A Harris's hawk appeared, dark brown and stately, and Ellie was gone. The raptor beat its wings, fanning the women standing nearby. This was no glamour but the actual transformation of matter. The bird shot up into the sky. Sarah remained lying in the grass.

"Whoa," Sylvie said. "I've never seen that before. Flying. That's not the same as when Minerva and June changed into cats. They were still them, and they were on land."

"Isn't this supposed to be impossible?" Shondra whispered.

Minerva looked upward, keeping track of Ellie. "What about the energy this takes? How do they do it?"

"It's a different kind of magic," Maggie said. She was impressed the sisters had this specific ability, but a witch wasn't chosen to be a Bast unless one had remarkable talents. "Ellie is drawing energy from Sarah who's drawing energy from the Earth."

They watched the raptor wheel against the twilight sky, pushing through layers of magenta and purple. Its silhouette stood out against the golden and generous moon. The group looked on in awe.

A gunshot rang out, and the hawk tumbled from the sky. Their amazement turned to alarm. Amanda tried to get under the plummeting bird, but it was coming down behind the house. On the ground, Sarah trembled and turned gray. The hawk kept falling.

Maggie backed away from the group. Looking upward, she breathed out and said, "*Ventus*." From Maggie's exhalation, a wind was conjured, and she used her arms to push the gust upward until it cradled the hawk.

"Amanda with me," Kissa said. "The rest of you stay here with Sarah."

Maggie was already in the backyard by the time the two warriors appeared. As it fell through the air, the hawk was on its back, wings outstretched, and its head hanging limply to one side. How could the violence have escalated so quickly? They couldn't endure another death. Maggie heard Gia cry out.

The hawk strayed dangerously close to the school.

"She's going to hit the building," Kissa said.

"*Ventus*." Maggie said again and steered the hawk toward the grass and away from the school and the concrete pad fronting it.

It struck the ground with a soft thud. The raptor lay on its side, one wing coated in blood. "She can't return to human form if she's unconscious," Amanda said. She gathered the creature and took her around front, placing the hawk next to Sarah.

"Is she okay?" Minerva asked. Everyone crowded around, expressing their concerns as they peered over Amanda's shoulder.

While they had been focused on Ellie, Shondra had the foresight to seek Dr. Williams's assistance. The women gave the doctor room. After examining the bird, the doctor rummaged through her medical bag, found an ampule, broke it open, and held it near the hawk's head. Ellie materialized.

"Oh, thank the goddess," Sylvie said. The others relaxed when they saw Ellie was alive.

The warrior tried to sit up. She put too much weight on her injured arm, groaned, and lay back down. Sarah came out of her fugue and kissed her sister's forehead. The bullet had gone through Ellie's arm, which Dr. Williams and Shondra, acting as Dr. Denny, cleaned and bandaged.

"It's not too bad," the doctor pronounced. "Nothing damaged. You'll need to sit the fight out though."

"I'm fine," Ellie said. She struggled to sit up, and Shondra put a gentle but firm hand on the woman's shoulder. Ellie relented and stayed down.

Maggie had clearly heard Gia cry as Ellie plunged from the sky, and she wondered if the Arch-Magica's glitter show hadn't actually been protection for Ellie. Had the child sensed something was going to happen to the warrior? Could her baby be capable of something that sophisticated? Gia was less than a month old.

With Ellie not seriously injured, Kissa turned to Sarah. "What did you see?"

"There are people with guns lined up along the wall fronting the road," Sarah said. "They're also along the west wall like you said, Kissa, but the hexes and sigils are holding them back. There's no one by the river or the back of the property." Sarah continued with her observations. "Esther is standing in the bed of the truck."

Kissa walked to the driveway and peered down its length. "That's their tactic then. Attack us with magic within the walls," she said. "If we try to escape beyond the walls, they will use physical force."

Kissa walked back to the group. "Shondra, can I ask you to see Ellie inside, please?"

"No way. I'm seeing this through." Ellie sat up, this time waving away anyone trying to stop her.

Dr. Williams gathered up the first aid items and pronounced that Ellie would live. "But she needs to avoid any direct confrontation. No more flying. No gun wielding. No hand-to-hand combat. Now, I need to get back upstairs to Gia." The doctor turned and hustled back into the house.

"Ellie, you can stay near the house. Sit on the porch and keep watch," Kissa instructed.

The warrior started to protest but Kissa stopped her. "No buts." Ellie grumbled but complied.

"I'm sure the property is secure, but let's break up into pairs and spread out along four quadrants," Kissa said.

As they separated into groups, a boom reverberated across the landscape. Minerva clamped her hands over her ears as if expecting the sound to repeat. Sylvie and Amanda ducked to avoid flying debris. Kissa pivoted and headed for the driveway. The others followed.

Esther's voice was clear and strong, spelling in their direction.

"Can you feel that pressure? She's using Roxanne's Push," Sarah said. The others felt it too.

They came to the top of the knoll and stopped, getting their first, in-person, look at Esther Goode, Noah Corwin, and the Abecedarians. In their white robes and hoods, Maggie thought the cultists looked a cross between the KKK and the Inquisition. The costume played a part in their messaging. A bearded man stood next to Esther in the bed of the truck. "That's Noah Corwin," Maggie said. She remembered him from their last confrontation—when she thought he'd died. She continued toward the gates.

"Mom, stop. Where are you going?" Minerva started after her.

Maggie turned and held up her hands. "Just wait there." She needed to talk with Esther. Maybe alone the two of them could come to an agreement.

As she approached, she took notice of who was doing what. More acolytes stood around Esther than Noah Corwin, and they helped her down from the truck. This said something very important about what was going on.

"What do you want, Magica?"

The rogue witch wasn't what she expected. Even Maggie was susceptible to the stereotype of the wicked witch, but the woman was Maggie's age and even handsome. "Esther, I'm not the Magica tonight. I'm coming to you woman to woman. What is it you want?"

"Witch, you will not address us." Corwin stepped in front of Esther, and Maggie saw a glint in the woman's eyes. "We are here for the book and the girl."

"I'm speaking to Esther."

"Silence," the man roared. "You will do as I—"

Esther extended her hands. Flames danced at the ends of each finger. The witch then jerked her wrists and fire shot out at Maggie.

Instinctively, she brought her arms together like bellows, and a rush of air met the fire. "Esther, please. What are you doing?"

Esther pushed past Corwin and went straight to the gate, grasping the bars, her hatred drilling into Maggie. "So many things I want to say you," Esther said. "Look at your house and your children and all your people. I'll take them all from you before this ends."

"But why?"

"Woman, get away from that devil," Corwin commanded.

Esther stood at the gates, ignoring Corwin. "This isn't over. This is the beginning."

Why wasn't Esther asking for Heather? "Heather's inside and she's safe."

"Maggie," Sylvie yelled down to her.

Maggie turned to look back at her group. A mass slammed into her pushing her to the ground. Her ears rang. Esther had taken a cheap shot. Hands took hold of Maggie and guided her back up the drive. She struggled against them. Familiar voices reassured her everything was okay. She glanced from side to side and saw Amanda and Sarah.

"Mom, are you okay?" Minerva asked.

Maggie nodded.

"Well," Kissa said, "what did the witch have to say?"

Maggie thought of Esther's threat to take everything from her. "Nothing." There was no need to alarm everyone when all Esther was trying to do was intimidate her. "I tried to negotiate, but Corwin interrupted us." Maggie remembered the malice in Esther's eyes.

"Now what?" Sylvie asked.

"We counter. Which spell, Magica?" Kissa asked.

Maggie ignored Kissa calling her Magica. "Hornsby's Repelling. Everyone know it?"

"Feel up to it, Mom?"

She did. Her ears no longer rang, and her mind had cleared.

The women formed a line and held hands to magnify their power. Maggie recited the words of the call, and the seven followed with the response. Elizabeth Hornsby had been a witch during the Battle of Gettysburg. It was her innovative phrasing that helped win that battle and ultimately the Civil War. Maggie hoped it would do likewise for them, on a smaller scale of course.

"Let me check," Sarah said. She leaped upward and hung in the air. "I think it's working. Esther's stopped. I don't feel the push anymore. She's talking to the men around her. Wait. She's—"

A blast pushed all eight women apart, sending them flying.

Shondra cried out as her head cracked on the driveway. She sat up and blood dripped into her eyes.

Everyone else lay spread across the grass.

"Goddamn," Sylvie muttered. "She tricked us. We could've gotten really hurt."

"That was a Stop-Spell," Minerva said.

"A powerful one at that," Sarah said. "Magica, something stronger?"

Maggie thought about it. "Let's use the Perez Cyclone. A taste of their own medicine." The women formed a circle, arms interlocked. "Shondra and Minerva, will you serve as the gate?" They nodded. As the group recited the words in unison, they turned widdershins, starting slowly, building speed with each full rotation. Leaves and grass clippings got caught up in the small cyclone forming in the middle of the circle. As the witches turned faster and faster, the cyclone grew taller.

"Now," Maggie said. Shondra and Minerva dropped their hands and the gate opened. The cyclone took off down the driveway, Maggie walking after it, guiding it with her hands. The other witches followed her. The cyclone rattled the fence gates but didn't bring them down. Maggie made sure that wouldn't happen by controlling the speed and size of the cyclone.

The men covering the entrance toppled aside like bowling pins. It then swept over the truck. Esther's feet were knocked out from under her, and she landed hard.

Esther struggled to her feet and turned her back to them. Instead of countering with her own spell, Corwin grabbed her arm, pulling her to the truck's cab. The other Abecedarians piled back into the box trucks, and all three vehicles drove off.

"What the fu—" Sylvie said. "Are they giving up? What about Heather and the book?"

"I don't understand." Shondra looked around as if searching for something she'd lost.

"That was the most underwhelming fight I've ever been in," Amanda said. She and Sarah went down to the gate. "There's no one here," Amanda yelled back.

"Magica—" Kissa started to say.

Maggie blanched. "Oh no." She turned and ran for the house.

Ellie stood up as Maggie rushed by her and exploded through the front door. She bounded up the stairs.

The door to the nursery stood open.

Maggie rushed to it. Mother Esme lay in the doorway, blood bloomed around her head like a scarlet halo. Maggie stepped over the woman and headed to Gia's crib.

It was empty.

"Maggie." Dr. Williams crouched near June, applying pressure to her side. Blood-stained June's blouse and a puddle of red formed beneath her.

"Where's the baby?" Maggie turned looking for Heather.

"Maggie," the doctor said.

"Where's Gia?" Maggie's anger slammed into everything in the room. Pictures fell from walls. Books flew off shelves.

Kissa grabbed her arm. "Magica." Maggie turned her rage to Kissa, who rebuffed the spell by crossing her arms in front of her face.

"Where is my baby?" Maggie threw aside pillows and blankets.

"Maggie!" Sylvie yelled.

Minerva and Amanda bent over Mother Esme. Amanda checked for a pulse. "She's dead."

"Where's Heather?" Maggie screamed.

Minerva crouched next to Mother Esme and took hold of the dead woman's hand. "Heather took the baby," she said.

"They tricked us." Maggie collapsed to her knees. "They took Gia. They took my baby."

PART 3

Chapter 26

Heather had been a Trojan horse. The cult's mission had ne-ver been about the book or their runaway member.

Maggie swung between anger and despair. Waiting and watching the clock made her feel helpless. She couldn't just sit there. She had wanted to go after Gia immediately, but Kissa stopped her. The Sisters of Bast would go in search of the baby, and Maggie should call her friend Benson Scott. The police needed to come. There would be questions, lots of scrutiny, but he would know how to handle this from the law enforcement side. It was better that she and the sisters weren't there. The warrior looked regretful.

Now Kissa wanted Benson to be here. But it was too late.

Maggie blew her nose and threw the tissue into the growing pile in the trash can. Her eyes felt bulbous and inflamed from hours of crying. Emotions kept swamping her, and she struggled not to capsize under them. She could grieve, but she couldn't turn the pain inward and lose herself in it. Her gullibility and foolishness struck Maggie the hardest. Believing the girl a victim of abuse, her heart had gone out to Heather. As the Magica, how could she have been so deceived? How easily the girl lied. At every turn, she gave some plausible reason, and they all bought into it. No, that wasn't true. She had believed Heather's stories. Everyone else voiced their suspicions. Minerva didn't trust her at all. Benson wanted to remove her from the house. Sylvie wanted to lock her up, and Kissa had the handcuffs ready. If only she had allowed Heather to be restrained, she would never have taken Gia.

The Amber Alert kept going off on everyone's phones. The bleating reminded Maggie of her failure. Law enforcement officers from various agencies were spread between the nursery and the road outside the property, all collecting evidence and had been at it for hours. She recognized the local and state police from the murders, but now the FBI was here as well.

When Maggie had tried to enter the nursery with Benson, she was stopped and told she should wait downstairs. People taking prints and photographs moved around in a choreographed dance. Their thoughts projected everything from sympathy to disgust, but all their feelings pointed to Maggie being careless, maybe even neglectful. A few even saw her as a suspect in her own daughter's disappearance. Benson told her to wait in the kitchen.

Poor Mother Esme was dead, and June was in the hospital with a knife wound. Shondra accompanied her. The police had questioned all of them and were now upstairs with Benson. They should never have sent him away. If he had been in the nursery, he would've stopped Heather. June had been in no shape to deal with someone as manipulative and dangerous as Heather Goode. Five murders and now a kidnapping. This made them all suspicious to law enforcement. Maggie looked at her watch. When were all these officers going to leave so she could go and search for her daughter? Waiting on them was making her sick.

While the police did their part, the women pieced together the events leading to Gia's kidnapping. "I touched Mother Esme's hand," Minerva said, "and I saw what happened. When Dr. Williams left to assist Ellie, Heather took advantage of the opportunity. From Mother Esme, well...I felt something hit her head, but because she didn't see it, I didn't see who did it either."

"It had to be Heather," Maggie said.

"No, here's the thing. Mother Esme was looking at Heather who was holding Gia when she was attacked from behind. I saw it through Mother's Esme's eyes."

"Are you saying there were Abecedarians in the house?" Minerva just shrugged at her mother. She didn't know for certain. Maggie turned to the doctor.

Dr. Williams filled in the rest. "When I returned from helping Ellie, I saw Mother Esme in the doorway, and I did what all of you did. I ran into the room to check on the others. I didn't see Heather or the baby. June was lying on the floor, and when I saw blood, I started rendering aid. That's when someone knocked me unconscious."

"So you didn't see anyone either?" Maggie asked.

"No. I'm sorry."

Minerva shivered. "You could've been killed too. June could've bled to death."

"I can't believe this happened. How did the cult members get past all our barriers and protections?" Maggie's head throbbed from crying. She needed some ibuprofen and a hot cup of coffee. Minerva poured a cup and brought it to her mother, along with several pain-relieving tablets. "Who am I kidding? They got in because I let her in. Everyone tried to warn me."

"Maggie, one of your strengths has always been mothering," the doctor said.

"How can you say that?" Maggie's voice hitched in despair. Minerva and the doctor winced. "One child is dead and now one is kidnapped. What kind of mother am I?" She covered her face with her hands.

Minerva sat next to Maggie and hugged her. "You're a great mom. Seriously. But you're also the Magica."

"I used to think about renouncing it and letting it pass to the next one, but now that Gia's the Arch-Magica I can't do that. I won't do that." She put her head on the table and cried. "Our friends and family have been murdered. My baby's been kidnapped. I'm a fool."

"No, Maggie," Dr. Williams said. "You were duty-bound."

"I was too empathetic. I saw her as an abused daughter, but you knew right away, Minerva. You were suspicious. That's why you didn't want her in the house."

Minerva put her arms around her mom. "You were just being a good mom."

"Maggie?" Benson stood in the doorway. She surprised herself by rushing into his arms. She couldn't figure out why this man brought her so much comfort.

"Is it bad, with the police?" Dr. Williams asked.

Benson spoke while still embracing Maggie. "They're not happy but don't suspect anyone here. Right now, they're seeing this as an aggrieved mother who wanted a newborn to replace a lost child, but since the abduction is tied to the same people who committed the library fire and murder and then the murders of the other women, your daughter's abduction is considered serious and of high priority. Maggie, this isn't staying out of the news. Every law enforcement agency in this state and all the surrounding ones will be actively searching."

"I'm sorry, Benson. I should never have sent you away."

"Don't do that, Maggie." He hugged her tighter to him. "Like you said, the Basts have their ways. I don't blame Kissa for not wanting me around. Betrayal makes people suspicious of everyone. The Basts are more than qualified to handle situations like this. Unfortunately, we all thought this was about a book and an abused girl. I take the blame as well. Four murders should have been a warning that this was much more serious than we understood it to be."

"What happens next? They've been here for hours. When are the police leaving? I can't sit around here waiting," Maggie said. "Gia's a newborn, and she needs my milk. The supply they took from the fridge will only last two days. She's so small. She needs me." Maggie was aware she sounded frantic.

"Once all the agencies are through collecting evidence, they'll leave. These things take a long time. They'll be asking you questions all day. In fact you might have to go down to the station today as a technicality. You probably can't go searching for Noah and Esther Corwin until tomorrow."

Maggie recoiled, stepping away from Benson.

"What?" Minerva and Dr. Williams blurted simultaneously.

"Benson, did you say Noah and *Esther* Corwin?"

He nodded. "We discovered that Esther Goode and Noah Corwin married thirteen years ago. Noah Corwin is Heather's stepfather."

Maggie heard the pieces clicking into place, everything finally making sense. Maggie thought about the timeline. She needed to sit down. "Then Esther married him about seven months after the stillbirth of her child. Heather was seven at the time."

Dr. Williams, who had been leaning forward, fell back in her seat as if deflated. "This doesn't make sense. A witch marrying a cult leader who believes all witches should be put to death. Why would Esther do that?"

Everyone went silent for a few seconds.

"Well," Minerva said, "Mother Esme did tell us that Esther requested to be separated from the community. She was angry about losing the baby. Did anyone give her a hard time about it?" They all looked at one another.

"Something drove her to the Abecedarians, and it had to do with the stillbirth," Dr. Williams said.

"Here's another thing," Minerva said. "It's odd to geographically have Magicas so close to one another. Let alone a Magica giving birth to an Arch-Magica. That's only happened a couple of times in our history. Magic makes sure they're located in different parts of the world."

"It's safer that way," Dr. Williams added.

"Well, not so much anymore." They waited for Minerva's explanation. "I did a project on the phenomenon in college. Well, not about the Magicas specifically. Anyway, Magicas are never born in areas of great female persecution. Geographical variety amongst the Magica had been increasing over time, but once again, the number of dangerous places for women has been increasing around the world."

An insight into Minerva's state of mind sprang to Maggie's attention. Was Minerva's heightened empathic sensitivity being triggered by world events and not just personal ones? Maggie wished she had the time to talk to her daughter.

"Why do they want Gia? What advantage does it give them?" Benson asked.

"If—" The word caught in Maggie's throat. "If we don't get her back, they can raise her to be a powerful tool, even a weapon. Magic doesn't discern between good or evil. Magic left to its own devices is untamed and selfish. That's why witches are trained."

"Doesn't sound any different than basic human nature," he said.

"That's true. Forces that powerful need to be molded and directed to become agents for good. Without a moral and ethical code those forces are dangerous," Dr. Williams said.

"So they could make Gia do bad things in the name of their beliefs."

Maggie nodded. "That's what cults do. Right?"

A uniformed officer appeared. "Mrs. Mills-Towne, sorry to interrupt. Sir, we're about finished here. The Captain would like to see you."

"I'll be back as soon as I can, Maggie."

Hearing that all law enforcement would be clearing out soon energized Maggie. Playing the victim helped the various agencies conduct their investigations, but now it was time for Maggie to take charge. No, for the Magica to take charge. She had decided it was time.

"This means we'll head out to begin our own search. Minerva, if you don't mind, call Samuel and tell him they need to stay with the Grandparents for a few more days. Don't tell him about Gia."

"Got it, Mom."

"Dr. Williams, I don't know how long you'll be staying."

"I'm here until Gia is found."

"Let's check the room where Heather was staying. We can use the bedclothes or other objects to scry."

"I sent word out to all the witches about what's happened," Dr. Williams said. "Everyone has or is going to start their own search scries. I'm worried that Esther will make it difficult to find the baby."

Maggie shivered at the thought of Gia out there, helpless and in the possession of people who were unhinged. Her stomach lurched, and Maggie found herself running to the sink to vomit. She crossed her arms on the sink's lip and waited for the nausea to settle. This was just like when Richard and Michael were murdered. How could she allow these horrific things to keep happening to her family?

The doctor rinsed a towel in cold water and placed it on Maggie's forehead. "I know you want to do everything in your power to find your daughter, but you recently gave birth. You need to heal."

Maggie removed the compress and looked at Dr. Williams. "Thank you. I do have a favor to ask of you." The doctor nodded. "Could you please contact thirteen witches that you trust to come here?"

The doctor frowned. "Are you sure?"

"I don't have a choice. This has gone on too long, and now look where we are." Because of Richard's and Michael's deaths and the toll it took on her family, she had been too hesitant to call on the Magica. Maggie now regretted that choice. "Will you bring together a coven for me?"

Dr. Williams tried to make an argument for waiting, but Maggie's face expressed her steadfastness. The doctor relented. "Okay, but it's nearly noon. The coven won't be able to get here until tomorrow."

"Good. As soon as all thirteen witches arrive, I'll perform the ritual to call forth the Magica." Cold pricked Maggie's spine at the thought of inviting it in for the first time in two years.

This time she would have better control over the entity.

Chapter 27

Law enforcement vacated the property just after noon, but Benson was right. Not only was Maggie's presence required at the station, but everyone who was at the house at the time of the kidnapping was asked to make an appearance. Maggie kept the Sisters of Bast out of it. Dr. Williams called Sylvie, telling her she needed to meet them at the police station. The five women spent hours being questioned by the police and completing paperwork. By the time they returned home, it was late. The four warriors were already at the house, and they'd ordered Chinese food so it would be there when the others got back. Even in crisis, life needed attending.

Since they hadn't eaten since the previous day, the women dug into the food. Sylvie heaped her plate with fried rice and sweet and sour shrimp. The Basts made her portions look small as they piled on ribs, fried wontons, Kung Pao chicken. When Dr. Williams noticed Maggie not eating, she made her a plate of plain white rice and stir-fried vegetables, knowing her digestion couldn't handle anything more right then. They gathered around the banquette table. Too hungry and tired, everyone remained quiet and focused on their food.

Shondra pointed to an open spot at the table. "Come on, Maggie. Sit down. Eat."

Maggie paced around the kitchen island like a racetrack. "I can't. We lost an entire day when we needed to be out searching for Gia," Maggie said. "I think I'm going out now."

Everyone discouraged her. "It's too late and dark," Kissa said. "And we have no leads. We can't just drive around. We tried that today." Sarah,

Amanda, and Ellie, with orange chicken sauce smeared on one cheek, nodded in agreement.

"None of us have slept for over twenty-four hours either," Dr. Williams said. "That's not safe for either our mental or physical health."

Maggie wrung her hands. "I can't sleep." They didn't understand. A mother separated from her newborn was the greatest ache. When she thought of Gia with that monster Esther, she wanted to scream. "No, I have to go. I can't sit around as if nothing's happened. You don't understand what it's like."

Sylvie stood. "You're not the only one suffering. We all are." She threw her napkin down and stormed from the room. Everyone around the table put down their forks.

Maggie covered her mouth with her hands, ashamed for saying something so horrible. "I'm sorry. I'm feeling crazy right now."

Dr. Williams left her food and went to Maggie to speak with her privately. "Listen, I can give you a mild sedative." Maggie started to protest, but Dr. Williams held up her hands. "Wait. Please listen to me as a doctor. You're not going to do anyone any good if you're exhausted and distraught. Let yourself sleep tonight. Plus, the thirteen arrive tomorrow morning. You need to be ready to accept the Magica."

The doctor was right, but eating and sleeping felt selfish when her baby was out there with dangerous fanatics. Maggie looked at the women gathered at the table shoveling food into their mouths even though they all looked like they were about to fall asleep over their plates. The idea of waiting until morning stung Maggie, but it made sense.

"Come on." Dr. Williams led her to the table.

~

In the slate gray light of early dawn, they met once again in the kitchen. Dr. Williams made coffee, and Minerva had toast and butter ready for the group. Sarah and Amanda yawned and rubbed sleep from their eyes. Sylvie and Shondra sat at the table with cups of coffee and maps spread out before them. All the Basts were dressed in their battle gear. Kissa told

Maggie that yesterday they couldn't pick up either a physical or magical trace of Heather or the baby, which meant the Abecedarians had planned the abduction well in advance, and Esther had used magic to erase all traces of themselves.

"How's that even possible?" Minerva asked. "Only the Magica has anywhere near that level of magic in them."

They all looked at Maggie for an explanation. Her own answer startled her. "Esther is using the powers drained from the murdered women."

"Fuck no!" Sylvie bellowed. "I'm going to kill her and I'm going to kill her slowly." She paced the room like a caged animal.

"It might need to come to just that," Kissa said.

The gate's buzzer rang. The thirteen had arrived.

Dr. Williams and Shondra led them to the school to prepare. The Sisters of Bast decided they needed to stay close to the house and not go out until the Magica was ready. In her office, Maggie pulled crystals and herbs from the apothecary drawers. She didn't know where Minerva was, and she worried the emotional toll on her oldest would cause her to withdraw.

"Why not get the power you need from us?" Amanda asked. Kissa was looking over Maggie's books.

Maggie set her tools on the altar. "If I needed the Magica for a small assignment, I could tap into just about anyone. But this is big magic, which means I require a number of powerful witches to be more effective. And the Basts need all their powers to find Gia. When I tap into the coven, I'll be drawing primarily from them, but the Magica will need a little magic from every witch on the planet."

Ellie, sitting nearby and holding one of Gia's blankets, asked if they would feel it.

"Maybe. Only the thirteen asked to make the ritual coven will feel the draw on their powers. You and other witches might feel nothing. If a witch is trying to do big magic right now, then she might be slightly off." Maggie didn't add that what she asked of the thirteen would hurt them, and they would forever be changed. The last time she had called forth the Magica three covens of witches had been summoned and drawn upon over the six months Maggie searched for the murderers of her husband and son. No witch asked denied the Magica and none complained afterwards. Service to one's own was considered the highest honor.

"There I have everything. I'm ready to start the ritual," Maggie said.

Minerva entered Maggie's office. "Mom, you need to see this now." She held out her phone.

Maggie and Kissa leaned in to look. It was a YouTube video of their gate being cast live. At the bottom of the video was the call name of Rockill's local TV station, WRKL. The camera swung away from the reporter and surveyed the large group congregating outside the gate and more marching down the road.

Sylvie appeared. "What's going on?"

Everyone was trying to crowd around Minerva. "Am I the only one with a phone?" Sylvie and Amanda pulled out theirs.

"It's not just this tv station. See the other news outlets? And look at the number of people with their phones out, which means they'll be posting to their social media too."

Minerva groaned. "Look at the signs they're carrying."

BURN THE WITCHES.
SATIN LIVES HERE
PROTECT ARE CHLDREN FROM WITCHS

"Great. What's next, pitch forks and torches?" Sylvie said.

Sarah snorted. "They can't even spell."

Dr. Williams and Shondra appeared. "What's going on?"

"Listen." Ellie held up her hand. They silenced their phones. Ellie went to the front door and opened it. The others followed. Drifting over the stonewall, the crowd's voices sounded like water rushing toward them, all chanting, "Stop the witches. Save the children."

Maggie bristled. Her infant daughter had just been abducted, and these nonmagicals were trying to lay blame on her. Guilt and fear were crushing her, and she didn't need this stupidity at her doorstep.

In the video a man raised a megaphone to speak: "In this house live witches. Every day they commit blasphemies against the Lord, Our Savior. These witches engage in orgies. They drain the blood of abducted children to keep them immortal." People in the crowd gasped, while a few women wailed.

"He's talking about a blood libel," Amanda said.

"This is just a distraction instigated by the Abecedarians to keep us in here and from searching for Gia," Kissa said.

Sylvie paced the room. "This is the modern version of a witch hunt. Spread a lot of lies on the Internet and let it take hold. Then all the believers in their lies begin to harass the targets. Idiots."

"Gullible," Amanda added.

Maggie shook her head. "Look." She pointed at Minerva's screen. "Those are the children's teachers."

A reporter approached one of them, Mrs. Madden, who in addition to Luka had also taught Samuel and Becca & Betsy. The reporter asked the teacher what she was doing out here.

Mrs. Madden wiped her eyes. "I'm their teacher. And I'm afraid for the children. I know L— I mean one of the boys hasn't been in school for a week. What happened to him?"

Becca's math teacher sidled up to the microphone. "Neither have two of his sisters. And now a baby has been 'kidnapped.'" She did air quotes to insinuate that there was something more going on.

"I called the school," Maggie said. "I informed them they were with their grandparents this week. Both those women sent them homework."

"I'm afraid," Mrs. Madden said, her eyes red and watery. "You know what witches do to children."

The decision to send Luka and Becca & Betsy to their grandparents had been a sound one. Maggie didn't want her children to see the people they trusted treating them like monsters.

Sylvie threw her arms up. "Unbelievable. These people are crazy."

"Being manipulated," Sarah said.

The camera pulled away from the teachers and panned the crowd. "Those are our neighbors." Minerva pointed out the older couple who lived down the road from them. "And there's the mayor of Rockill with his son Pent. He's talking to the man with the megaphone."

"I'm calling the police," Sylvie said.

"Wait." Kissa pointed to figures in the crowd, some wearing khaki uniforms, others dark blue. "They don't look like they're trying to get rid of these trespassers."

"Sometimes the police are on the side of conspiracy nuts," Minerva said.

"Don't any of those people know how to think for themselves?" Sylvie asked.

"This kind of thing has been going on for millennia. Jews. Women. Native Americans. Black people. Japanese. The outsider, those seen as different, has always been the preferred target," Minerva said.

Maggie considered what Minerva had been trying to communicate all this time. She was impressed her daughter was so aware of world events.

Kissa put away her own phone. "That is the mission of the Sisters of Bast, to fight these ideas and attacks around the world."

"Look," Amanda said.

The man with the megaphone instructed everyone to pray with him. The crowd bowed their heads and quieted, waiting for him to begin the prayer.

"I don't want to hear another word from that guy." Sylvie covered her mouth, whispering a spell through her fingers.

The man lifted the megaphone to speak, but it crackled and then cut out. He shook it, trying to get it to work. He looked up at the house, and on Minerva's phone screen it seemed he was looking directly at them. He tossed away the megaphone and spoke to the crowd.

"Well, that was creepy," Sylvie said. "Do you think he might be one of the Abecedarians?"

"Ah, good point," Kissa said. "The Abecedarians not only instigated this but also are agitating the crowd."

Maggie was done with the distraction. "Sylvie, please call Benson and tell him what's going on here. Everyone else, it's time for the ritual." Maggie gathered up her materials and led the way.

Sylvie held her hands up to stop her. "You can't do the ritual outdoors. They have drones." One was buzzing above the front lawn as they spoke.

"We'll do it in the school's great room. It will be a little dangerous, but we don't have a choice." Maggie wasn't sure if the ritual would even work indoors. Magic possessed mass and big Magic needed space. She had to try.

They congregated in the great room of the boarding school. With the drapes drawn, the coven of thirteen stood in a circle, Maggie at the center. Each woman wore a red cloak, hoods over their heads, while Maggie's was just a serviceable brown one, her head bare for now. She would need the hood later to shield her face once she transformed. Around her neck Maggie wore the ruby necklace presented by the Mothers of Hecate to the new Magica when she came into her powers. Even though it was seen as beautiful, Maggie knew the true purpose of the gem. She put her hand to it and felt its power.

Candles provided the only light. The thirteen witches joined hands. Maggie wondered if she should send everyone not involved away, but she knew they wanted to see her become the Magica, their symbol of strength and hope. She couldn't deny them this moment.

Using white and red chalks she drew the symbols around her. Each witch then stepped forth and placed a crystal specific to their abilities on one of the thirteen glyphs. The crystals served as not only the connection to the Magica but also as an anchor to the world, preventing the Magica from sucking all the power out of them as Esther had done to Lavinia, Lucy, Jinny, and Susan. Maggie set a large, clear quartz before her. This would protect the witches in the room and around the world from being drained.

"Great Mother and all the Goddesses," Maggie intoned, "I am your vessel. Fill me with the spirit and power of the Magica."

The candlelight grew intense, but oddly the room grew darker. Objects disappeared into this murk. Soon no one could see the person standing next to her, each alone in her own void. The air thickened as a force descended into the room. Maggie watched as the entity materialized. Because of its powerful energy, it was the only thing that could penetrate the gloom, and all heads turned in its direction.

Maggie's knees buckled, and she went down. The muscles in her legs cramped and stung, but she raised herself to her feet and held her arms to the sky. Two bolts of electricity hit Maggie's hands. The others in the room gasped. The thirteen stood silently.

The energy traveled through her body. Maggie's skin shimmered and shifted from white to beige to dark brown to pink to black. Every time she blinked her eyes changed color as well. The Magica was a compilation of every Magica that ever existed. While this entity resided within her, Maggie would carry all the memories and emotions of every Magica. This collation of past experiences made the Magica wise in a way that was almost dangerous.

The ritual was almost complete. "Great Mother and all the Goddesses, I draw the power from these thirteen witches who offer it freely."

Each of the thirteen stretched out both arms, right palm stacked upon the left, and thirteen bolts shot forth from them into the Magica. She allowed their power to fill her. When she lowered her arms, the coven collapsed to the floor. They would remain in a semi-comatose state until she returned their powers.

The Magica stepped out of the circle. She pulled the hood over her face, protecting the other women from the change in her appearance. "Let's find the Arch-Magica," she said.

Chapter 28

Benson saw the crowd swarming around Maggie's driveway gate, blocking anyone from entering or leaving. He had important information to relay to Maggie about the whereabouts of baby Gia, but this mob needed to be dealt with first. He nosed the car through the crowd, trying not to hit anyone. Cars lined both sides of the road from the stop sign a quarter mile back all the way down to where the road ended at the Hudson River. Unable to go any farther, he stopped in the middle of the road and got out. The other law enforcement vehicles behind him were forced to do the same. Not a single permit had been pulled for this event, meaning that everyone gathered was breaking the law. He knew events like this could turn ugly and violent, and they needed to clear the area in front of Maggie's property.

He couldn't believe the size of the crowd. It appeared as if almost every citizen of Rockill had shown up for this, but there were also people who were from other places. It had the air of a carnival. A group sold bottled water from the back of their car. No less than three groups had set up tables to sell t-shirts with repugnant sayings. Several people weaved through the crowd selling bags of chips and candy bars.

All around him people carried signs accusing Maggie of drinking her own children's blood, while others mentioned God's punishment for witches. Even children carried signs attacking Maggie and calling for her death, which Benson saw as a form of child abuse. Take your kid to a peace march supporting civil rights or an anti-war rally but forcing one's kids to be involved in nasty propaganda was flat out wrong. This wasn't a protest. This was an attack on innocent people, a family who was trying to deal with their own tragedy. Shame on all of them for behaving irrationally and cruelly.

Other people's tragedies didn't need to be another person's entertainment. Maggie didn't need this. He looked at his watch. He had to get up to the house and talk to Maggie, but stopping this insanity was his first priority.

The police officers and Sherriff's deputies who accompanied him went into the crowd. A group had been designated to head for the gate and make sure no one got through. The others were to encourage people to leave of their own volition or be arrested. Searching the crowd, he spotted a Rockill city police officer who hadn't come with them. The man saw Benson approaching and tried ducking out of sight.

"Officer, stop right there," he commanded.

The man put up his hands as if he was being arrested. His glazed eyes barely registered Benson, darting from him to those in the crowd. The man's nametag read Penny.

"Officer Penny, do you know what you're doing could get you fired? And put your hands down."

"I heard that children were in danger out here. That's why I came. To save the children." He pulled a square of paper from his pants pocket and handed it to Benson, a flyer decorated with lightning bolts and children crying tears of blood. A clear message stood out in bold at the center of the paper.

WITCHES ARE KILLING OUR CHILDREN. SAVE THE CHILDREN!

Maggie's home address was at the bottom. A printed flyer indicated that this wasn't some sudden uprising. This was planned, and most likely by the Abecedarians. He'd seen this type of messaging before. Who could argue against saving abused children? It sucked in easy prey, sentimental and emotional types who didn't stop to think and who just reacted out of manipulated empathy. If a person did try to present a rational argument and proof that their claims were false and ill-conceived, they would accuse that person of collusion and participation in said abuse. Witch hunting came in many forms.

"Officer Penny, do you know what's happening to that family up there?" He pointed toward Maggie's house. The officer shook his head. "That woman's infant daughter was abducted. What do you think she's going through right now?" He waited for the officer to speak, and when he didn't, Benson repeated his question more sternly. "I asked you a question. Tell me what that woman is feeling right now."

The officer blinked several times. "She's scared. She wants her baby back."

"And?"

"She's angry about what we're doing down here, accusing her of harming her child. All she wants is for her daughter to be brought back to her safely." Officer Penny shook his head as if coming out of a daze.

Benson wondered if the man had been drugged or spelled, not by Maggie but by that other witch who had kidnapped Gia. Or maybe it was just plain old susceptibility to misinformation due to lack of critical thinking. "What is your situation now, Officer Penny?"

The officer blushed. "I'm sorry, Sir. I got caught up in all this." He waved his arm at the crowd.

The sudden reversal of the officer's state of mind surprised Benson. "Officer Penny, I need to get up to that house and help that family. I want you to go through this crowd and find the law enforcement officers who also succumbed to this nonsense and question them like I did you. Then I want all of you to help the officers who are out there now doing the right thing. Clear all these people out of here. Can you do that?" Officer Penny nodded his head, turned, and entered the crowd.

Benson pushed his way through. Men sneered as he passed. Women hissed. Their hostility made him touch his gun through his suit jacket, reminding himself that he wasn't unprotected and had every right to keep the peace. He came across the mayor, who bowed his head and ducked behind a large group who had doused themselves in red corn syrup. He understood why Maggie and her kind needed to hide their true selves. This was a carnival of the disturbed. He spied something alarming and went off to investigate.

A group had found the pyre Samuel had taken apart and hidden in the bushes. Several women gathered dry grass lining the road and then spread it over the logs at the base of the pole. Another man took out a lighter. He bent to light the kindling.

"Stop. Police."

Startled the man fumbled the lighter, and the flame barely touched the dried grass before it went up with a whoosh. The flames crawled through the stacked logs and up the pole like a hungry animal.

People in the crowd screamed when they saw the burning pyre. Others snatched the opportunity to add to the madness.

"Burn the witches! Burn the witches!" The chanting spread as quickly as the fire did.

He got his radio out and let dispatch know they now needed the fire department out here as well.

A sharp pain spiked Benson's left shoulder. Another hit his lower back. He reached around to rub the two spots. A rock came hurtling at his head, and he ducked. Several more rocks pelted him. He couldn't believe it. They were stoning him like some Jackson story.

He drew his gun. He didn't want to, but he had no choice. The rock throwing stopped. In the distance, the wail of sirens told him the fire department would soon arrive to put out the fire. He holstered his weapon and rubbed his shin where a fist sized rock had hit him. He was going to have a few bruises.

Getting these people to leave wasn't proving to be easy. They looked intent on staying and making their point. He forged on, now on the lookout for more troublemakers. Anger and hatred came off each person like a stench. He felt uneasy weaving through the crowd, but he stayed alert. A man in the bed of a truck was spouting off nonsense through a megaphone. Benson wished he knew more about the Abecedarians, but they had no pictures or even names of their members. He suspected this guy might be one of them. The man instructed the crowd to pray, but when he started the prayer, his megaphone spluttered and died. Benson grinned, wondering whose handiwork that was. He brought out his radio and informed the police officers that prayer man was to be taken in for questioning.

Storm clouds boiled up over the horizon, rolling in their direction. Lightning bolts chased one another across the gray sky. Worried faces turned upwards, and parents hustled children back to their cars. A large group of elderly folks stumbled back onto their bus from the senior center. Thunder crackled like a metal sheet shaken. The rain came down on the mob all at once, no sprinkles announcing the deluge. People screamed at the stinging pellets, dropping their signs as they headed for shelter.

Benson's hair and suit remained dry. The man leading the group prayer hopped down from the back of the truck and gave him a hard stare, as if accusing Benson of being in cahoots with the witches. That was fine by him. Three officers approached prayer man who looked surprised. He wasn't close enough to hear, but he could see the man heating up in a one-sided animated conversation, while the three officers remained calm. For a second, he worried the man was swaying the officers.

They motioned for prayer man to turn around to be handcuffed. Good. The guy could stew in a jail cell for a few hours waiting for Benson to get around to talking to him. Right now, he needed to get up to Maggie's. He found his car untouched right where he had left it and drove it up to the gate where he punched in the code Maggie gave him.

The house was empty, but he heard noises coming from the school. Not wanting to interrupt, he took a seat in the kitchen to wait. It wasn't long before the back door opened, and Sylvie entered the kitchen. A woman in a cape followed, the hood pulled over her face.

"Maggie?"

The hood fell to the side revealing a woman who looked like Maggie but with noticeable differences.

He stared. "Your eyes are so light, like sea glass."

"Benson, do you have information for us?"

"And your hair is so red."

"Yeah, yeah," Sylvie said. "And what big teeth she has. Information, Benson."

"I'm sorry for staring, Maggie," he said.

"Magica," Kissa corrected him. "She is the Magica."

His face flushed. He glanced at the Magica and then looked away. Confusion overwhelmed him. Before him was the woman he felt himself falling for, but she wasn't. She was something else. It was more than the change in her hair and eye color. This woman, the Magica, carried herself differently than Maggie. An unnatural power emanated from her, something too big for an average person to possess, even a witch.

The Magica studied him, and he gave her a smile. She returned it with her own grin. "Benson, I'm still here."

He felt a weight lift hearing her voice, but he couldn't approach her as if she were wholly Maggie. And at the back of his mind he wondered if this was something he could live with. Sylvie drummed her fingertips impatiently on the table.

"Oh yeah, the reason I'm here," he said. "Cameras showed a group of women going into a grocery store. They bought diapers, formula, and other baby items."

"How is this relevant?" Kissa asked.

"Let me show you." He held up his cellphone.

In the video, five women dressed in old-fashioned dresses moved through the store together. They stopped in the baby aisle and loaded a cart and then proceeded to a checkout lane where they paid cash.

"They look uncomfortable, nervous and shy, about being in a store," Amanda said. Everyone agreed that their behaviors were suspicious.

"Is there footage of them in the parking lot? The vehicle they left in?" the Magica asked.

He detected motherly worry in her voice. It would have troubled him if there hadn't been. It helped with the idea that this being and Maggie were one. "Let me show you." He pushed play on the next video. "It's an old van. No front license plate. We also have stills of the rear plate which is mud covered."

Sylvie leaned in. "If the rear plate was also missing, that would attract a cop's attention."

"If it is acceptable to the Magica, I propose that the Sisters of Bast pursue that van," Kissa said. "Benson, I believe you may have more images of this van."

"Yes, I can give you what the police have. From intersection, road, and other cameras, we know the general direction the van traveled."

"Which is?" Sylvie asked, impatience undercutting her tone.

"Most likely heading back into the Catskills."

Minerva looked at her mom and the others. "Do you think they went back to their compound?"

"No, the police have checked. The cult's not there."

Sylvie grunted. "So maybe they're holed up in another deserted resort."

"But that's a large area, and they could be anywhere," Minerva said.

The Magica had removed her cloak while everyone was talking and fetched a hoody and black leather jacket from the coat closet in the laundry room. "Let's follow Kissa's plan. Sylvie can accompany the Basts and follow the path of the van. Minerva and I will go to that grocery store and speak with security. Dr. Williams is going to stay with the thirteen in the school. They will need monitoring." She pulled the jacket on.

Minerva cleared her throat. "If it's okay, I want to go with Kissa."

"It might get dangerous."

"All of you were doing important magic at my age." She hesitated before speaking. "I need to get out into the world."

"Are you sure, Minerva?" Magica asked, taking her daughter's hand in hers. Minerva nodded.

Her gesture touched Benson. What was he thinking? This woman was still Maggie. If he was falling for her, then he had to understand this part of her too.

"Kissa, Sylvie, how do you feel about this?"

Sylvie shrugged. "Fine by me."

"Don't worry, Magica. I will take care of your daughter. No harm will come to her," Kissa said.

These women didn't need him anymore, plus there was Kissa's rule about not working with men. "I'll just go back to the station and see if there are any new developments."

"Benson," Kissa said, turning her full attention on him, "I want to apologize to you and to the Magica. I made a grave mistake having you sent away. The baby would never have been abducted if we had stuck with Maggie's plan, and Mother Esme would still be alive. I am very sorry."

Kissa's apology took him aback. He didn't know what to say but eventually found the words to address her. "Thank you. I know everyone was trying to do what they thought was right. You didn't have any idea about what the Abecedarians had planned."

"Still, Maggie is the Magica. I should have trusted her decision." Kissa bowed in the Magica's direction. "Please forgive me, Magica."

"Of course, Kissa Hassan."

Living in the male dominated world of law enforcement, Benson had never seen women from this perspective. These women were brave and smart, warriors and intellects. Maybe women only appeared weak because the system put them in that position. If they hadn't suffered centuries, no millennia, of oppression, they would be different. They would be like these women before him. He understood Minerva's wanting to go into the field with Kissa. It was her way of fighting back that fear and dependency instilled in females by society from birth. This was no weaker sex, only a subjugated one, and he felt ashamed of males for doing irreparable harm to females.

Ellie stood. "What are we waiting for? Let's find the baby Arch-Magica."

The women broke up into their two groups, while he headed back to the department. These women were their own heroes.

CHAPTER 29

Magica found Dr. Williams and Shondra in the school and explained the plan. The doctor told her not to worry; she would care for the witches. The thirteen came out of their trance twice a day, to eat and care for themselves. Each wake-state lasted only fifteen minutes, and someone needed to be there to assist them. Shondra was going to the hospital to watch over June.

Sylvie and Magica packed the Land Rover with a variety of magical tools and overnight bags. Before they left, she called the children and their grandparents, but for the call she needed to glamour herself as Maggie. Even though it wasn't a true physical switch, the short-term spell alleviated the pressure she felt as the Magica. She hated to use a cliché but she felt like herself for a few minutes. Being a witch possessed of magic was very different from magic possessing a witch. She loved her magic and being a witch, but if it had been her choice, she would have chosen not to be the Magica. She worried for Gia's future as the Arch-Magica. It was already proving to be treacherous.

She dialed her in-laws' number and girded herself to explaining how her newborn had been kidnapped by a stranger she'd allowed into her home. When the call ended, Magica released the glamour. A sadness, deep and raw, overtook her. She flinched as images flashed through her mind: *a baby wrapped in a blanket, a woman holding a bottle, a crib lined with stuffed animals.*

Magica stumbled, putting a hand out to grip the side of the vehicle.

Gia.

Her daughter was communicating with her. Magica tried to chase down the contact, but it was gone. She hoped the images were real time. Knowing her baby was safe and being cared for should have eased her mind, but it only intensified the pain, like someone squeezing her heart. Guilt swept in on a second wave of horrible emotions. It was her fault Gia had been kidnapped, and Maggie could never forgive herself for not seeing what was going on right before her.

Sylvie came up behind her. "How'd the call go? Whoa, what's wrong?" She reached out to help Magica but dropped her arms to her sides.

"I saw Gia. She sent me images, letting me know she's okay."

Sylvie's eyes grew wide. "Holy shit. She's just a couple weeks old. Is that normal—even for a witch baby?"

"No." Magica righted herself.

"It's because she's the Arch-Magica. Right?" Magica nodded. "Did you see her location?"

"Just an ordinary room." She got into the backseat, while Sylvie slid behind the wheel.

Sylvie turned and squeezed her eyebrows together. "Not going to ride shotgun?"

"I need room to do some of the spells."

"Ok, that makes sense. Are we ready?" Sylvie shifted into drive. "So what about the kids? What did my parents have to say?"

Dealing with people as the Magica wasn't easy, the majority of her feelings, especially those connecting her to people, were tucked away with Maggie. Blunt would be a good description of the Magica's feelings, like a knife with a dull blade. Trying to capture the sharpness of real emotions and then relay those to others was difficult. To retain a semblance of humanity, she allowed Maggie's emotions and ideas to surface when needed. And sometimes Maggie's personality took over, regardless of the Magica's wishes.

"Becca & Betsy cried when they heard about Heather's deception. Samuel took it in his worried but level-headed manner." In this respect he was much like his father, and Maggie could count on Samuel in times of trouble. He was her rock after Richard's and Michael's deaths. Even when she couldn't be the adult during the horrific ordeal, Samuel could be, which she knew wasn't fair to him. They were a family, and he embraced his role and responsibility within it.

Her father-in-law, much like his grandson, took the news in a practical way. "Your dad kept asking about police and what they were doing to find Gia." Magica went silent.

Sylvie looked up into the rearview mirror. "And my mom and Luka?"

Magica started to speak, but Maggie's emotions threatened to spill out. She cleared her throat. "Not well. Your mom turned pale and disappeared from the camera. Luka is angry." Even though he didn't voice it, she knew he connected Gia's abduction with the deaths of his father and little brother.

Sylvie changed the subject. "So we're starting with the store where the women were caught on the surveillance camera."

Magica knew what her sister-in-law was thinking. "Gia's okay, not hurt. They're taking care of her."

Sylvie gripped the steering wheel. "Doesn't make it any easier."

Magica had to tap into Maggie or come off as uncaring. "No, it doesn't." Then she realized that Sylvie was also referring to her own situation.

"It's going to take an hour to get there," Sylvie said.

The atmosphere in the vehicle turned somber, and Magica realized not talking was going to be worse than talking about what Sylvie was experiencing.

"I'm sorry about Lucy and the baby."

Sylvie stared straight ahead, concentrating on the road.

"Sylvie?"

The 5,000-pound vehicle slid to a stop on the highway's shoulder as Sylvie braked hard. She threw the Land Rover into park and rested her forehead on the steering wheel. Magica reached out to her friend, resting a hand on her shoulder. At least, Sylvie wasn't shrugging her hand away. A tremor shook Sylvie, followed by tears. They remained in that position until Sylvie cried herself out. Only then did Magica lift her hand away. Out of the center console she dug up some tissues.

Moments like this, it didn't matter if a person was a nonmagical or a super witch. Hurt was hurt. "Sylvie, I can take some of the pain away, if you want."

Sylvie shook her head vehemently. "No way. I need to feel this. I need to carry this with me. Just like you're carrying the pain of Gia's abduction.

We have to feel this because that's where we'll get our strength to find your baby and stop Esther."

Those were wise words.

After she wiped her eyes and blew her nose, Sylvie put the car in drive, signaled, and entered the highway. "Thanks," her voice hoarse from emotion.

Magica just gave her a nod.

"Did Benson send you those videos and the still shots of those women from the store?"

Magica pulled out her phone and found what Sylvie was asking for. "The stills are helpful. Look."

Sylvie glanced at the phone, then turned her attention back to driving. "Other than the Little House on the Prairie clothes and long hair, they seem pretty normal. I was expecting a more distinct cultish look."

"What? Like black robes and rope sandals?" Magica examined each picture, memorizing their faces.

"It's out of character for them to be shopping in a store and driving a van," Sylvie said. "Guess they needed modern conveniences like disposable diapers and formula. And they couldn't be bothered with a horse and buggy, too slow when you're kidnapping babies."

"While you're driving, I'm going to track them."

"I can pull over and help."

"That's okay. I can tap into the thirteen." Magica spread a map beside her and held a lapis pendulum over it. She focused on the women's faces. They appeared in her mind—shopping for baby items, paying, and then driving away in the van. The van disappeared once it turned onto the street. This told her nothing that the video camera hadn't picked up. Frustrated, she tried again.

"Fuck."

Sylvie glanced over her shoulder obviously shocked by the expletive out of Magica's mouth. "What did you see?"

"Nothing. Sorry about the profanity."

"That's kind of weird, difference between Maggie and the Magica. How you're the same and not the same."

Sylvie wanted to quiz her on these differences, but now wasn't the time. "We'll talk about it one day. I want to focus on this." Magica sat back, watching the passing landscape. Some trees were still dressed in scarlet and orange, but most were denuded from the storms. The sky remained blanketed with gray clouds, threatening another storm. "With the exception of that one day, we haven't seen the sun since Heather arrived at my door," she said.

"Hmm? You're right. Is there significance to that?"

"No," Magica said. "An observation. Maybe it mirrors our state of mind." If she could take back the events of that night, she would, but there was no way to travel back in time to change anything.

Sylvie signaled right and exited the highway onto a surface street. "I have a question. Is that normal, not being able to track someone?"

"No." Sylvie's question made Magica sit up. "No, it isn't." They knew some of Esther's power came from stealing the magic of the four murdered women.

"Then how is it being done?" Sylvie stopped talking realizing what the answer was. Her face turned red. "You don't think she'd use the baby's powers?" The Land Rover picked up speed. "What kind of witch would do that to a baby?"

"Ease up, Sylvie. We're in a town." Sylvie blew threw a stop sign. "Gia's healthy. They're not hurting her. I can feel it." The Land Rover raced along the city streets. Magica got a glimpse inside of her sister-in-law's head. "Sylvie, they're not draining her."

Sylvie lifted her foot off the gas. "She's really okay?"

"Yes. She's strong. You weren't in the room when Gia threw magical glitter over Ellie."

"Holy crap."

"Even the Mothers were shocked. They'd never seen a baby, Magica or otherwise, display such powers. Sometimes they can coax a favorite toy over to them, but that's about it. Heather saw it too. She probably told her mother about it."

"When I get my hands on Heather, she's going to be sorry," Sylvie said.

"We don't fully understand the extent of Heather's involvement. She might still be a victim in all this."

"Is that Maggie speaking?"

Magica was caught off guard by Maggie's conviction that Heather could still be a victim. She didn't voice this to Sylvie. "There's the store."

Sylvie parked the Land Rover in an empty spot. "I've got a question. If you got cut off during the scrying just now, do you think you'll have the same problem trying to pick up any signals from their presence in the store?"

"I don't know, but we have to try. Leads are slim." They exited the vehicle and headed for the entrance.

"Witch!"

They stopped. A woman rushed them with her shopping cart. "Baby killer." It toppled over before it reached them. Sylvie kept the magic discreet.

"You're that woman from the news. The one whose baby went missing."

"Baby killer. Where is she?"

A crowd formed, and Sylvie and Magica hurried back to the Land Rover. Fists beat on the rear window. "Shit. We're stuck." The crowd prevented them from backing up, and they couldn't pull forward because a car occupied that parking space. "I didn't know we needed to make a getaway."

Magica looked back at the group. "I could freeze them or set off an explosion."

"Hold on."

A man appeared at the car blocking them. He looked at the mob attacking the Land Rover and made the choice to get into his vehicle and make a quick retreat.

"Luck is on our side." Sylvie drove forward through the open space, across a sidewalk, and then bounced down off a curb onto the street. She looped around several blocks before parking at the back of the store. They waited. "I don't think the crazies know I fooled them. Let's go."

Three employees sat smoking outside an open door. Magica met the eyes of each person as she and Sylvie entered, with not one of them attempting to stop the women. They did seem to be in awe of the woman with ice green eyes and her leather wearing partner. Magica made so they would forget them as soon as they passed.

Sylvie pointed to a staircase, and at the top SECURITY was stenciled on a door.

A woman in a uniform answered after Sylvie knocked firmly. Her eyes grew wide, followed by a panicked look, realizing she might have made a mistake opening the door to these two. She tried closing it, but Sylvie stopped the door with her foot.

"We're not here to rob you or anything. We need your help," Magica said.

"We're looking for these women," Sylvie said. Magica held up the phone.

The woman backed away from the door making room for them to enter. The security station was small with one wall a bank of monitors displaying various parts of the store and the parking lot. Another wall contained a large rack of DVRs, computer servers, and other security monitoring systems. The main feature, though, was a one-way mirror overlooking the store.

"I saw what that crowd almost did to you up front. I was gonna call the cops, but you drove away," the security specialist said. "The cops were already here this morning. I don't want any more trouble."

Sylvie explained she was in security as well. This calmed the woman, and she started to speak freely. "The police said the people in those pictures might've kidnapped a baby, a newborn. I even heard they think the mother might be in on it. All kinds of sickos out there."

"It's my baby," Magica said.

The specialist hung her head. "Aw, shit. I'm sorry."

"It was a cult that took the baby," Sylvie said. "Got it? Some crazies squatting in the abandoned resorts up in the Catskills. So we would appreciate it if you squelched any conspiracy theories you hear."

The woman stood up, steel in her eyes. "Sure. So how can I help?"

Something about the security officer made Magica wary. Her name tag read Holder. Magica glanced at Sylvie, letting her know something wasn't right.

"Can you show us video of that day? Maybe the parking lot, before they entered the store?" Sylvie asked.

"Sure. Got it right here because of the cops who were here." Holder pressed play on the digital recording. The van sat in the parking lot, farthest corner. Two women occupied the driver and passenger seats. The other three must have been in the back.

Sylvie leaned in, pointing at the figures. "They're nervous. See. Trying to psych themselves before going into the store. They're not use to doing this because they belong to a cult, the Abecedarians."

She was right. The women were engaged in a serious discussion, their hand movements spoke to uncertainty and fear. Magica tried to get something off them, but digital was not a favorable medium for magic. "Do you know them?" she asked Holder.

"No."

The answer registered as a lie to both Sylvie and Magica.

"Sorry, I've got to take care of something." Holder stepped over to the monitoring equipment and fiddled with some switches.

Something had shifted with the security specialist. While Sylvie concentrated on the video, Magica made her way to where the guard was standing. "So this looks like quite the complex system for a grocery store."

"A little bit. The store's had a couple of robberies, and one night a man came in and shot a cashier." Holder focused on the monitors displaying different parts of the store.

"Did the cashier die?"

"No," Holder said. "But she sued and won, a lot. Store figured its cheaper to have all this and me." She took a few steps away from Magica.

"Holder, what's wrong? You were eager to help us, but now you seem reluctant. Do you know something?"

Sylvie watched the interaction from her peripheral vision.

"Nothing's wrong. I just have to get back to work."

Magica took hold of Holder's forearm. The woman not only pulled away physically but also managed to yank her thoughts away. While the Magica could have easily bulldozed through the woman's protective measures, backing off was in everyone's best interest. Holder didn't know what she was.

"I'm sorry," Magica said. "I need to find my baby." She held Holder's eyes for three seconds.

"No harm, no foul." Holder rubbed the spot where the Magica touched her.

She wrote her mobile number on a slip of paper and handed it to the woman. "If you hear something, please call us." She then leaned in. "And if there's something else on your mind, something personal that you've wondered about, call me." Magica held the door open for Sylvie.

"What the hell?" Sylvie clunked down the stairs, Magica right behind her. "Don't you want to go onto the floor and see if you get a reading?"

"No." Magica got into the passenger seat.

Sylvie stood outside the driver's side, looking at her as if she'd lost her mind.

"Get in," Magica insisted again, and this time Sylvie complied.

"The guard knows something. It was when you named the Abecedarians. I felt something turn in her," Magica explained. "And that's not all. She's got some witch in her, but she doesn't know it."

"Really?" Sylvie looked back at the store. "So why didn't you force her to tell you what she knows?"

"I thought about it, but I sensed getting her on our side was the smarter thing to do. She knows the truth about Gia. Holder could go either way."

Sylvie nodded her head. "You mean good witch or bad witch."

"Yeah, let's see where her conscience leads her. But I also let her know to call me if she wants to learn more herself."

"Sure, I get all that, but we need to find Gia now. We don't know what the crazies have planned."

Magica felt stung. "I know. Gia comes first, but we can't sow anger and hatred in our wake. The public is against us as it is. That woman knows something about the cult."

"Still, what if she chooses bad witch?"

Of course her sister-in-law was concerned, having just lost her wife and child. Maggie understood all too well. She had suffered not only the abduction of her newborn but also the loss of a husband and a toddler, but she remembered the nightmarish hell she created when she went on a rampage searching for their killers. People died then. People were dying now. "I'm trying to be cautious and safe. We don't need any more dead people."

Sylvie smacked her thigh. "I know that, but we're working at a snail's pace here. I say we go in and get that information out of that security guard."

"No. We need her on our side."

Sylvie grumbled. "Sorry. I know I get hotheaded."

The women turned quiet, each staring out their side windows. She loved her sister-in-law, but Sylvie's temper could jeopardize finding Gia. Sylvie pulled out of the lot and headed for the highway.

They didn't get far before Maggie's phone rang. She answered, listened, and then asked several questions before disconnecting.

"Well?"

"Pull in over there." Maggie pointed to an upcoming gas station on their right. "I've got some information to tell you."

CHAPTER 30

MINERVA WONDERED IF SHE'D MADE A MISTAKE.

Back at the house, the decision to accompany the Sisters of Bast made sense. She meant every word of what she said. Her life as a witch was a sheltered one. Her mom, her aunt, the Basts, they had all been doing important work by their early twenties. What had she done? Homeschooled instead of going to high school because she couldn't deal with the sensory overload. And when she chose a college, her pick was Vassar, literally across the river, and though she did board there her last two years, she lived at home for her freshman and sophomore years. She didn't ski, skydive, mountain climb, or even paddle board. Adventurous wasn't even a word in her vocabulary.

Choosing to accompany the most badass witches in the world in their search for Gia was out of her comfort zone, but the ask tumbled out of her before she could clamp a hand over her mouth. Maybe the recon mission with June and Benson had given her a taste for excitement. Look at her, recon mission. Who says stuff like that? That mission didn't end well though—stepping into a trap, knocking herself unconscious, and then having him carry her out of the compound.

Carey most likely chose her because she would make a sensible wife and mother. Cute but not bombshell beautiful. Educated but not too ambitious. Pragmatic. Reliable. What scared her more than going on a mission with the Basts was her boyfriend's proposal. Sylvie and the Sisters showed her another side of life as a witch. The house was full of strong, beautiful women. Witches owned their lives. If they married men, witches didn't become subservient or come in second. Her own mother and father were equals. She wanted that kind of relationship and wondered if she could have that with Carey. Hell, she couldn't even tell him she was a witch.

"Want some?" Sarah held up a pack of gum. Minerva declined. "I thought you were asleep. You were so quiet." Sarah popped the square into her mouth.

"Just thinking," Minerva said. She sat in the back of the van next to Sarah, while Ellie was buckled into a jump seat at the very rear. Amanda drove, and Kissa rode shotgun.

"Hey, Minerva, you want a tour of the van?" Ellie unbuckled and went over to Minerva's seat. "The two front seats can pivot and face the interior of the van. Look at this," Ellie said. She pressed a button and a round table pushed up from the floor, a telescoping leg raising it. "We can work around this table or eat. Come back here." Minerva unbuckled her seatbelt and followed.

Ellie opened a cabinet revealing a compact kitchen. "And over here is the bathroom."

Minerva peeked in and saw a shower, toilet, and sink. "Where do you sleep?"

"There are two bunks over the driver and passenger seats that lower. And…" She pressed a button and panels on the left lowered into two bunks. "Go ahead press the button."

Minerva did and the bunks raised themselves back into place. She ran a hand over the panels. "These are also cabinets."

"Yeah," pleased that Minerva had noticed. "Can I show her, boss?" Kissa granted permission with a thumbs up. Ellie pressed her forefinger to a smooth black pad. The cabinet doors popped open to an arsenal.

"That's like a movie," Minerva said gazing at the array of weapons.

"I know. Pretty cool," Ellie said.

"Yeah, cool," Minerva whispered. Guns, knives, and things she couldn't recognize sat in their own secured compartments. Her desire to help the Basts deflated. She was out of her league. The Sisters of Bast didn't need her, and she wondered why they agreed to take her. How could she have imagined that she was qualified enough—or at all—to go on a mission with these four warriors? She felt like a silly, ineffectual schoolgirl.

"What's wrong, Minerva?" Sarah asked.

She felt so embarrassed she wanted to cry. Badasses don't cry, but she was no badass.

"Min?"

"I don't know why I'm here. I've never used a weapon," she confessed.

"Minerva, you don't need to use weapons to be here," Kissa reassured.

"Never fired a gun?" Ellie asked.

"I've never even touched one," Minerva said.

Ellie removed a gun from its niche. She checked to make sure it was unloaded. "Hold out your hands. Both of them." Ellie placed the weapon on her palms.

The gun was heavier than expected. She had never felt anything so serious before. The metal felt oily but also like cold velvet. "It feels like a snake." During a visit to a zoo, she had run her fingers over the skin of a little yellow snake. It felt beautiful and awful at the same time. That was what the gun felt like, and it frightened her.

"Yes, a snake is a good comparison. A gun is cold-blooded and only comes to life in the hands of its handler," Sarah said.

"What do you think?" Ellie asked.

All eyes were on her. Kissa turned around in her seat to watch, even Amanda peeked into the rearview mirror. "It's scary and powerful," Minerva said.

"That's how most serious things are in this world," Kissa said. "If you want to determine how serious something is, think about how much it frightens you. Not everyone needs guns. We can train you but think about what kind of person you are first. Do you want that?"

The gun certainly frightened her. Kissa was right. "It's not me." She handed it back to Ellie, who returned it to the cabinet. "I think I'm another kind of person. I admire the four of you and what you do for the Witch World. You're all brave and badass." The four women laughed.

So what kind of witch are you, Minerva?

All she knew was that she didn't want to follow her mom around or sit on the sidelines as all the grown-up witches attended to the matters at hand. She didn't know how she was going to contribute to the Sisters of Bast and the search for baby Gia, but she felt compelled to be here, that same force was nudging her along. She needed to get out into the world and figure out her purpose.

Kissa's phone rang and she answered. When the call ended, she told Amanda to pull over. "The Magica received information about the possible whereabouts of the Abecedarians. We need to plan."

The van's headlights illuminated a bullet-riddled *No Tres-*
passing sign hanging askew on a chain-link fence. Like the abandoned resort,
the gate sported a new padlock. With a smirk, Ellie held up her hands, wiggled her fingers, and hopped out of the van.

"She's a master lock picker with those magical fingers," Amanda explained.

Ellie had left the sliding door open, and the cold November night air
rolled in. The open door framed the woods like the dark themed Thomas
Cole paintings Minerva had seen in Hudson River Valley museums, all black
smudges and shadows. She stared into the forest, imagining something lea-
ping out of it and into the van.

The van lurched forward startling her. Ellie pushed open the gate and ushered the van through. She then hopped in, sliding the door shut. They continued
down the road pockmarked with potholes, weeds creeping out of cracks. Tree
branches sounded like nails on a chalkboard as they scratched the van's sides.

Kissa winced. "Abandoned places cost me a fortune in paint jobs."

Sarah laughed. "The baddies should have the courtesy of at least trim-
ming the hedges."

Their levity in this moment of uncertainty wasn't lost on Minerva, but
all she could feel was trepidation. The trees ended and before them was a
parking lot. In the distance brick buildings loomed in the dark, a defunct
manufacturing site. The place didn't look ramshackle like the abandoned
resort did. Someone was maintaining this place.

"No one's come out to confront us," Sarah said. "Either they have no
security or have some other nefarious plan."

Amanda glanced about. "I don't see anything nefarious." She looked at
Kissa who gave the go ahead to proceed.

"Wait."

The van shuddered to a stop, making everyone grab a nearby surface.

"Do you see that?" Minerva pointed to a bright red light embedded in
the road ten feet from the van.

Amanda and Kissa tilted forward in their seats, straining to see. "I don't
see anything," Kissa said.

"Don't you see the bright red light set into the road?"

Ellie grabbed the door handle to investigate Minerva's claim of a red light.

Minerva grabbed the back of Ellie's shirt. "Don't do that." She didn't know exactly what was happening, but it was the proverbial bad feeling. "It's dangerous. I don't know what it is, but I can sense it."

"Boss," Sarah said, "Min could be seeing a hex mine."

"Esther seems to be dabbling in all sorts of magics," Amanda said.

"You seem to be sensing them," Ellie said."

"Hmm, not the mines," Sarah said. "She's sensing the emotion of danger. When they were laid, the terrorists likely left residues of their own emotions. Never thought an empath would be helpful on a mission."

The doubt of her own worth to this mission lessened. Maybe she would be some use to the Sisters of Bast.

"Okay, we will make our way around them," Kissa said. She unbuckled her seat belt. "Let's switch places."

It took several seconds before Minerva realized Kissa was speaking to her.

"Is that so she can get blown up first?" Sarah joked.

"Very funny," Kissa said.

She now knew why they joked so much, but Sarah's comment still troubled her. "Is that true? Will we get blown up?"

"Could, and rather badly," Kissa said.

Minerva finally understood the gravity of what the Sisters of Bast did. They joked but this was no joke. They understood the seriousness, and now she did too. "I don't think I'm qualified to do this." How quickly she felt her confidence deflate.

"But you're the only one who can see the red lights," Amanda said.

Minerva looked around at all the Sisters who were dressed in leather and combat boots. She wore jeans, a sweater, and a rain jacket. "Can't someone do some magic so that one of you who are more experienced can guide us through the mines? I don't feel like being responsible for everyone's deaths."

Kissa touched Minerva's shoulder. "We were all inexperienced at one time. This is how you become experienced. We trust you." The other Sisters murmured their support.

Minerva's shoulders ached. "I know you mean well, but I'm not you, any of you. I don't have super abilities. I can't even manage everyday living. I possess no real purpose."

"Whoa, hold on their, Minerva," Sarah said.

Kissa looked aghast. "You are the daughter of the Magica."

"That doesn't have anything to do with me," Minerva blurted.

"Of course, it does," Kissa said. "Your mother has had the Magica since birth. She carried you, as well as your brothers and sisters. What she has she passes to all of you. Something of the Magica must have transferred to you. You need to discover what that is, but you won't know what that is until you get out into the world."

Minerva sat back in the passenger seat and stared at the red light before her. Kissa's argument was one she had never considered. Minerva bit her lower lip. When was she going to stop being so afraid?

"Now." She hadn't meant to say the word aloud, but it felt good. "Now." Three time's a charm. "Now. Okay, I'll give it a try."

After they cleared the first red light, the Basts congratulated her, and Minerva felt the thrill of success. She just might be good at something after all. She spotted another light and guided Amanda around it. More red lights popped up. Minerva helped Amanda negotiate all of them. It felt like a slow-motion slalom course. At least no one had been blown up.

Amanda drove forward. Minerva spotted something odd up ahead.

"Hold on. There's a problem."

They were coming up on two red lights, one on the left and another on the right. Minerva considered the distance between the two. "How wide is the van?"

"Almost two meters," Amanda said.

"American here. What's that in feet?"

"A little over six feet."

Minerva tried to guess the distance between the two red lights. She explained what she was seeing.

"Maybe we can back up or go left or right," Amanda suggested.

"I would need to see the road all around the van."

Amanda brought up all exterior camera angles on the console monitor.

"No, we're surrounded by red lights."

Sarah chuckled. "Like being in shark infested waters."

Minerva wondered what it would feel like to be blown up. "We don't have any choice but to go forward." She sighed and closed her eyes, needing a few seconds of quiet. The red lights appeared in her mind. Then there was a cut away to a frontal view of the van. Even though she was still inside, she was seeing the van as if she were outside standing in front of it. "Go forward," she instructed.

"Minerva, your eyes are closed," Amanda said.

"I know. Go ahead." She felt Amanda hesitate, but eventually she put the van in drive.

The position of Minerva's perspective had changed. She was now on the other side of the red lights and low to the ground. The van moved toward her.

"A little to the right."

Amanda adjusted the direction of the tires.

"Keep it steady."

The tires were now inches from the hex mines. From her position, Minerva gauged whether the tires were going to trip or miss the mines. "Drive forward. And don't turn the wheel. Keep it very steady."

The tires were now parallel with the hex mines. "Keep going." There was less than an inch between the tires and the red lights. "Keep going."

The tires rolled past. Minerva exhaled. "Okay, those were the front tires. Now for the rears."

With a few adjustments, all the wheels cleared the hex mines. Everyone in the van exhaled, and Minerva opened her eyes.

"What was that about? I thought you said you didn't know how to do any of this mission stuff," Amanda said.

Minerva shrugged. "When I closed my eyes, it was like seeing the world from outside the van, like a drone."

Kissa gave her a wide smile. "Job well done. So now let's find these bastards and get your baby sister back."

Minerva felt pleased with herself. She wasn't the inept girl she thought of herself as. Her abilities expanded the more involved she became. She was glad she was there to help the Sisters of Bast, but she was still worried about what waited for them in the building.

CHAPTER 31

Benson shuffled a few files around, pretending to look busy and important. "Your name is Paul Miller. Correct?" The man's fingerprints were in the system, and he was wanted in several states for fraud and assault.

The man shrugged.

Paul Miller appeared reticent to divulge any information. Playing bad cop with Miller wasn't going to work. "How rude of me. You want a coffee?"

"No." Miller's voice squeaked when he spoke, and his right leg was shaking, causing ripples in Benson's own coffee cup. At the mob outside of Maggie's home, the man had come off as so self-assured as he incited the crowd with his megaphone. It was a different case now.

"What are you arresting me for? I didn't do anything wrong."

"Let's see. Gathering without a permit. Trespassing—"

"I wasn't trespassing. I was on the road."

Benson flipped through a file. "Actually, that's a private road owned by the occupant of the house. So you were trespassing." He paused to pretend he was studying a document. "Inciting a riot. Disturbing the peace. Oh, and conspiracy to commit murder and attempted murder."

"What?" The man shot out of his seat, but a chain from his handcuffs to the table restrained him, jerking him back into the chair. "I didn't attempt to murder anyone."

Picking up a remote control, Benson turned on a television screen mounted in the upper corner of the room, near the ceiling, and out of reach of most people.

The video showed Paul Miller, megaphone in hand, speaking to the crowd: "You know what we're going to do? We're going up there and rescue the children from the pedophiles and cannibals. Then we'll erect some pyres or gallows. Whatever you handymen out there can construct." The audience laughed. "Then the plan is to round them all up and burn and hang'em. How's that sound? Are you with me?" The crowd cheered and responded with a collective YES!

The screen turned black. "I think the DA will call this a pretty clear-cut case."

The man's eyes grew large at the mention of the DA. "It was just talk. My first amendment right."

"Wrong, that's not how the first amendment works." Benson could see the man was thinking about how he was going to fare in all this. He gathered his files and stood to leave.

"Wait."

The doorknob was in Benson's hand, but he stopped.

"I have information. Can we make a trade?"

"Is it good?" Benson asked. Miller nodded. He counted to five in his head before he spoke. "I'm not sure if I have the authority to cut deals. Let me go check with my boss." He shut the door behind him, leaving the man to worry.

Benson stood outside the door and breathed out through his mouth, releasing the tension building up inside of him. He couldn't blow this. The life of Maggie's baby was on the line. Ten minutes would be a good amount of time to leave the guy to mull things over. He dropped the empty files on his desk. He needed a fresh cup of coffee, and his stomach grumbled, angry at having missed lunch. Next to the coffee machine, he found a grocery store cake butchered into squares.

"Hey, whose birthday is it?" Someone yelled *mine*. "Happy Birthday! May I?" The birthday boy gave him a thumbs up. Benson grabbed a fork and speared a slice onto a paper plate. He took the cake and coffee back to his desk. When he finished, he looked at his watch. He'd given Miller enough time to decide on what he was going to say.

When he opened the door, the man perked up and peered around Benson, expecting to see another person. "What happened? Where's your boss?"

He went around to his chair. "Well, she wants a bit before she talks to the DA." He folded his hands on the table and waited.

The man squirmed. Benson observed Miller glancing from wall to wall, even looked over his shoulder a few times. He tried to stand again but with the same result. "Okay, I'll tell you something, but you swear you have to protect me. Or they'll kill me."

Benson leaned in. This was what he was waiting for, but he needed to act nonchalant. "You're in a police station. I don't think anyone will get you here."

Miller slunk low in his chair, like he was trying to hide. "You don't know what she can do. She killed those four women and just sucked them up."

"Who are you talking about?"

The man's eyes darted about the room. "Esther Goode."

He held up a finger. "Mind if I record this?"

"No," Miller exclaimed. "I mean no way." He kept shaking his head, emphasizing his decision.

"Can I take notes?" He took out his notepad. Not that Miller had any say whether he took notes or not, but he wanted the man to think he had some control. "Are you saying you saw Esther Goode kill four women?"

"Shh." The man trembled. "She'll hear. But yeah, I did. And she's gonna do it again today."

Benson perked up. He hadn't expected to hear this. "Someone's going to be killed today? Who?"

A little froth formed at the corner of Miller's lips. "The witches. She's gonna take their power today. She's got the kid, but she needs to stop the witches coming after it."

He needed to alert Maggie, or Magica.

"You think I'm crazy, talking about witches."

He kept his eyes on his notebook. "I assume you're talking about people who you think are witches."

The man jerked the chain. "No, man. Real witches with power and stuff."

Benson's ears felt stuffed with cotton, and he shook his head. "You mentioned a kid. I presume this is the kidnapped baby?"

The man rubbed his own ears. "Yeah, she took the baby. Well, her daughter did."

"And by 'she' you mean Esther Goode. And by 'daughter' you mean—"

The man interrupted. "You're going too slow. Bring me your boss. Someone who can move this along before it's too late."

"What's being planned?"

The man threw his head back and sighed in exasperation. "Aren't you listening? She's gonna kill all those witches today when they go out to that place. It's a trap."

"Where is this place you're talking about?" Benson's ears felt clogged again.

"Where's your boss?" Miller demanded.

"Hold on a second. I'll check." As soon as he exited the room, he took out his phone to call Maggie and warn her.

The explosion blew out the wall behind Benson, ramming him into the floor. His phone sailed across the room, disappearing under a cabinet. His ears rang. All he saw were feet running back and forth. Benson turned his head back to the interrogation room.

The walls dripped red. Only Paul Miller's hands survived the explosion, still chained to the table.

Benson groaned. Above him the ceiling cracked. He struggled to stand, but his legs wouldn't obey. He needed his phone to call Maggie. He tried pulling himself across the floor.

And then it all came crashing down on him.

Chapter 32

"No use hiding the van," Amanda said. "If they're here, they know we are too."

The four selected their weapons. Ellie proffered a small pistol to Minerva. She declined.

"Well, you need something," Sarah said. She chose a knife that fit in Minerva's hand. "And you'll need this." She handed over a black leather harness. "Fasten this to your thigh. The weapon will be accessible, and you're less likely to cut yourself."

Minerva followed Sarah's instruction. The handle felt heavy in her palm, but she couldn't imagine using the sharp, pointy part to stab or cut anyone. She sheathed the blade.

"Well?" Sarah said.

"Yeah, not bad. I feel a little protected," Minerva lied. The knife, like the gun, frightened her.

They left the van and headed for the first brick building. "Ellie, take lead," Kissa said. "And, Minerva, you're going with Ellie."

"What? In front?" Minerva's insides went ice cold. It was one thing to point out hazards within the safety of the van, but outside of it they were exposed.

"Your new-found ability might be helpful here," Kissa said. "We need to keep a look out for all manner of things."

She didn't know if she was up to it. Ellie didn't wait. She took point. It didn't give Minerva time to think, and she had to scamper after the tall woman. Plus, she wasn't about to go against Kissa's orders.

Ellie approached the building diagonally, heading for a wall with no windows, and the others followed. Ahead, a strip of purple light stood out to Minerva. She touched Ellie's arm and shook her head. Minerva got in front of Ellie and led them around the trap. They followed the perimeter of the building until they came to a door. Minerva examined it for any signs it had been tampered with. She grasped the handle and pulled. It opened onto a dark hallway. She was going to step forward, but Ellie stopped her.

"That was too easy. Do you see any traps?"

Minerva looked at every surface in the hallway. "No, we're good."

"Let me go first. No magic doesn't mean there aren't baddies in there with guns," Ellie explained.

Minerva's eyes widened. She hadn't thought of that. She assumed Esther being a witch would primarily use magic.

Sarah grabbed a brick lying in the grass and propped the door open. Ellie led the way, moving her gun from side to side. There were four doors, and each Bast checked one. None opened. Ellie signaled they should go forward.

The door Sarah had propped open slammed shut, turning the hallway mine-shaft dark. All four turned on flashlights.

"That brick wasn't going anywhere," Sarah said. "Someone closed that door on us."

Amanda went back to the door and found it locked. "This is a trap. Maybe we should kick down the door and get out of here."

From further in the building, there came a faint sound like crying. "Did you hear that?" Minerva asked. She went after the sound.

"No, Minerva, wait," Kissa ordered.

"Do you hear that? It's a baby crying." Minerva couldn't wait. Her little sister needed her.

The Basts chased after her, their lights illuminating the way. The hallway turned right and then opened onto a cavernous room with rows of windows on two sides. If it had once been a manufacturing plant, no machinery remained—just broken concrete and a few dark oily patches. Every move they made echoed back to them.

As the only object on the vast, vacant floor, the child seat stood out as a grotesque incongruity. Minerva hesitated. The baby cried out again. She knew it was a trap but controlling the empath in her was difficult. She couldn't take it anymore. She ran to the car seat, fell to her knees, and pulled aside a blanket.

A doll.

Minerva's excitement deflated. The crying started again, mocking her. She smashed the doll on the concrete floor. When it continued crying, she smashed its head on the ground once more trying to get it to shut up. If she had only been more insistent with her mother, had explained what was going on with her emotions, Heather could have been expelled from their house that night, or at least had Benson deal with her in the morning. Then none of this would be happening.

A choking sound made Minerva turn around. Ellie and Amanda were grasping their throats. The oily patches they stood on started to shimmer.

"They're traps," Kissa yelled.

Lured by the source of the crying, Minerva missed the signs. Esther had used a key emotion to override the need to be cautious.

Sarah reached out to the trap, wanting to rescue Ellie.

"Don't touch them. You'll be locked into it," Minerva said. She didn't know how she knew this. She just did. "Kissa, Sarah, we're going to hold hands making a circle around them. Ellie and Amanda, you do the same."

Outside the circle Kissa and Amanda followed Minerva's lead. Within the black circle Ellie and Amanda took one another's hands and used their magic from the inside.

Amanda's eyes started to bulge. Ellie gasped. They were suffocating.

"Minerva, this isn't working," Sarah said.

Doubt crept in, trying to make Minerva question her ability to handle the situation. No, she knew she had chosen the correct spellbreaker. "Keep going."

Come now, girl. What do you know? You're surrounded by greater talents than you have.

Minerva glanced from Kissa to Amanda. Who had spoken to her? Both women were chanting, eyes closed. Minerva looked around. They were the only ones in the room.

The women in the trap were gasping. Amanda fell to her knees.

You're killing them.

Minerva's fingers tried to slip from Sarah's hand, but she held fast.

A sound like ice breaking signaled it was failing. The magic cracked, leaving a gap for the two women to slip through. Without waiting for Minerva's cue,

Sarah reached in and yanked her sister out by her tactical belt. The momentum too great, Sarah lost her footing and stumbled into the trap herself.

The magic Minerva and the others had raised vanished. The spellbreaker fell apart, and Sarah's fear hit Minerva like an electrical shock. Ellie crawled toward her sister, but Kissa stopped her.

Amanda's eyes bled. She clawed at her neck trying to breathe. Sarah put her arms around her friend and tried to share her breath with her. The black circle's magic wrapped itself around Sarah and Amanda and sucked them through the cement floor.

Now you've done it, Minerva.

"No." Ellie scrambled to where the black circle had been. She pounded the concrete floor. "Not my sister. It should have been me." She directed her anger at Kissa. "You stopped me. I could've saved her."

"You would have been lost as well." Kissa kneeled beside Ellie, urging her to come away, warning that it may still be active. But Minerva knew it was spent.

"I don't care," Ellie snapped. "My sister."

Minerva crossed her arms over her chest and turned away as Ellie's emotions threatened to engulf her. It wasn't just loss, but the loss of a twin. Minerva needed to distance herself from the riot of anger and pain. She shouldn't have run headlong after the crying baby. She should've watched for traps. In focusing on her own emotions, she had failed those around her and now two people were gone.

"Where did they go?" Minerva asked. "Are they..."

Kissa shook her head. "I don't know. I've never seen anything like that."

Minerva lay crumpled on the concrete floor.

"We need to get out of here now," Kissa ordered. When Ellie and Minerva didn't get up, she barked her command. "Get up now!"

Minerva stood, wiping her mouth with the back of her hand. Ellie ignored her superior. She lay spread across the spot where her sister and friend had disappeared, maybe even killed. "Now, Ellie." The warrior struggled to her feet. Kissa pushed Minerva to the front. "You're leading. Watch for traps."

This was penance for screwing up. If any more appeared, she would go down deservingly. They made it back to the main hallway without any surprise attacks. Minerva pushed down on the latch, remembering it was locked.

"Get out of the way," Kissa said. "Stand back." Her magic blew the door open. Kissa gave Minerva a shove. There was no time to stop. They took the same path around the building and back to the van. Kissa opened the sliding door for them.

"Do you see any traps?" Kissa asked as she put the van in drive.

Minerva scanned the road. "No."

"We need to warn Magica and Sylvie." Kissa floored the gas pedal.

Two shots rang out.

The van swerved and rammed into a light pole. Minerva who had started climbing into the passenger seat was thrown back.

The gun blasts kept coming.

Minerva squeezed her eyes shut. This isn't the time to hide. If she didn't act, they would all die here. The shooting paused as a group of five shadowy figures ran toward the van. She had maybe a minute.

Now, Minerva.

Ellie lay sprawled on the van floor, shot and bleeding but still alive.

Kissa's head rested against the driver's side window. Minerva placed her hand on the woman's neck. No pulse. She needed to administer CPR, but Kissa was upright and buckled into the seat.

Minerva looked up to find the shooters closing in. She needed to get Kissa out of the seat. The seatbelt buckle wouldn't open. Minerva yanked, but the buckle resisted. She jerked the belt again, but nothing happened. She gave up and her hands fell back into her lap.

What was she going to do?

The shooters were now seconds away. There had to be a way to stop them. The van held plenty of guns, but she didn't know how to work them. Maybe the dashboard had buttons for lasers or a machine gun. She punched buttons on the console. No luck there either. All those weapons, and she was helpless.

The knife.

She pulled the blade out and used it to slice through the strap.

Minerva grasped Kissa by the armpits and pulled. The woman's head flopped to the right exposing the gaping wound on the left side of Kissa's head. Minerva jerked away, gagging at the sight of brain matter sticking to the driver's side window.

What was she going to do? Ellie was shot, and Kissa was most definitely dead. Minerva started shivering.

The sliding door clicked as someone tried opening it. Why hadn't she thought it sooner? She slapped a warding spell on the doors and windows. Now what? She needed to do something. Nothing came to her. She couldn't figure out what to do.

Ellie was shot. Kissa was dead. Ellie was shot. Kissa was dead.

The shooters beat on the sides of the van.

Ellie was shot. Kissa was dead.

Minerva moaned, rocking back and forth. Grief and terror churned within her. Her moaning grew louder. When the emotional pressure within her became intolerable, Minerva opened her mouth and wailed. Her body had stored every emotion she'd ever experienced or been exposed to. Now it was all being released.

The shooters dropped their weapons and covered their ears. Even when she stopped wailing, they still shuffled about clasping their heads.

Minerva took advantage of the moment. She wrestled Kissa's body into the rear and then flung herself into the driver's seat. She started the van and stepped on the gas. The cult members skittered out of the way.

The engine coughed and spluttered, then stalled.

"No. No."

The shooters lifted their rifles at her.

"You will start." She pushed the button. It flashed for three seconds.

Then they opened fire on the van.

CHAPTER 33

MAGICA GLANCED AT THE MOBILE PHONE AGAIN. NO TEXT OR PHONE call from Minerva, Kissa, or Benson. The last contact she had was with Kissa three hours earlier, telling her the location of the ABCs. As for Benson, Magica had no idea where he was. Magica felt Maggie sinking into despair.

"What's going on?"

"No one's responding to my calls or texts."

Sylvie glanced over at her. "Minerva's with the Sisters of Bast. I think she's well protected. And we're about thirty minutes away. Don't worry."

"I don't worry. These are Maggie's feelings."

Sylvie grimaced. "It's kind of strange. You don't have feelings as the Magica?"

"Of course, I have feelings. I'm not a monster. The worry you see emanating from me is Maggie's worry though," Magica explained.

"So what are you feeling then?"

"Concern."

"Isn't that the same as worry."

"No," Magica said. "Worry is a hyperbolic projection of negativity onto the future. Concern comes from knowing the facts of the situation and weighing them against realistic outcomes."

Sylvie snorted. "Hmm, sounds like semantics to me."

"It isn't," Magica insisted.

The phone rang, Minerva's name on the screen.

"Minerva?"

Her daughter's voice cut out for a few silent seconds.

"Mom!"

"Minerva."

Again, an empty gap interrupted them.

"Minerva."

"Mom...help..."

This time the call dropped off. Magica redialed but the phone rang and rang until Minerva's voice mail kicked on. "She said she needed help."

"Shit," Sylvie said. "Don't worry. We'll be there in about fifteen minutes. And you know she's alive."

Magica grimaced. "I misjudged Holder."

"Maybe you didn't."

"What do you mean?"

Sylvie gripped the steering wheel, staring at the road before her. "What if Esther got to her, planted that information in her head?"

That idea stunned Magica. It was exhausting how Esther kept getting in front of them.

A vehicle without headlights passed them.

Sylvie braked hard. "Was that them?" She didn't wait for confirmation but u-turned the Land Rover. She flashed her lights to get the driver to stop. Instead, the driver floored the van.

"Minerva was driving." Magica and Sylvie gave each other a look.

The van shimmied across the road. "She's going to roll that thing," Sylvie said.

"I'll stop it."

Magica put her hands onto the dashboard. She didn't want Minerva to come to an abrupt halt. The van needed to decrease slowly. "*Retardar*," she whispered.

The back of the van rushed up on Sylvie, who swerved onto the shoulder to avoid a rear-end collision. The van rolled to a stop.

Magica bolted from the Land Rover. Wards covered every opening, but she disposed of them with a wave of her hand, like shooing away a pest. The driver's door opened, and Minerva stumbled out.

"Mom." Blood soaked her sleeves and chest.

"Minerva, what happened?" Magica ran her hands over her daughter. She couldn't lose Minerva too. "Have you been shot?"

Sylvie slid open the back door. "Maggie, it's Kissa and Ellie." Both women lay on the floor, a puddle of blood growing around them.

Magica climbed into the back and placed her hands on Ellie's chest. A weak life force warmed Magica's hands. "She's alive, barely."

Sylvie climbed in to tend to Kissa. "Oh shit." Sylvie said. "Oh no."

Within Magica, Maggie wanted to crumble in despair, but Magica pushed away her host's emotions. Minerva came around the front of the van, looked at Kissa, and turned away.

"Can you?" Sylvie nodded at Kissa.

"No, that's beyond even the Magica's abilities," she said. "But we can still save Ellie. Let's get her to the Rover." It took the three women to carry Ellie to the cargo hold. "I'll need to keep in contact with Ellie, but with the power of the Magica and the thirteen, she should live." She put her hands over Ellie's heart.

A shock slammed Magica into the side panel.

Sylvie scrambled into the cargo hold. She stuck her hands into Magica's hair, feeling around for injuries. She pulled back her hands. "No blood but you might have a bump."

"Mom?" Minerva looked at her, the whites of her eyes standing out in the growing darkness.

Magica sat up, rubbing the back of her head.

"What was that?" Sylvie asked.

"Esther. I felt her come between me and Ellie. She blocked the thirteen from helping me," Magica said. "There's no way that Esther should have been able to do that." She placed her hands on Ellie again and pushed back at the obscene powers being used by the rogue witch.

"Minerva, were both women shot in the van?"

Minerva nodded.

"Look. There aren't any bullet holes in the windows," Sylvie said. "The bullets were runed. This might be a problem."

"Okay, let's get going," Magica said. "Minerva, I know you're upset but you'll need to drive the Rover. And Sylvie, you drive the van. We need to hang onto Kissa's body for now. I need to keep Ellie alive and Esther away."

"Hey, wait a second. Aren't we forgetting something? Minerva, where are Amanda and Sarah?" Sylvie asked.

In the driver's seat, Minerva shuddered. "They—" her voice cracked. "They disappeared. I think they're dead. They fell into a trap. I tried to help."

"Okay, let's talk about this later," Magica said. She didn't need for Minerva to get upset right then. "Just focus on the road." It would take hours to reach home.

Magica kept her hands and mind focused on keeping Ellie alive, but the rogue witch's growing powers angered her.

Who did Esther think she was, the Magica?

CHAPTER 34

Dr. Williams assisted them getting Ellie into the downstairs bedroom because Minerva appeared to be succumbing to shock. Unable to remove her hands from Ellie's body, Maggie told Sylvie what she needed from the cupboard in her office. The doctor was prepared to stay and help.

Minerva, pale and with a sheen of sweat on her upper lip, folded herself into the room's armchair and hugged her knees to her chest. Shock had set in as soon as she put the van in park. The ordeal now over, Minerva's body and mind were shutting down.

Something troubled Magica, a lump in her gut told her to send the doctor away. "Thank you, but I think you should return to the thirteen."

"Are you sure?"

"Dr. Williams, I've got that 'Something is rotten' feeling. And I'm afraid for your safety." Magica cocked her head. "You've been relatively unscathed through this whole ordeal, and I'd like to keep you that way in case things go terribly wrong."

"I could argue that I'm a doctor and I know how to remove bullets, but I'm going to listen to you." Magica was relieved to have at least one person put herself entirely in her hands and not argue. Dr. Williams excused herself to return to the school. She greeted Sylvie in the hallway.

Sylvie placed the box of items Magica needed on the bed. "Doc isn't going to stay and help?"

"I asked her to go back to the school. Can you take Minerva upstairs, please, and get her under some warm blankets."

"Yeah. Prop her legs up too. First aid stuff. Got it."

Maggie looked her sister-in-law over for signs she might be breaking down as well. If there were any, she hid them, or more likely punched them down into some dark recess of her soul. Other than looking a little ashy, Sylvie appeared intact. Either way, Maggie thanked the goddess she could count on her sister-in-law. Minerva let herself be guided out of the room. She moved like an elderly woman.

With one hand, Maggie set out the items for the spell. First, she placed the clear quartz at the center to amplify the magics. At each of the eight major compass points she placed a corresponding crystal. She picked up the shaker of silver powder. If she shifted some of the power of the thirteen into Ellie, the warrior's recovery should be nearly instantaneous.

Magica proceeded with the ritual. As soon as she sprinkled the silver, two bullets pushed out of Ellie's body. Magica waited for her to return to consciousness. The minutes passed, and Ellie remained silent. Magica picked up a bullet and examined the markings etched into the metal. Kill runes. Ellie was lucky to be alive, but healing would take longer than expected. She created a silver field that enveloped Ellie. This was all she could do now. The spell and silver combined with the power of the thirteen would work to heal Ellie in time. Magica hoped. With Esther, she couldn't be sure what the rogue witch would stoop to.

She needed to wash her hands. The image in the bathroom mirror startled her. The Magica's hair, usually a fiery red, appeared dull, her skin was pale, and a grayish film lay over her eyes.

Minerva wasn't just in shock. Magica grabbed the canister of silver powder and hurried upstairs.

Sylvie was exiting the hallway bathroom. "Look at my hair and eyes."

Magica swept past her, heading for Minerva's room. Her daughter was convulsing, frothy saliva bubbled from her mouth. "We've been poisoned." Maggie performed the healing ritual on Minerva. Sylvie brought a wet wash towel and cleaned her niece's face. At the end of the spell, Magica sprinkled the silver, and the same magical shell appeared around her daughter.

Minerva continued to froth at the mouth, and then her skin went stone gray.

"Maggie, whatever you're doing it's not working."

"I know." She drew a little more power from the thirteen.

Sylvie turned and went downstairs. When she came back, she held out a bottle. "Dr. Williams recommended Atropa belladonna."

Of course, the spelled atropine tincture would counteract the spelled poison. Magica administered the tincture. Minerva's gray complexion dissipated until her daughter appeared only pale.

She handed Sylvie the canister of silver and the atropine. "Do the spell on me, and then I'll do you."

"How did Esther do this? And why?"

She shook her head. "I don't know, Sylvie."

"They could have all been exposed to something at the factory and then passed it to us. Or maybe the kill runes poisoned Ellie and then us."

Magica shook her head and shrugged. "Anything's plausible at this point. As to the why, I think Esther is trying to slow us down, if not outright stop us."

Maggie administered the belladonna to Sylvie.

"Esther knows you'll stay here and take care of Minerva."

Magica went to Ellie and gave her the remedy. "Well, Esther misread our ability to figure this out quickly."

"Maybe it was all the time she needed."

Maggie wanted to say 'for what' but Magica held it back. "I'm going to make coffee."

Sylvie volunteered to go out to the school and check on the thirteen and see if Dr. Williams needed anything.

It felt strange to be sitting at the banquette in an empty kitchen in the middle of the night with only the drip of the coffeemaker in the background. She thought of how they'd failed to rescue Gia again. No, she, the Magica, had failed. It was her responsibility and thus her fault.

The Magica's obligations to the Witch World harmed her family. Her infant daughter kidnapped. Sylvie lost her wife Lucy and an unborn daughter. Then there were Lavinia, Jinny, and Susan—three good, kind women. And Mother Esme. Maggie kept expecting her to appear with a warm smile. And now Kissa was dead, along with Sarah and Amanda. Ellie had a life-threatening injury, and Minerva was in shock. And they'd all been poisoned.

She wanted to cry, felt the buildup within her, but she wouldn't allow it. Those would be Maggie's tears. She was the all-powerful Magica, revered by the Witch World. She couldn't just give in to despair.

All the magics in the world can't stop bad things from happening. People like Esther rise up to create mayhem and disorder. And good people don't always prevail. Hell, good rarely prevailed. Good had to persevere because evil just kept chugging along. And what was it Esther and the cult wanted from all this? Power? Revenge? A reckoning?

All Maggie wanted was her baby back.

At every turn Esther alluded them. It was as if the witch was tapped into Maggie, watching her. Maggie looked around the room for cameras. No, a rogue witch wouldn't have to use nonmagical technology. Not to mention the house was protected with an excess of wards, and still somehow Esther found ways to best Maggie and the Magica.

Despite all that, she was the only person left to stand against Esther.

Meanwhile, Esther possessed an endless supply of mindless drones to call into action. Cult members she could weaponize. And their followers viewed Noah Corwin as some kind of savior against an imagined foe.

Esther felt wronged and cheated of the power, but it was never hers. If her baby had lived, she would have been the next Magica. Esther had no claim to that. Magica sat up. The thought hovering in the shadows of her mind was almost too terrible to acknowledge.

But there it was. And if this idea turned out to be true, she would be forced into a dire position—the one every Magica dreaded.

So few witches knew the primary purpose of the Magica. To prevent Magic from falling into the wrong hands.

Maggie only discovered this truth once the Magica officially passed to her. She was the self-destruct for all magics. The world had come so close many times throughout history. During her induction ceremony, Maggie had asked the Mothers how Magic would be destroyed if she had to activate the fail-safe. They had no idea only that the necklace was the key. Obviously, it had never happened. They surmised that perhaps all Magic could just disappear, leaving witches and supernaturals as mortals. Or the destruction of Magic could result in the destruction of all their kind. For this reason, the threat to Magic needed to be so grave, the kind that would endanger every person and thing on the planet, before the fail-safe of the Magica could be invoked.

Ultimately protecting Magic rested in the hands of the Magica, and no one else.

The back door opened, and Sylvie and Dr. Williams entered the kitchen. "I'm just stopping by to get a fresh cup and then I'll head back," the doctor said. The coffee was ready, and Sylvie poured cups for the three of them.

"Sylvie told me about the Sisters of Bast. We took a few minutes to care for Kissa's body. We wrapped and placed her in the school's big freezer. We'll contact the Sisters of Libitina, and they'll know the best way, medical and legal, to deal with the remains." Dr. Williams reached out for Magica's hand. "I'm sorry. I know you and Kissa knew one another well."

Magica sipped her coffee. "I was thinking that Esther always seems to know what we're doing or manipulates us into a situation of her doing. When Heather was here, she was the spy. But now?"

"It's Gia," Dr. Williams said.

Both Magica and Sylvie looked surprised.

"Esther's exploiting the mother-child connection to spy on you." Dr. Williams was so nonchalant about her claim, as if it was the most obvious answer—and it was. "And can you imagine how much stronger that bond is with you as the Magica and she the Arch-Magica?"

"We suspected Esther was tapping into Gia's power but not that she was accessing specific powers. I've been checking in with Gia several times a day," Magica said.

Dr. Williams sipped the hot brew. "And she's been checking in with you."

"And Esther's been watching these interactions like watching a movie."

Sylvie stopped stirring sugar into her coffee. "Holy shit. Did you know this?"

"No."

"But you're the Magica," Sylvie said.

Magica huffed. "All powerful witch doesn't mean all-knowing witch or infallible witch or perfect witch."

Sylvie threw up her hands in defense. "Yeah, got it. Sorry."

The doctor gave Magica a sympathetic look. "You're just too close to this. Perspective requires one to step back and take the long view."

She was right. The same thing happened when the Magica went looking for the people who had ended her son's and husband's lives. She kept missing the details. Because of her short-sightedness so many people had been hurt or killed. Magica knew this had to stop.

"So what's next? Where do we go from here?" Sylvie asked.

"Have you seen my phone?" Magica patted her pockets.

"It's probably in the Land Rover. Want me to get it?" Sylvie asked.

Magica stood. "Thanks. I'll do it. Can you two check on Ellie and Minerva?" She tugged on her coat and boots before heading out into the cold night.

Sitting in the driver's seat of her car, she scrolled through her phone looking for calls from Benson. Maybe he had helpful news. It was strange that there was neither a text nor voice message from him. She pressed the call icon.

"Hello?"

A woman's voice surprised Magica. "I'm sorry. I think I have the wrong number."

"Wait. Are you calling for Detective Benson Scott?"

"Yes, I am," Magica said.

"Are you a relative of Mr. Scott's?"

Magica's stomach tightened. "Is he okay? He's not d—"

"No. He's alive, but there was an explosion at the police station. He was hurt. I'm Nurse Renny. We're trying to find Mr. Scott's family to inform them, but it seems he has no emergency contacts."

"I'm sorry. I'm not a relative." She paused trying to figure out what their relationship was. "I'm a friend, Maggie. Is he okay?"

"Mr. Scott is in recovery. You can come by tomorrow during visiting hours."

"Yes, I'll do that. Please take care of him." Recovery? She put the phone down and then smacked the top of the steering wheel with the heels of both hands. A scream lodged at the back of her throat. The explosion was no accident. Of that, she was certain. Every person who had a relationship with her ended up hurt or dead. This had to end. The thought of any more people suffering was intolerable. She was done putting people in harm's way.

She started the vehicle and put it in drive.

The Magica would stop Esther and the cult and get Gia back.

Alone.

CHAPTER 35

Magica pulled into a parking lot behind a big box store. Her decision to leave was spontaneous. Sylvie would be angry with her and chase her down, and Magica knew she didn't have much time before her sister-in-law caught up with her. If the bond between herself and Gia was so strong that Esther was able to know her every move, then she needed to fix that and quickly.

A wind hit the Land Rover rocking it from side to side. A weather alert warned an early winter storm was approaching with possible snow for higher elevations. The Land Rover's four-wheel drive could handle it, plus the chains were in a storage compartment in the cargo hold.

What she wasn't prepared for was to do magic. Spontaneity meant no preparation. No potions, no crystals, no witch tools. But what had she told Benson? Witches didn't need those trappings. They existed to harness and focus energy. She had all she needed at her disposal. The thirteen were still active in the boarding school. She could also draw on witches across the East Coast, but they all hated when the Magica did that without asking first. She heard plenty of complaints from irate witches, even back when she had been searching for her husband's and son's killers. Witches suffered from self-centeredness just like the nonmagical population. The Witch World wasn't all nature-and-nurture, everything will be just peachy. Take Esther for example.

Magica dreaded the action she was being forced to take, but it was something that had to be done to stop Esther. As a mother, Maggie felt the terror of having a child abducted, but as a witch with the ability to connect to her child, she experienced some comfort knowing they were taking good care of the baby. She had to sever the bond between herself and her little girl to stop Esther from tracking her. A rock dropped in Maggie's gut knowing how fearful Gia would become once detached from the comfort of her mother. What made this especially dangerous would be Esther's reaction when she discovered what the Magica had done. Would Esther hurt the baby in retaliation? Magica needed to put her plan in place and prayed to the goddess it would work.

The Magica would control the narrative from this point on.

She got out of the car. The evening's temperatures had plummeted, and she smelled the snow predicted to fall that night, but she needed space to perform the separation spell. She reached out to the goddess and made her request. Miles away, the thirteen groaned in their sleep, deeply affected by the spell. A few snowflakes fell on her face, feeling like cold tears. The ritual didn't take long, but in its final seconds, Maggie heard Gia's cry for her mother. And then the baby's voice went silent.

Magica got back into the Land Rover. She felt Maggie's despair, but they could now focus on the plan without worrying about being given away. Esther wouldn't have the upper hand this time.

The separation spell was also a message to Esther.

As Magica started the engine, Maggie cried. The lack of connection made her baby feel dead.

∽

"Come on," Magica said aloud to the car ahead of her slowing in the blizzard. She didn't have time to waste on some person who didn't know how to drive in inclement weather. Heavy snows pummeled the Land Rover as she drove further into the mountains, but she controlled the weather by parting the snowfall in front of her vehicle, keeping the windshield clear. Of course, the driver in front of her didn't have that ability, but she needed to make better time. She pressed the car horn.

Brake lights came on catching Magica off guard. She veered for the breakdown lane, tires crunching on wet gravel. The car speeded up and pulled over. Now she had done it. Her impatience was going to result in an altercation. A hand popped out of the driver's window. At first Magica thought the driver meant to give her an obscene gesture. Instead, he waved for her to go around.

As she drove past, she gave the driver a very short honk as a thank you, and apology for assuming the worst in people. When dealing with evil, it was too easy to assume everyone was bad. She glanced at the navigation screen. It would be another hour before she reached the abandoned factory. She gripped the steering wheel and pressed on the gas. The storm wasn't going to get in her way.

She reached her destination in better time than expected. The paved road off the highway led to a parking lot where she paused, putting the Rover in park. The mines and traps Minerva had negotiated were gone, the magic holding them in place having dissipated. This was a good indicator that any other spells or binds Esther might have laid were also gone. She doubted the rogue witch could have anticipated Magica's return to this spot. She drove on and parked as close as she could to the old building.

She scrutinized the tree line for anything moving. What would be out on a night like this? Monsters, she told herself. Just monsters.

Inside the factory, the storm reinforced the darkness within. She tossed a few light balls into the air as she followed the hallway to the main floor. Before crossing the threshold, she scanned for traps like the one Sarah and Amanda fell through. Magica spotted a scorched spot and kneeled at its edge, a dimension trap. This must have been the place where it happened. The dark patch didn't emanate any signs of life, but that didn't mean they were dead.

"Got a Schrödinger's cat problem," she said. The two women could be dead in another dimension or alive in another dimension. Two options that told her nothing and gave little hope.

Magica needed the time to set up the confrontation between herself and the cult, and she couldn't have done it connected to her baby. This entire time Magica and her people had played defense. Now, however, she was going to have the upper hand.

She surveyed the space. Broken bottles and bits of iron littered the floor. The machinery that once filled the factory had been removed. It was just one cavernous place with nowhere to hide. Maggie got busy setting hexes and laying down magic traps. The rogue witch couldn't fault her a few protections. In fact, it might be even more suspicious if Maggie didn't set up any spells or binds. Too many though and Esther might get defensive and end up hurting Gia. Maggie seethed. Let her try and that will be end of that bad witch.

Dr. Williams's warning echoed in her head: it was the bond between the Magica and Arch-Magica making Esther dangerous. How much did Esther know about Maggie's other children? Did Esther know their whereabouts? This was why the Sisters of Bast and even so many of the Magicas didn't have children. Unfortunately, they were a liability and always at risk. Still, she wanted her family back together, and Gia safe at home with all her sisters and brothers. She wouldn't give up her children for anything in the world.

It was time to summon Esther.

Magica found a clear spot on the floor. Using light, she etched a circle around her and cast a protective spell. She reached out to Gia. The baby startled awake at the astral presence of her mother and cried. Maggie felt someone circling the baby.

Meet me at the abandoned factory now. Bring the Arch-Magica.
Let's make a trade.

She knew Esther would bring more than the baby with her. The entire cult would be at her disposal, ready to destroy Maggie's team. The rogue witch would be caught off guard when she saw Magica alone.

No more of Maggie's people were going to be hurt or killed. But would it be enough? It had to be. She couldn't afford for this confrontation to go wrong, but if it did, she touched the ruby necklace, there was the fail-safe.

But even as the Magica, she didn't know if she had it in her to destroy all magic.

Chapter 36

Magica heard cars sooner than she'd expected. Several in fact, meaning Esther wasn't coming alone but had the Abecedarians in tow. Nothing less was expected. Magica hoped for a peaceful exchange, though what that exactly entailed remained a mystery. She and the others had speculated as to what Esther and Noah Corwin wanted, but only they could reveal what their end game really was.

The door opened. Out of the gloom of the dimly lit hallway Heather appeared. This surprised Magica. The girl's skin looked grayish, her hair limp on slumped shoulders. Even when she showed up on Maggie's door wet and shivering, Heather seemed like a lively young woman. Maybe the kidnapping had been hard on her. Maggie still believed Heather a victim in Noah and Esther's plan, and the empathy Maggie initially felt for Heather was still there.

Heather stopped in the doorway and cast her eyes to the ground, and Magica felt her remorse. "I'm sorry."

"Silence," Noah Corwin commanded as he and Esther entered, followed by the cult members who had discarded their robes for more practical clothing, which signaled there would be no peaceful exchange. Corwin established a command position along the wall nearest the door. Esther stood to his right, while Heather receded into the background. The cult formed a horseshoe around their leaders, ready to close ranks and protect them from the Magica.

Gia wasn't with them. "Where's my daughter? I told you to bring her."

The old man bristled. "The Devil's mistress does not dictate to Noah Corwin. If you want to see your daughter again, you will do as I say."

Maggie held her words, but the hubris of Noah Corwin, a man with no real power telling her, the all-powerful Magica, what to do was ironic. She wanted to send a bolt of lightning into his forehead.

"You have been brought here for one purpose," Corwin said. Beside him, Esther remained quiet, head bowed in deference. Heather had her arms crossed and kept looking toward the door.

"Since the first witch Pandora entered this realm, evil has seeded this world. Woman has tainted this planet with her wiles and blood."

"Seriously? You're going to give the bad guy speech?" She'd heard this speech too many times.

"Quiet!" Corwin raised his hands. "Our Heavenly Father, we now bring the answer to return this world to the Edenic Garden it should be." Corwin pivoted and brought a finger down to point at Maggie. "You wear the ruby, Magica. You will use it to initiate the mechanism to end all Magics in this world, relegating them back to Hell and Satan."

There it was. The thing Esther and Corwin had created all this mayhem over, and they used Gia to lure her here. That he knew about the ruby and that she could do such a thing as end all Magic took her aback. The true purpose of the Magica was known by only a few. Did Esther know? Were there other witches in on this whole thing?

"What say you, Witch?" Corwin eyed her like a crow with its head cocked to one side.

He couldn't be serious. There had to be another way to get Gia back without destroying all magic.

"Enough."

The word fell on Maggie's ears like a hammer, but it wasn't Noah Corwin who spoke. It was Esther.

"Like the Magica, I'm tired of your speeches." Esther took a step away from her husband. "I do thank you, Noah Corwin, for bringing the Magica to me. It has taken years, but the moment has arrived."

"What do you speak of, woman?" Corwin swiveled his great birdlike head toward Esther.

"It's over." Esther pulled a lightning bolt from the charged air. It sizzled white in her hand. "You're over."

She slammed the bolt through Corwin, killing her husband.

Esther did what Magica had wanted to do herself.

Only problem was, now she had no idea what any of this was all about.

CHAPTER 37

Corwin's corpse smoked. The smell of cooked flesh wafted through the room.

Magica stood stunned, choking on the stench.

Neither the Abecedarians nor Heather showed any shock and remained rooted to their spots.

Esther winked at her "How did you like that, Magica? You wanted a lightning bolt, and I supplied it."

She couldn't understand how Esther read her mind. The bond between herself and her baby had been severed.

"I knew you were going to figure out the bond. So I spelled it to prevent it from happening. I know. You felt the bond break. Right? You felt the baby's fear." Esther laughed. "I manufactured all of it. I'm not impressed with the whole Magica thing. Your powers seem kind of measly compared to what I've been able to do by sucking a couple witches dry."

"The Magica is to be cautious and judicious with the magic bestowed upon her," she said. "Too much magic used in one moment disrupts the balance of life on this planet."

Esther shook her head. "Even to rescue your baby you held back? What kind of mother are you?"

Questioning her ability to mother infuriated Maggie, and Esther continued to goad her.

"You let so many people die, Magica How many more are you willing to sacrifice in your quest for caution and judiciousness?" Esther motioned for someone to come forward.

Acolytes led two people through the door—Minerva and Ellie. The Abecedarians had gone to her house and abducted them.

"Where's Dr. Williams?"

"And the thirteen?" Esther said. "Well, the doc was strong. She used a powerful barricade spell on that school building. I couldn't get to them."

Magica was relieved to hear this news.

"So I had my people burn it to the ground," Esther said. "In fact, all the buildings, including your beautiful house."

"You killed all of them?" Magica moved towards Esther.

"Uh-uh. No, stay where you are." Esther signaled, and another cult member entered carrying her baby.

Gia. Maggie wanted to rush Esther and grab the child, but Magica restrained her. "What is it you want?"

Esther smirked. "I take it all these people have value to you?"

Magica didn't acknowledge the question. She needed to get Maggie under control, or the witch's emotions would oust the Magica within Maggie.

"I considered sending a couple of Corwin's people down to Florida to bring back the rest of the family. You know, make this a big family reunion. Isn't that what you love more than anything in the whole world, Maggie, family?" Esther chuckled. "So we're going to make a trade. And I'm going to be magnanimous in my offer."

The rogue witch swept her hand towards Minerva and Ellie. "In exchange for their lives, your infant's, and the rest of your family's, I ask for one thing."

Magica waited to hear the demand, but Esther stayed mute. "What is it you want?" Esther was playing games.

"Very good! I want you to give Heather the power of the Arch-Magica," Esther said. "It is rightfully ours."

"That's crazy," Magica said. "The power of the Magica belongs to no witch. It was intended for your daughter who didn't survive." She gave those words a twist like a knife pushed into Esther's heart.

"Shut up!" the witch screamed. She turned toward Minerva and Ellie. "You want me to kill them now?"

"No. I apologize," Magica said. "Let them be." She looked at their faces. They shouldn't be here. This was her fight.

"Yes, it is," Esther said.

Because you can read my mind, I could never take any action against you that you couldn't put down.

Correct, Magica.

You will kill all of them.

Not the Arch-Magica. She will live with me. I will be her new mama. Esther grinned, amused by their magical tête-à-tête.

"Just to get this one thing straight, Esther. You need me to do the transfer because you don't possess the power to do it yourself?"

Esther waved her hand dismissively. "You're still the Magica, and I'm just some lowly rogue witch. Are you going to get on with it or do you want me to kill that one?" An ABC pulled Minerva away from the group. Ellie made to tackle the man but was stopped by the other acolytes. Minerva, still too ill, slumped to the floor.

Magica sent a tendril of comfort to her daughter but felt a tug on her magic. "Stop, Esther. She's not well."

Esther leaned forward and whispered, "You have the power to end all this right now. Give Heather the power of the Arch-Magica."

Could she even do the thing Esther was asking? And what would her daughter's life look like magicless? Even without being the Arch-Magica, Gia was born a lineage witch. How does a witch live without her magic? And the other consideration was Heather. The girl didn't seem strong enough to hold that much power. Maggie ran through all the possible scenarios but came to the same conclusion.

"That's right. There isn't. So what do you need to do the transfer?"

"I just need to hold Gia's and Heather's hands. I will act as the conduit."

Esther took the baby from the Abecedarian, cradling Gia against her breast. Maggie flinched. There was something grotesque about Esther's version of motherhood. Losing a child had warped her. Magica glanced into the woman's face and found Esther scowling at her, her mouth grim with fury. She thrust the baby toward the Magica, retaining her grip on the infant. Gia let out a startled cry at being handled so roughly. Maggie wanted to dart forward and take Gia. Esther drew the baby back, a warning.

She took her baby's hand. Velvety fingers curled around hers, and she choked back tears. All she wanted was her baby back home. Even Magica ached at robbing Gia of her birthright.

Heather placed her hand into the Magica's free one, and she gave it a squeeze. Poor girl. Magica began the transfer. The raw, undeveloped power of the Arch-Magica flowed through her. It was a power that wouldn't be activated until Maggie died or relinquished the Magica within her.

She shook her head when she realized how stupid she'd been. In her concern for her baby, one fact slipped past her. Esther needed Maggie dead for this to work. The transfer faltered.

"What's going on?" Esther screamed. "Finish this."

Magica stared hard at Esther, allowing her mind to consider all the ways she would kill the rogue witch. Esther grimaced. "Stop your fantasies and get on with it."

Magica smirked but resumed the transfer. She tried not to think about her ordeal. With so much magic flowing in the room, maybe a little ward would go unnoticed. Too focused on the Magic transfer, Esther didn't respond to Magica's thoughts, and she took the opportunity to place a shield around herself, the baby, and the other two witches. It wasn't a lot, but it could slow down anything menacing Esther had planned.

"How does it feel to lose this power?" Esther said.

Magica turned her pale green eyes on the rogue witch until she relented and looked away. But she finally understood what this was all about.

The transfer stopped like a switch being flipped off. Magica staggered backward, releasing Gia's and Heather's hands.

Gia squalled as if the extraction of magic hurt her. The sound made Magica flinch. "Let me have her, Esther."

The rogue witch pulled Gia away. "Not yet. We need to see if this worked."

Magica stepped back and balled her hands into fists. She was tired of Esther's games. If the witch didn't start reciprocating, Magica would make her sorry. A flash drew her attention to Heather.

The young woman bloomed like a midnight flower. Her tired skin glowed, and the black patches under her eyes disappeared. Her hair grew shiny and her lips deepened to red. "Mother, I'm the Magica." The girl beamed.

Magica reached out to take Gia.

Esther grasped the baby's neck and legs, making Gia cry in pain, and flung the baby into the air. Maggie screamed, scrambling to reach the baby before she hit the factory's cement floor. Esther's throw propelled the baby's body into a long trajectory, and the baby went rigid and screamed.

Ellie leaped into the air. All six feet three inches of her stretched forward and upward, her long arms reaching.

Magica pushed herself in Gia's direction but felt like she was moving through quicksand. She wasn't going to reach the infant in time.

"*Tempus tardus*," Maggie screamed, drawing the energy up out of the earth to fill the room.

Time, if not completely stopped, slowed. The second hand of the analog watches worn by a few of the acolytes took fifteen seconds to click from one second to the next. It was not a spell Maggie could hold for long without severe consequences.

Both the baby and Ellie hung suspended above the ground. It took Gia a full minute to reach the point in which she intersected with Ellie. The woman's hands grazed Gia as she kept moving through space. Ellie's fingers snagged the baby's clothing, drawing her in like a football.

The Abecedarians as nonmagicals couldn't move. Magica signaled Minerva who understood what her mother needed. Min raised her arms and a spell exploded from her. The cult members were blown backward into a concrete wall. The energy drained from the room, releasing time from the Magica's spell.

Ellie came crashing down, but she tucked the baby into her and rolled onto her side, protecting Gia.

Magica reached Ellie who held the baby out to her. She ran her hands over her daughter's tiny body making sure she wasn't injured.

"Mom, look!" Minerva yelled.

Maggie twisted around to see Esther's hands wrapped around Heather's head.

The young woman's eyes rolled back into their sockets, showing all white. Her mouth gaped open in a soundless scream. And then Heather's body convulsed. Esther gripped her daughter's head tighter. Her glowing skin started to char. Esther was draining the Arch-Magica power out of her own daughter.

They all stared in horror. Magica had to stop this. She gathered a mass of remnant energy still lingering in the room and heaved it at Esther.

The witch stepped aside, pulling Heather with her like she was nothing more than a rag doll. Undeterred Esther continued to squeeze her daughter's head, extracting the last magic out of her. It took only minutes for Heather to be drained. She then dropped her daughter's husk to the ground.

Magica rushed Esther, but the floor opened in multiple spots. Esther stepped into one of the portals and disappeared. Seven acolytes, all women, followed suit.

The Magica threw herself onto the spot where Esther escaped, but the portal had closed.

From the hallway doors could be heard banging open, and voices announced themselves as the police. Law enforcement officers poured into the main room. The remaining Abecedarians tried to flee.

Magica looked up to see Benson and Sylvie running to her. Ellie came over with Gia, putting the baby into her mother's arms. Benson hugged Maggie to him, the baby squeezed between them.

"What happened?" Sylvie walked over to Heather's desiccated corpse.

Around them, the officers arrested the cult members, leading them away.

"Esther killed Noah Corwin and Heather," Magica said, drawing Gia closer to her.

"Good god." Benson took off his jacket and covered the young woman's body.

"I can't believe Esther did that to her own daughter," Ellie said.

Minerva hugged her mother. "I'm sorry, Mom. You were right about Heather."

Magica nodded. "Can we go home, Benson? Or do you need us?"

"We've got this," Benson said. "Take your family home."

Home with her family was all Maggie wanted.

Chapter 38

Maggie's house buzzed with the normalcy of homework and laundry. She sat at the banquette folding towels. Samuel was preparing a pot-roast with potatoes and carrots, while Becca & Betsy squabbled over the different answers they'd come up with for the same math problem. In the family room, Luka sat next to Gia's bassinette, rocking her and telling stories.

Her baby seemed to be fine despite the horrific thing Esther did to her. The police insisted Gia be taken immediately to the hospital for a thorough examination, and Maggie didn't argue. The doctors found her to be uninjured and healthy. Still, Maggie worried. That's what mothers did. Well, most mothers. Some, like Esther, were monsters. Maggie held herself to a measure of responsibility for Heather's death. She hadn't been wrong about the young woman, and maybe if she'd taken the time, she could have turned things around before the situation got worse, so much worse.

The house hadn't burned to the ground as the rogue witch had claimed to have done. Once Sylvie realized the Magica had skipped out on her own, she called Benson. He talked his way out of the hospital and led a squad of law enforcement officers to the house. Before he could get there, Esther and the cult attacked, kidnapping Minerva and Ellie. Sylvie escaped. She'd been the one to show Benson the way to the abandoned factory.

The school and house had been set on fire. Dr. Williams and the thirteen saved the school, but it needed significant repairs. When Benson and his people arrived, they put out the fire that had taken hold in a small section of Maggie's house—her husband's study. She and the children salvaged what they could. The contractor and his crew boarded up the hallway leading to that room. Maggie tried not to cry.

Both Sylvie and Ellie chose to head back home to grieve with their families. Maggie's heart ached for everyone they had lost.

She gathered the folded towels and went upstairs to put them in the linen closet. Minerva's door was shut. Maggie knocked.

"Come in, Mom." Minerva lay in bed, a book in her hands.

Maggie sat on the edge of the bed. "You okay, Min? Don't you want to come downstairs with everyone?"

Her daughter sighed. "I'm tired. I need time alone to recharge."

"I know it's difficult to be an empath but don't isolate yourself too much. Okay?"

Minerva nodded.

Maggie stroked her daughter's hair as she had often done when Minerva was a little girl. "I want to thank you for helping me with the family while I was pregnant. As the oldest you always get stuck in the role of alternate parent. That's not fair, but it is family."

"You're welcome, Mom. I think I needed my own time as well to figure things out." Minerva drew her knees to her chest and gazed out her window. "Honestly, life kind of seemed to be moving faster than I was comfortable with. Carey is going to ask me to marry him."

This was what Sylvie had been alluding to. This is what was upsetting Minerva this whole time. "What are you going to do?"

"I'm going to say no. That's crazy. Right?" Maggie started to speak but stopped. She needed her daughter to tell her own story. Minerva continued, "He's handsome and rich and so good to me, but, Mom, I never told him about us, about being witches. I talked to Aunt Sylvie, and even Benson, about this, and it made me see that if I couldn't bring myself to reveal the truth to him then maybe he wasn't the right person for me." Minerva stretched out her legs like a satisfied cat. "Do you think I made the right decision?"

Maggie squeezed her daughter's knee. "You're an adult. You need to do what's right for you."

"Well, I've made some more decisions. I don't want you to be mad."

"Min, I'm not going to be mad. You're an intelligent level-headed woman, and I know your decisions are going to be sound. So hit me. What other decisions have you made?"

Minerva reached into the top drawer of her nightstand and brought out a stack of papers. "I want to go to San Francisco at the start of the New Year. There's this nonprofit I want to work at." She handed Maggie a letter. "But I also got admitted to Stanford Law School. I'm not going right away though. I want to get some real-world experience first. The nonprofit helps persecuted witches around the world. That's what I want to do. I want to make a difference. But, Mom," she paused and took Maggie's hands, "I know Esther's out there and she wants to—"

When Minerva couldn't say it, Maggie filled in, "—kill me."

Minerva nodded. "I'll stay and help you fight her. You'll need help keeping the family safe. Plus I know you want to find Esther and get Gia's magic back."

Something within Maggie expanded, a bubble of love, that moved up and through her. "Sweetheart, I love you, but you need to go. You've discovered your strengths these last couple of weeks. You're not some shy wallflower. You're a warrior." Minerva's eyes watered. "I've got this. Don't worry."

Did she really have this? Her daughter was an adult. Why was she still giving her platitudes like she couldn't handle the truth? "Wait, Min. I need to start being honest. You're not a child. It's not going to be easy. I've only ever wanted to be a good mother because mine wasn't. In trying to give you kids the best childhood, I've glossed over the bad parts we've all suffered. I now realize that even good mothers mess up. They're not perfect. They make wrong choices. And that's okay because that's how we better ourselves.

"So yeah, I'm afraid. I'm afraid of Esther. She killed her husband. And then did the most heinous thing a parent can do—she killed her own child. Esther frightens me, and I have to stop her. I also need to get Gia's magic back if that's possible. All of that is on me. You need to live your life and find your way."

Maggie pulled Minerva in and hugged her until her daughter melted into her arms. For a few minutes, her eldest became an infant once again, and Maggie remembered all the times she cradled and carried her little girl. This would be the last time they would ever share as mother and child. Maggie was grateful for this moment.

CHAPTER 39

A PLEASANT MURMUR FILLED THE ELEGANT RESTAURANT—FROM THE gently flowing water of a fountain to the voices of patrons leaning in to whisper their dreams and desires to one another. At the center of every table, an amber glass bowl held a candle, casting a mellow light. She could see why Benson wanted to try out Fork & Honey.

Maggie felt self-conscious though. They had shared so much in the past month but knew so little of one another. She studied his face, trying to read his emotions. He looked happy, and he had asked her out on a real date. She wasn't going to assume anything though. Maybe this was the grown-up way of ending things.

The bad mother complex occupied her thoughts as well. After everything that happened, leaving Minerva to care for the children while she went on a date wasn't easy. She tried talking herself out of going, but Minerva convinced her they would be safe, that life had to go on.

The waiter poured Maggie a Hudson Valley cabernet the color of rubies, which made her think of the Magica. Hopefully, Maggie wouldn't need her anytime soon.

Once they were alone, Benson raised his glass. "Here's to date nights."

His choice of words surprised her. Date night was a term used by couples who wanted to keep the romance alive. Still, she didn't know what to make of it, but it did appear that he wasn't going to break up with her.

"I want to apologize again for everything you went through," Maggie said.

"Please, no more." He set his glass on the table. A scar slashed his right cheek, adding to the ones he already had. She lifted her hand to touch his face but drew back. He captured her hand before it returned to her lap and gave it a squeeze. "I'm fine, Maggie. And the scar, I think it makes me look tough."

She grinned at him apologetically.

"I'm glad I was there when this started, but I wish I had said no when Kissa had me sent away."

"I was part of that decision too."

"You fought for me." Benson released her hand. "And I'm sorry about Kissa and her team. Ellie's okay?"

Maggie thought of Kissa dead, and she had to consider that Sarah and Amanda were as well. Maggie took a sip of wine. "Thank you for saying that. She came to like you. I can't believe she's gone. I mean, she was the strongest of us." Maggie paused, afraid of crying. She composed herself and continued. "Ellie is coming back after the New Year to stay with us for a while." Maggie lowered her voice. "Esther's going to come for me. To gain all that power she needs me dead because it's not like I'm going to relinquish the Magica to her."

"Don't worry. I'll be here."

A server brought out their plates, laying a dish of roasted duck and pureed root vegetables before Maggie and salmon with quinoa for Benson. "Looks as delicious as something Samuel would make. It's a good thing your son can cook, or we would have all starved these past few weeks." She agreed.

Maggie looked out across the dining room. The restaurant presented a picture of serenity. Oiled dark wood gleamed. Smooth piano jazz poured from discreet speakers. People dressed up, sipping cocktails, and talking about their careers. This was the world of normal people, non-magicals. Oh, they had problems. She wasn't going to romanticize them, but none of them had a problem affecting the entire world.

"Esther said something to me during the transfer. She said, 'How does it feel to lose this power?' She believed that's all I cared about, losing the power of the Arch-Magica, which isn't my power. In fact, I've never been comfortable with the power of the Magica. I considered giving it up, but there wasn't one in waiting. Then when I learned that Gia would be the next one, well, I knew I would be stuck with it for the rest of my life. I would never foist it onto someone who didn't want it." Maggie shook her head. "How could Esther ever contemplate misusing her baby's power? And now my baby's? The idea is monstrous and unethical."

"What I'm about to say is horrific." He looked directly at her before he continued. "Maybe her baby died because the power of the Magica knew there was something wrong with Esther. Sorry, I know that's horrible to think." He looked away from her.

"I never considered that." She took a long drink of her wine., taking the minute to think about how she wanted to respond to Benson's idea. He didn't speak and allowed her the silence to contemplate his idea. "Horrible, yes, but also true. We live in a sanitized and safe world, or at least we try to, and because of that, we've lost touch with the cruel indifference of nature, and for us, magic. So either Esther possessed her character issues before her pregnancy, or they developed after the death of her husband. Doesn't matter which one because the Magica knew Esther would exploit that power for her own uses."

"Unfortunately, a baby died."

Maggie sighed. "Like nature, magic isn't nice. It's protective and self-interested. Magic is dangerous. And it can't be allowed to get into the wrong hands—" Maggie faltered.

"What's wrong?"

She closed her eyes. "I let magic get into the wrong hands."

"Hey, you did what you could do."

Her thoughts drifted to the bigger problem. The one thing she hadn't told him...or anyone. She had the fail-safe to consider. Esther had to be watched. The only problem was no one knew where she was. This scared Maggie more than if the rogue witch had been galivanting across the countryside wielding black magic. Esther off the grid meant she could be doing anything—plotting some diabolical event affecting the world or planning on having Maggie killed. This left her at an impasse. Esther was dangerous, and Maggie had to be prepared to end Magic, even if it meant the end of all witches and supernaturals. That's how dangerous magic in the wrong hands was.

"Maggie?"

"Hmm? Sorry. Just thinking."

"Do you want dessert? Apple crumble pie with ice cream?"

"Can we share one?"

They finished off the pie together, but Benson wanted to end with a port. He had more questions for her.

"If the Magica entity abandoned Esther's baby, why doesn't it do the same with Esther?"

Maggie shrugged. "It might not be able to. Esther made herself extremely powerful by draining the powers from the witches she murdered. She could've found a way to bind the Arch-Magica power to her."

Benson left his chair and took the one closer to her. "I know this is going to hang over us, but on date night let's not dwell on this anymore. We'll set aside another time to deal with Esther. Date night is for fun."

"So after everything I put you through, you want to keep going with this?"

His eyes went soft and dreamy as he took her all in. He kissed her hand. "Yeah, I do."

"Next date night we take the kids bowling. Or we can stay home and watch scary movies. Okay?"

"Whatever you want, Maggie Towne." Benson put his arm around her and drew her close. "Can I kiss you?"

"You better."

CHAPTER 40

Maggie stood outside the house watching Benson drive away in his sporty car. The evening had been lovely, but she was tired. The Yuletide tree twinkled in the living room window, and she couldn't believe another holiday was upon them.

The lights were on in the kitchen. She entered through the back door, taking off her shoes so as not to wake the children. Samuel was sitting at the banquette with his schoolbooks spread out on the table. She tossed her coat and purse on a counter stool.

"Hey, Mom. How was your night?" When he looked up at her, Maggie remembered him as a baby and a little boy. His independence and gentleness had surprised her. She didn't know small children could be like that. He was the reason why she wanted more children.

She kissed him on the head. "It was fabulous. But it's also fabulous to be back home. So what are you doing up?"

Samuel shrugged. "Gia was super fussy, and it tired Minerva out. I told her to go to bed, that I'd stay up and watch over the children and wait for you to come home."

She loved this person. "Thank you. Are you staying up or going to bed?"

He motioned to the book in front of him. "I'm going to finish this first."

"Okay, don't stay up too late. I'm going to check on the kids."

"Night, Mom."

"Goodnight, my love."

She stopped at Becca & Betsy's door first and listened to them breathe. She turned the doorknob and peaked in. Their beds were side by side separated by a nightstand. A soft light filtered into their room and touched their faces. Maggie stood between the two beds and watched her girls sleep. They had been babies once and then little girls—laughing one minute and then falling into some serious endeavor the next and always together. She knew that couldn't last forever. Becca would soon have her own interests and friends. Maggie hoped it wouldn't break Betsy's heart too much, but their sisterhood would bring them together later in life. That's how things went. She blew them kisses and then closed the door quietly behind her.

Out of respect for her privacy, Maggie stood outside Minerva's door and didn't go in. Her oldest child. So sweet that first child. So much a miracle. To think that Maggie, a homeless child who had grown up in poverty, could bring this tender creature into the world. When she held Minerva in her arms for the first time, she thought of caring for this tiny thing, nourishing her, protecting her, and she cried as she thought of her own mother's neglect. Why hadn't her mother loved her like Maggie loved her children? She wiped the moisture from her eyes. "Goodnight, baby girl."

Goodnight, Mom. I love you.

Maggie grinned. She couldn't express that amount of emotion and not expect Minerva to pick up on it.

Luka's room was last. His door was open because Gia was sharing his room with him, for a little while at least. Luka insisted on it. Her crib was right up against his bed, and Luka had his hand pressed through the rails. Gia had hold of his index finger. It was a beautiful sight, her little boy and her baby girl holding hands as they slept, and it saddened her. Luka needed Gia nearby because he was protecting her. While she loved that he was like that, it made Maggie feel like a bad mother for not protecting all her children. Stop, Maggie. She reminded herself she was going to stop thinking in absolutes. While she could swear that no harm would ever come to her children ever again, she knew it was a promise she couldn't keep. All she and the Magica could do was be vigilant and try their best.

And Gia, her little witch with no powers. The rogue witch was still out there with the Arch-Magica's powers. At least, they weren't actualized. She didn't want to think about that woman right then. Maggie kissed her fingertip and touched each child on the cheek. Both Luka and Gia grinned, and their dreams filled with ponies and bright flowers.

Maggie went to her room but kept the door open in case Gia woke. After washing her face and brushing her teeth, she went to the dresser for her pajamas. The broken picture frame was still there and the replacement one still in the store bag.

All these weeks and she'd never gotten around to switching Richard and Michael's photo to the new frame. She would do it right then. She removed the photo from the damaged frame and placed it into the new one. There. That wasn't so hard, Maggie. She held the framed photo and her heart ached. The fact that her husband and son were no longer in this world was brutal. She had been granted extra time with Richard since his death, but it wasn't the same.

Their deaths hurt so much. It was a pain that dwelled on the periphery of her emotions but came back razor sharp when she wasn't expecting it. And there was so much guilt. No one tells you that your greatest regrets will be attached to death. At least with the living, you can make amends. There was no fixing things after death. And no one tells you that the emotion you'll feel the strongest after a loved one's death isn't grief or heartache. No, it's guilt because we wished we could have done more for that person when they were alive. Maggie pressed the photo to her chest and cried. Her husband's and child's deaths were her failure and her guilt to carry for the rest of the life.

"I am so sorry." She wept. "I miss you both every day."

Something touched her shoulder and when she looked up, she saw it was Richard. She grasped his hand and kissed it. "I'm so sorry, Richard. Tell Michael his mama loves him and misses him." Maggie's sobs shook her whole body.

He gathered her in his arms. "I'm sorry too, Maggie. I'll tell Michael what you said, but I'm here for the last time. It's time to let the dead go." He pulled her in tight to his chest and she rested her head on his shoulder. "I love you, Maggie Towne."

And then the feel of his arms around her disappeared. Richard was gone. Little Michael was gone.

She still had the other children. They needed her, and she needed them. They would all be okay because they were her family, and that was all she ever wanted.

She knew it wouldn't be easy. Out there was a rogue witch with super-powers Maggie needed to find and stop before she destroyed everything.

But Esther would discover that she should never have crossed paths with the most powerful force in the universe, and it wasn't the Magica.

It was a mother protecting her family.

The End

BOOKS BY E. S. MAGILL

SERIES
Magica: Book I- Rise of the Cult
Magica: Book II-Rage of the Werewolves

ANTHOLOGIES EDITED BY E.S. MAGILL
Wily Writers Presents Tales of Foreboding
Deep Cuts
Haunted Mansion Year One

NONFICTION
Reveal Your Wings

E.S. MAGILL UNIVERSAL LINKS

IF YOU ENJOYED THIS BOOK, PLEASE LEAVE A REVIEW.

DISCOVER MORE

https://bit.ly/m/esmagillwriter

Join the Sisterhood

(community, Sisterhood certificate, newsletter, and other goodies)

https://bit.ly/493lpQO

Explore the Website

www.esmagill.com

ABOUT THE AUTHOR

E.S. MAGILL FELL IN LOVE WITH ALL THINGS DARK AND WEIRD AT A very young age. Her genres are horror, dark fiction, supernatural suspense, and paranormal thrillers. She loves to create dark and imaginative worlds for her readers.

MAGICA: Book I Rise of the Cult is her first published novel. Her short stories can be found in anthologies such as *California Screamin'* and *Blood Lite III*. In addition to writing, she has edited several anthologies: *Wily Writers Presents Tales of Foreboding, Haunted Mansion Project Year One,* and *Deep Cuts.* She served as the Reviews Editor for *Dark Wisdom* magazine, where she also wrote the column "The Dark Librarian."

Her love of the craft prompted her to start a small publishing company, Scribes & Scribblers Publishing, where she creates nonfiction workbooks for writers. Mental Health advocacy is also very important to her, and in her nonfiction book *Reveal Your Wings* she writes about her 40+ year journey with depression and eventual cure.

E.S. Magill holds a B.A. and M.A. in English, specializing in the postmodern gothic. Retired from teaching middle school English, she now spends her days writing, reading, and binging all things dark & fantastic. She considers herself a life-long Californian but recently moved to Phoenix along with her also-retired husband Greg.

DISCOVER MORE AT **WWW.ESMAGILL.COM**

www.ingramcontent.com/pod-product-compliance
Lightning Source LLC
Chambersburg PA
CBHW071410300726
48976CB00006B/2045